# after
# fallen

## WHITNEY WALKER

After Fallen

Copyright © 2020 by Whitney Walker

First Edition

Published by Serendipity Stories

Whitney Walker
www.whitneywalkerwriting.com

Edited by Ella Medler
https://ellamedlerediting.yolasite.com/

After Fallen  is a work of fiction. Names, characters, places and incidents are the products of the author's imagination or are used factiously. The author's use of the names of real places, events, or public figures are not intended to change the entirely fictional character of the work. In all other respects any resemblance to actual events, locales, or persons, living or dead, is entirely coincidental.

ISBN: 978-1-7341895-4-4
eBook ISBN: 978-1-7341895-5-1

*For Claerie*

*Your limitless dreaming while wearing that million dollar smile is more inspiring than you could ever know.*

# CASSANDRA

*C*affeine, confidence, and red bottomed shoes. What more does a girl need to take on New York City? Technically, I guess I am not a girl, since I've been claiming to be twenty-nine for an undisclosed number of years now.

And, though I am in the city that never sleeps, I love every minute in my heavenly hotel bed, thus the venti Starbucks warming my hand in the cool morning air. My game time shoes are far from sensible for the walk to my office in the financial epicenter and there's a good chance I'll probably end up like Monica with her beautiful but painful boots. But, seriously? It's impossible to resist the powerful magic of Louboutin's with their bold flash of scarlet!

I could take a cab or an Uber, but with the traffic the commute is three times as long, and that seems a terrible waste of time. The last option is the subway, but hard pass on the chance of sitting in gray, sticky gum like the last time I traveled by train.

The sun is barely peeking through the skyscrapers enveloping Times Square when I leave the hotel, but even as early as it is, an energetic crowd is gathered to cheer on street performers. I push to my tippy toes outside the circle of people just in time to see two young men career through the air in synchronized double-flips.

They high five one another as the rest of us clap for their performance.

I turn in place to stop and smell the grease and meat from the nearby food carts. My stomach growls with delight. The dizzying array of lights dance frantically around dynamic, larger-than-life bill-boards advertising every well-known brand and playbills for all the popular Broadway shows are like a carnival.

I make my way through the triangle shaped, strangely traffic-free space, surrounded by cabs and double decker buses and listen to sounds of melodic honking.

I FEEL awake and alive by the time the whooshing heartbeat of money tells me I have arrived at the intersection of Broadway and Morris. I find myself face to face with iconic statue of the bronzed bull, its colorless beady eyed head formidable, tail raised, and poised to charge.

I love a good backstory and this sculpture has one. In the middle of the night, its creator placed it beneath the Christmas tree deco-rating the entrance of the New York stock exchange. City permit be damned, its imminent removal was rebuffed, and it quickly became an urban legend with international acclaim.

The bull's eighteen feet of height towers over my five-foot-four frame, but I feel just as powerful as it looks. And good thing, because with what I am about to do, I am going to need it. My lips curve upward into a coy smile as I place my fingertips to them and blow a kiss in the direction of my inspiration feeling plenty bullish myself.

THE COLD NOVEMBER wind whips me through the revolving door of the reflective blue building. My work has helped grow the company from a fledgling startup into a mergers and acquisitions powerhouse. During my first business course I developed an addictive shopping habit. Not the typical one for clothing, shoes, or accessories, but for companies. I knew I was destined to buy them, no patience for building them.

I breeze into the warmth of the lobby, bustling with worker bees and executives alike even at this early hour. Each step of my high heels echoes off the stark marble space, punctuating my arrival.

I slide my license across the security desk. Arthritic boney fingers retrieve it, then peck my name into the keyboard as I check my watch impatiently.

"Good morning, Miss Lewis," the shaggy haired older man offers along with my identification and a security badge. As many times as I've been here, I should probably know his name too, but I wouldn't be able to pick him out of a lineup. I'm nice out of necessity, not for pleasure always hearing, but not always heeding, my mother's voice in my head. *Regardless of your mood, Cassandra Anne, good manners, good manners are very important!* Don't forget the exclamation point. It's a song in my head, playing on repeat. So very annoying, mother. I give a curt nod with a forced smile and head to the elevator. And my next victory.

WHILE I SAUNTER down my red carpet of sorts, the aisle way between two rows of cubicles, their inhabitants take notice. All ages, styles, and genders peer over the tops of their mini dungeons. Would I have survived to age thirty-two had I been wasting away in one of those? Doubtful.

On the walk I somehow obtain a sidekick. A young woman wearing the definition of mousy with pride as evident in the vintage glasses John Lennon round and the athletic knee socks accompanying the green plaid corduroy skirt hitting in the most unsexy just below the knee length. Regardless, she has bravely decided to accompany me to the conference room.

"Miss Lewis, I'm Paige. I've got some information on the Morpho deal you might want before your meeting. It could get you more dough than you could bake with for a lifetime." She giggles behind her hand.

I shake my head, trying to unsee and unhear her awkwardness. She hands me a folder. She could have emailed instead of accosted me.

"Thank you," I offer with a tiny, terse smile.

She bounces on her toes excitedly.

*Waiting for me to anoint you with a gold star?* She isn't leaving.

"I'd love to pitch with you someday, Miss Lewis. Can I fetch you a coffee? Make your copies? What can I do for you, Miss Lewis? I'd like nothing more than to be on your team."

The word "team" makes me cringe. Hell. To. The. No. I answer her request congenially, but honestly, "I'm a solo act, Paige. But thank you for the offer."

She looks dejected, but I wouldn't want to offer any false promises. Yes, I realize that hordes of people work behind the scenes to prepare details and data for me, but no, I'd never consider a supporting cast for any pitch. Those are on me, and me alone.

MY MEETINGS TODAY will take place in a historic bank vault converted into a conference room. What could be more apropos to garner funding for my client to acquire their archrival and nemesis? The door is circular, solid metal two feet thick, and houses a complicated looking locking mechanism.

The length of the left wall is lined with original safety deposit boxes stacked floor to ceiling. Each now empty box is tarnished dark metal, heavy and leaden, a number in elegant font on the front and a skeleton keyhole.

I imagine what used to be held here. Power, wealth and secrets inside an impenetrable fortress. It's no wonder I love this room.

A long mahogany table runs through the center of the rectangular shaped room with leather chairs along each side. I relax into the one at the head of the table and spin three-hundred-sixty degrees in the swivel chair, dizzying myself in the intoxicating smell of its leather and the lingering mishmash of men's cologne from prior meetings in the confined space.

Soon, I will make an irresistible offer to the investment bankers around this table. If they prefer attempting to negotiate over playing nice, I have two more potential meetings just like theirs in the next six hours. I can't lose today. Not that I ever do.

My phone skitters across the table with the vibration of an incoming call. I contemplate ignoring it, but if there is something my father knows, it's shrewd negotiating. Maybe I can get a pointer or two.

"Dad."

"Morning, Princess."

My spine bristles at the word and I promise myself. Next time. I have to tell him how much I hate that nickname. "How are you?" I don't want for an answer but it's the right question to ask, "I'm about to start a meeting."

"That seems to be your whole life."

"It is. And?"

"Well I hope you stop to smell the roses. Don't let that relentless pursuit of perfection get in your way of having any fun, Princess."

*Like you, Dad?*

"Taking names and kicking ass is my fun. No half measures here, Dad. Learned from the best."

He sighs at the backhanded compliment, "That's not what I meant. And, about that. There is always more to the story. Try to remember that when you slay your next victim."

"I'll try," I say half-hearted because I've just spotted said victim on approach, engaged in a conversation with Paige. What could they be chatting about? I wonder what she could have to offer. "I have to run."

"I'll make it brief. Thanksgiving. That's why I am calling. Please consider coming home. You know your mother makes a mean turkey dinner."

Yes, I do. But her Betty Crocker meets Julia Child aptitude had never been enough to deter him from missing in action status.

His second sigh is deeper than the first, as if he knows exactly where my head may have just gone. "We really need to spend some together, Cassandra. We need to talk."

5

*Which means I'll need a better excuse than usual for the hard pass on a weekend in Boston.*

"I'll let you know."

SMILING, I give the chair one more spin around. Fast. Dizzying. See, Dad? I'm not a complete bore. Then I smooth my skirt over the curve of my hip, and run a hand over my perfectly straightened hair. I plaster my most welcoming smile form cheek to cheek, greet my guests with a firm handshake, and an extra blink, or several, of my upturned, enhanced eyelashes.

Sliding the presentations compiled by Paige in front of each man, and the one woman who flank me on three slides, I begin to share the story of Morpho with my captive audience.

"The company founder decided on its name after a trip to Costa Rica, where he is looking forward to spending his time as soon as you all help him retire." I deliver this with a light laugh and pause for dramatic effect, "The beautiful blue morpho butterfly is one of the rainforest inhabitants there. When it flies, its wings flash from brilliant blue to dull brown. This makes the butterfly continuously appear and disappear. I doubt I need to explain how this applies to Morpho's competitors?"

I read the crowd. Engaged. Waiting for more.

"You could say that Morpho has undergone quite a metamorphosis from its inception. That's where you come in. I am offering you the right of first refusal to partner with Paragon on their acquisition of Brimstone. No story to tell there, perhaps right now they wish they would have chosen a less foreboding name. Perhaps they missed the foreshadowing. Are we ready to take a look at the numbers?"

I am peppered with questions from around the table, then accused of having lost my marbles. Newsflash people, no one liked playing childhood games on the playground with me either.

A stare off, or down, or something of the sort takes place with the elder in the room, a man of large stature and few words. Does he really think I'll blink? His gaze retreats to the paper in front of him. I glance at my watch. Seven minutes. I've been plenty generous. Time's up.

With a sweeping gesture of my arm, I push up the sleeve of my jacket, tapping the face of the Shinola across my wrist with my fingertip. Though a glaring reminder of a time I'd like to forget, it was one of the first made by the brand and its gold lattice and navy alligator band made it too pretty to pawn.

Head nods around the table have nominated one poor sucker to negotiate with me. I'm not in the mood, and they're not in the position to do so. "We think your offer is substandard, Miss Lewis," he delivers with plenty of confidence.

"Thank you for the consideration. I appreciated your time today." Stoic, I stand and reach right, collecting the presentation from in front of the woman, then man next to her. His dropped jaw resides somewhere in the neighborhood of his flubbery neck.

"I'm offering you more than your competitors. Tomorrow, you'll either be with me, or reading about Everhard in the news."

With the mention of their archrival comes the arm fold and clench of the jaw from the elder at the table. One would think his seasoning would have allowed plenty of time to perfect his poker face, but not so much.

I'd love to give the business to Everhard just for the name alone, to make up for the lifetime of taunting the founder has undoubtedly endured. However, this company will garner more press, and in turn, more notoriety for my company. And for me.

Eyes dart around the table, speaking silently to one another. I continue to retrieve the packets of paper in front of each seat, nonchalant. I take my time lining up the edges on the table and cradle the bundle in my arm. I walk to the door and gesture with my arm to exit. No one stands, but several are wriggling in their seats.

The elder gentleman leans forward in his chair then steeples his hands on the in front of him on the table. I take my own power stance and widen the distance between my two feet.

He presses his palms flat to the table with a smacking sound.

Clearing his throat, his raspy voice is insistent, "Two point five and we have a deal."

All heads swivel toward me. Once again, I sweep my arm toward the door, "Good day."

Eyes dart back in his direction. His head hangs, resigned.

"Draw up the contracts?" My assumptive close hangs in the air while several people look uncomfortable in their chairs, awaiting his answer.

"You drive a hard bargain, Miss Lewis."

"It's an opportunity not to be missed, sir."

I glance at my watch again. I need time to cancel the next meeting if they accept. Plus, I'm impatient. "And I need to end this meeting."

He lets out a little growl, then a huff, glancing around the table again. Three other men give nods of the head. Two others shrug. It's a quorum of concession.

"We're in."

I love my job.

Happy this is one more thing to check off the to do list, it's not cause for champagne or a victory dance. Today was like taking candy from a baby, tomorrow will be another story.

# CASSANDRA

*I*t may be the accidental jostle with my oversized, overpacked Louis Vuitton, or the fact that I am going to answer my ringing phone while packed like sardines on the plane's jet bridge to San Jose, but either way, I've just garnered one hell of an eye roll from the woman behind me. Love you too, sweetheart.

I know the call is an important update from my Paragon partner-in-crime, Sebastian. The "Bad to the Bone" ringtone he programmed into my phone himself after I missed, or ignored, his call one too many times gives him away.

"Hey there. What's up?" I calmly listen to his rampage. "You have to learn not to react. Don't let them get the best of you." I offer this sage advice, then pause to listen to his next diatribe of expletives on the subject of cleaning up what I left in my wake yesterday. "I already told them no, Sebastian. We'll go with Everhard then. We win either way. Don't let them get under your skin." I listen to the same old, same old, "Yes, I know you are nicer than I am. Maybe you should take up yoga, Sebastian. Learn to breathe before you rant."

One more sentence. The audacity. I take the phone from my ear and stare at it, confirming what I already knew. He hung up on me. I loudly reply, though of course he can't hear, "No, I do not need to take my own advice."

I step onto the plane right foot first, as always. No reason behind my superstition; it's just my thing. I am about to practice what I've just preached to Sebastian. I'd love to rant because I am in seat 10B. It's not first class and not an aisle, perks I'm accustomed to as a frequent flyer.

I can't recall the last time I saw coach, and I do center seats in coach like I do three-star hotels. Meaning I don't. However, the direct flight I had scheduled from New York had a mechanical issue. Now, I am ironically connecting through my hometown of Detroit.

I squeeze my suitcase into the overhead bin to the left and turn back toward row ten. At least it's bulkhead and there is no row of seats in front crowding us.

Oh, my.

Maybe the boardroom won't be my next conquest.

It might be 10C.

Or not.

No, no and hell no.

I know his type. Tall. Dark. Handsome. Heart-breaking.

I slide into my seat, my focused on anything that's not him.

Damn him. Without even knowing it, he's leveraging his height as an asset to win me over. I can tell he would tower over me even in my least sensible shoes. And by the way he fills in a plane seat, it's obvious his wide-shouldered masculine frame would engulf my smaller, feminine one.

And then it happens.

I try for a sneak peek, but my gaze is captured by a pair of entrancing eyes. The cloudy-at-sunrise soft blue where the sun begins to brighten the sky. It looks like someone took a magic marker to his eyelids and drew a permanent black line where his dark eyelashes begin extending. They don't stop. They are so long and full they nearly shield the blue beneath. Except, they are peering so intently into mine I can't miss their mischievous twinkle. It screams powerful bad boy and slayer of beautiful women. His hair only adds to his foreboding presence, 3:00 a.m. pitch-black. A bit wild despite his attempt to tame it with product. My fingers might like to try.

Maybe this one can handle me.

Fewer choices in men is a sidekick to the vice-president title. Men can't handle powerful women. It's just a fact, as hard and cold as ice. I've been called the same. This man is hot, however. Hot enough to consider letting myself thaw, at least for a flirtatious plane ride, since I'll never have to see him again when our four and one-half hours together come to an end. Panty dropping is as rare for me as the $3.93 million per carat blue diamond, and even the enticing and irresistible black hair, blue-eyed combination isn't worth the trouble.

It's not as if I haven't had chances, as there are plenty of male travelers in hotel bars ready for a no-strings-attached fling. I just never consider anything beyond the bay. Okay, maybe twice. But I've learned. Awkward sex with a stranger is a risk without nearly enough reward.

"You okay?"

I've just barely buckled my seatbelt and he is making conversation.

"Of course. What makes you think otherwise?"

"You seemed stressed getting on the plane."

I curl my lips upward, calculating my answer. "Just a little self-imposed stress. Never hurt anyone."

"Really? I've heard it might. Heart attacks? Ulcers? Whole host of other ailments. I hear taking up yoga is supposed to help," he quips, obviously having heard my conversation.

Has he just mocked me with my own line? I've heard enough airplane safety speeches to know that a little plastic bag is supposed to drop from the panel above in the event of a loss of cabin pressure. Considering his insult just sucked up my oxygen, surely mine will drop down any second now. A stranger has upended me, and we haven't moved an inch on the tarmac? Feeling hurt isn't something I'm accustomed to.

"Hey, I'm sorry. I didn't mean anything by that. I love yoga."

Did my dependable poker face just fail? Clearly, because he's just apologized. While his voice might be as smooth as the fine whiskey I'd recently acquired a taste for, thankfully I know what won't let me down is my well-honed ability to resist the temptation of acquiring a taste for this man too. The hangover isn't worth indulging.

HE EXTENDS HIS HAND, but I cross my arms, unsure if the action is to defend my pride, or if I am scared to be touched by this man who has somehow thrown me off my game in mere seconds. His eyes have me pinned in his gaze. Is the thing in the middle of my chest somersaulting in exhilaration? Or terror?

"Just a guess, but considering the Stella McCartney suit you are wearing, you aren't traveling for pleasure."

Apparently, my terse reaction hasn't deterred him from making small talk.

Come on, not fair. He has mad fashion skills, too? I blow out a sigh. Fine. I'll fold. I offer my hand.

He accepts it, offering his name, "Ryan Steadman," along with an irresistibly sexy smile complete with the slightest dimpled indentation just above the left corner of his full lips. So. Not. Fair.

I hold on a second longer than I probably should, "Cassandra Lewis."

What he says next is, "Nice to meet you Cassandra Lewis," but what my ears hear is, "Cassandra Steadman."

Yes, Cassandra Steadman passes the name test quite nicely. Wait, what? What the hell? No. No, and no.

My mind is sent careening back in time with that little faux pas of my brain.

At ten, I planned my double wedding with my cousin on a swing set glider. Disney World nuptials, nonetheless. We believed in the magic of both Disney, and love. At thirty-two, after a few not so serious boyfriends in high school, a commitment-free but fun collegiate experience, and the one who apparently wasn't, I've learned better. It is impractical, and weak, to believe in Disney-inspired fairytale endings despite my nickname of Princess, started by my father at three and adopted by my last ex-boyfriend.

At thirty-three, I'll take any of the Disney supervillain females over the pathetic princesses, despite my dismissal of all things hopelessly romantic being a character flaw in my mother's eyes. When she recently asked if I was ever going to get married, I answered I was already wedded. To my work. In return, the whites of her eyeballs rolled skyward to the universe or God or something. She asked in exasperation why she couldn't have a normal daughter, complete with air quotes on the word normal.

Her definition of success? Baby, and husband-rearing, I would argue that by her own definition she had not succeeded herself. Thus, no. No. And no. I don't return his pleasantry, but he doesn't take the hint.

"Are you a talker or an ignore-the-person-in-the-seat-next-to-you flier?" Ryan continues the conversation with a half of his lips raising crookedly into a smile. Darn it if it's not lopsided in the cutest kind of way.

"Depends on the day. I usually work." I've spent over one hundred thousand miles flying the friendly skies in the last twelve months. Not one movie or book to be enjoyed, but finance and business magazines weren't off limits. Most often Coldplay or Lifehouse was playing in my ears to drown out crying children or annoyingly loud talkers. From takeoff to touchdown, I worked on a phone, computer, or paper, productive every minute of every flight. It's how I rolled. Just a little white lie. "You?" I ask.

The flight attendant dressed in the unfortunate polyester uniform interrupts, leaning in slightly toward Ryan. "Is there anything I can get for you, Mr. Steadman?"

She doesn't ask me the question, or anyone else in coach. Why is he special? Is there more to know about this man? Of course, there is. I remind myself of the dangerous game where I know the rules and don't want to play.

Once, I'd thought I'd picked an equal. A fault of the female's XX chromosome, I fell hook, line, and sinker for the soulmate line.

Neither of us wanted marriage, but I did want to stop playing the field to avoid the dating horrors of my friends. Knowing better than to do so, I still planted roots in the Midwest. Instead of pursuing my own path out of school, I followed him. Right down into a devastated state, post-sixteen months of quick and dirty romantic bliss.

Ryan might be tempting - and so close to me in these seats his presence nearly engulfs the emptiness I've learned to ignore! - but good thing for me, my head has sworn off what the heart struggles to resist. I am only a few hours from a clean getaway. Headphones in, computer on, I do what I do best.

SNACKS ARE BEING SERVED, and though I'd like to laud myself as health-conscious, I still succumb to a Diet Coke-a-day habit, among a few other nutritionally deficient loves I've no intention of breaking up with anytime soon. When I remove my earphones to make my request of the flight attendant serving, it's as if Ryan has been waiting for the opportunity to strike up another conversation and immediately asks, "Is Detroit home or another stop?"

"Home. Now. I'm not from there. I grew up near Boston."

"You don't say." He smiles wickedly.

I know it's not the accent that has given me away because the fifty-one minutes south of the city where I grew up doesn't share its Bostonian flair. This means his judgement is based on personality. Fine with me. I'll own it. "Well, I've done my time in the Midwest."

He laughs heartily. "Done time? I'm sure you didn't mean to insult my upbringing with that comment."

"No harm intended." I don't clarify for him that it isn't the location that I have the problem with, just how I ended up in the location. "And where might you be from?"

"Detroit. Born and bred. Lived in Chicago for a while too but came back."

He looks away, a forlorn expression etching across his face, sadness replacing his smile. I'd like to ask what that is about, but this seems like a backstory in potentially dangerous territory, so I opt for humor instead. "No one is actually from Detroit. Or at least admits it. I am guessing you are really a suburb-dweller?"

A hand goes across his heart, "Ouch! Actually, I was born in a hospital in Detroit, and I did grow up in a Detroit neighborhood. I still live downtown now. My parents are snowbirds, so half-timers, but downtown in summer until the snowflakes fly."

Though Detroit is making news as an up-and-comer, the past few decades of this man's life didn't have Detroit as a city with a family-friendly reputation. I want to know more but he is poised to ask me another question.

"How did you end up in Detroit?" he asks with a curiosity and attentiveness I find foreign. And unnerving.

"It's complicated." I am technically in the suburbs, not Detroit. And I am not going there with him. I can divert this. "I live in Morganville, so I guess I'm the suburb-dweller. Detroit via Chicago. Like you." I pause, letting the similarity sink in. For both of us. "Northwestern undergrad then B-school at University of Chicago."

"I'm glad you didn't say Ohio State," he says, flashing his perfectly fit together, overly white teeth once again.

I can't stop looking at his lips forming words when I can imagine them forming a kiss against mine. It's distracting. "So, you know Morganville then?"

"I might be a little familiar with Ann Arbor," he says of the college town just next door.

I live just on its fringe. Still a cool small town, youthful vibe but separated from the beer-can and hedge-lined sorority and fraternity row by a zip code and expensive price tag on its houses.

"Familiar enough that I know I could date someone who doesn't share the same religious or political beliefs before I could a Buckeye." His smirk may be more appealing than his smile if that's possible.

"I know your type," I chide back. I'm referring to the good-looking, charismatic bad boy who has just found a way to drop in the fact that he is single.

"Fiercely loyal, willing to accommodate nearly all differences, but highly competitive?"

Did he just describe himself as my ideal man? Better not to dwell on that little detail.

"So where are you off to?"

The cart stopping in the aisle beside him forces him to lean slightly towards me. Several inches too close. I feel his energy course through my body like it's my own. I need some sort of a shield. Maybe that thing at the dentist when you get x-rays. Anything to protect me. I need to get out of here unscathed.

"A meeting," I answer curtly, lest I get sucked into any further wit and charm of the stranger.

"Okay then." He takes the hint and returns to reading his magazine. Out of the corner of my eye, I peek at the page and watch as he folds the top right corner into a triangle shape. I will choose to ignore the fact that I have dog-eared myself the same article in the same magazine in my bag under the seat in front of me.

Or maybe I can't ignore the fact.

I offer a better answer, "My work is confidential. My clients expect me to have a high level of integrity."

He flashes an understanding smile, "I could say the same."

This intrigues me. "Really? And what is it that you do?"

"Put things back together when people break them."

"Oh, like, you're a doctor?" I ask curiously.

"Nope. Businesses."

Now it's his turn to be secretive. It might be fun to make some secrets together with this man. "Can you tell me more?" I might as well ask, he could always say no.

"I take the leftovers and see what good can come from them after they have been disparaged and devastated."

Now I inwardly cringe. When I buy companies, I eat them for dinner and scrape the scraps in the trash. What's the phrase? Someone's trash is another's treasure.

Thankfully, we are approaching our destination, and soon my head will be out of the clouds and back to reality. I need my head in the game for the one that matters. The game of love isn't for me. And despite the collateral damage I might cause, I have a company to take over and sell for its parts.

As the plane door opens, I turn toward Ryan to say goodbye. "Nice to have met you. Good luck with your saving the business world, Ryan Steadman." His name melts in my mouth, like dark, sweet chocolate. A voice like whiskey, his name like chocolate. No, thank you. I'll stick with pink frosted sprinkle donuts and iced cappuccinos for my guilty pleasures. I'm just minutes to a clean getaway.

He reaches his hand out to shake mine once again, and I take his to be polite. This time it's his turn to hold on a second too long. His thumb strokes the top of my hand ever so slightly.

On the contrary, what I feel inside isn't slight in the least. I shudder involuntarily. My heart clutches defensively as his energy singes my core. I pull my hand away abruptly like I've just touched a hot object that burned.

My world is a highly controlled and calculated series of events. I know how to avoid scorching to my soul. Maybe I'm being overdramatic, or maybe I'm just smarter than most.

I reach for my bag on the floor in front of me, scoop it up into my lap to form a barrier from the smoldering embers, then escape onto the jet bridge. My feet on solid ground again, each hastened step puts space between Ryan Steadman and my heart that, for a moment, wanted to fall again but knew better.

# CASSANDRA

he blaring sound of my 5:30 a.m. alarm is more startling than it should be considering my body time should be three hours ahead. I had finally fallen into sleep after being awake much of the night, tossing and turning. The tossing had to do with today's presentation. The turning was for the lingering hangover of mixing those engulfing baby-blues and that dimpled smile with the chaser of his touch traversing lightning from my fingertips to the tip of my toes.

Where is he now?

Will he ever think of me again?

Did I leave the same mark on him he has on me?

Ugh! I pull the pillow over my head and stifle a groan.

I remind myself he fixes what I break. I'm the enemy! Yet, her I am padding barefooted across the room to retrieve my laptop from the credenza. Google just makes cyberstalking too easy! The white screen glows light in the dark room, and I type the only two pieces of information I know, Ryan Steadman and Detroit, into the search bar.

Author.

Doctor.

None of the pictures feature a more-than-attractive dark-haired, blue-eyed man. I try a few other variations on the spelling then head over to LinkedIn and try the same. I try the Ryan Steadman listings on Facebook, but no pictures resemble my Ryan. I wince. *My* Ryan? My brain is a hard-core traitor.

Oh well, at least my heart will remain protected and intact for another day. I close the laptop having wasted twenty minutes on a man who – thankfully! – seems to have disappeared into the ether.

FOR THREE POINT one miles I put one foot in front of the other. Each time my brain begins to drift to one man I am trying not to think about, I speed up the treadmill. By the end of the run I am wrung out, finishing at the torturous pace of an eight-minute mile. At least it gets me to the finish line that much faster. I'll have an extra three minutes in my perfectly scripted sixty-minute routine.

Hair blow dry and style is thirty-one minutes. Twelve minutes of makeup application, nine to dress, and finally eight minutes to pack my suitcase and purse with each item in its proper place. I'd like to think a place for everything and everything in its place applies to my head too, but my thoughts are more like a tornado with dirt and random broken, unidentifiable objects swept together into one big swirling disaster.

I take one more look at myself from head to toe in the full-length mirror on the hotel room wall. Today's suit is navy with pinstripes. I collect power suits like children collect seashells on the beach. Each one beautiful and unique. I feel my best in the tallest heels I can wear and still walk a straight line. I bought the suit to match these four-inch stilettoed navy suede Louboutins.

CECIL KNOWS how to make a girl feel good. Emerging into the sunlight through the front door of the hotel at precisely 7:22 a.m. I see his shiny, clean, black sedan parked in the valet loop. The trunk is already open and awaiting my luggage. When he sees me, he reaches up to remove his captain-like hat and puts it across his chest as if he's saluting the flag for our anthem. His nod of respect and smile is the greeting I've become accustomed to.

"Good morning, Ms. Lewis. You look mighty fine this fine today. Even more fine than when you arrived yesterday. I think California looks good on you."

Cecil's signature line.

He makes me like the state even more than the sunshine and beaches of the Pacific Coast Highway. His southern accent is a dead giveaway that he's been transplanted from the south. Alabama, in fact, and his geographically bred charm is endearing. He has the wisdom of a man who has lived a what-doesn't-kill-you-makes-you-stronger life and is happy to share life lessons and pearls of faith during our rides together.

He loads my suitcase then sees me into the back seat, watching me buckle my seat belt like a protective father. He softly closes the back door of the car and makes his way around to the driver's side.

"Cecil, you have to get that knee fixed." I tell him because it's painful to watch. He needs to have it replaced but is waiting for Medicare to kick in before he can afford to have the surgery.

"Aw, Ma'am you know this spring chicken ain't playing football anymore. I can get by until the time comes. As long as the world is turning, I'm all right. Better if the sun is shining like today."

Cecil knows my drill. I am preparing and rehearsing in my head. I'm always quiet on the way to the meeting, and he is my partner in processing and debriefing afterward. I offer him a smile however, as I lose myself in my thoughts.

We pass through buildings of sparkling newness representing the success the Silicon Valley of California stands for, hiding all the flaws and failures of those who have crashed and burned, like the company I am here to rescue today.

Not our final destination this morning, the car winds its way past the Paragon building where I'd worked with the team late into last evening, studying up on the players that would be posturing to turn me away today.

The team had done a thorough job of preparing the reports I'd scoured, backgrounds of the billionaires that were to play my judge and jury over the next few hours. There was always some element of surprise in these deals, as investors and boards come out of the woodwork with their own agendas, but I control what I can control. I've done my homework and feel ready to take on whatever curve balls come my way.

CECIL SLOWS the car to a stop in the circle drive of a blue-glass building, a welcoming rainbow prism reflection from the morning sunrise. I turn off the volume on my phone, tuck it back into my purse, raise my chin and step into the light as Cecil opens the door for me. I pull in a long breath of cool air.

"Knock 'em dead, Ms. Lewis," Cecil says with a tip of his hat.

"I plan to," I reply confidently.

Cecil lets out a deep laugh straight from the belly. "That's what worries me. It was just a figure o' speech, ma'am. Don't really do that."

"We shall see," I throw over my shoulder as I head toward the building. I watch the vision of myself in the glass as I approach. "You've got this, Cass," I say out loud and step, right foot first, through the front door.

The receptionist is a young woman who gives a nod as she holds up her index finger then points to the headset she is wearing. She peers at me from behind a marble counter of black swirled with gleaming silver sparkle. Everything is shiny, with extra sparkle, in the Valley. I am careful not to mar the shine with fingerprints she might have to wipe away. This is her castle, and I've stepped beyond the moat.

As she sizes me up, a large, welcoming smile spreads across her very pretty face. I hope it's genuine and not a trick to manipulate me into believing she might be nice before she sears me. At least I know to question her motives.

Blond hair bouncing off her shoulders as her head moves, I envy the flounce that looks like she's just had a blowout. Her Bohemian-style dress is white to pink ombre and flows with her as she moves swiftly behind the desk. She is conversing with someone on the other end of the phone while shuffling multiple sets of papers. Her southern drawl matches Cecil's. I wonder what about Silicon Valley appeals to her, or if she - like me - followed a special someone to find herself a fish out of water.

"Hello? Good morning," floats over the desk in my direction.

I greet the receptionist with as much sweetness as I can. She is my first test and I need a passing grade from her.

"You must be Cassandra," she says with an air of knowing.

"I am." I am not surprised she knows who I am, because this secret society of Valley gatekeepers know everything. They herald secrets with as much precision as those guarding the crown jewels. I play along though. "I guess you were expecting me?"

"I shouldn't tell you this, but *I* think it was a compliment. They told me to look for the woman who seems to walk on water, wearing Armani and an attitude." She's grinning manically, "They could put you in an ad for either. Or both."

"Thanks. I'll take it as a compliment," I reply, wondering who the 'they' might be.

"I couldn't wait to meet you!" she says enthusiastically, as if I am some sort of celebrity. "I'd usually offer coffee, tea, water, soda, crois-sant, bagel or muffin," she rattles off the list, "but I'm guessing you would pass. Too much potential for spillage or something left behind in the teeth."

She looks to her left and then right, puts both hands on the desk before me, and leans forward toward me. "I shouldn't do this either, but what the Sam's chickens."

I don't know about Sam's chickens, but I know that she is going to cross a line right now to help me.

"Laura Benifire is the front runner. But let's call her bonfire because everyone in the valley knows you can take her down in flames. Dick Wallace is in consideration too," she wrinkles her nose, "but does anyone trust a Dick?" She stifles a laugh at her own joke. "I doubt anyone is more prepared than you, if what I've heard is true, but thought I'd give you the G2 anyway."

"Thank you." I pause in surprise for this little gift. It's not military-grade classified data, but it's just as valuable to me. "What's your name?

"Charlotte."

She outstretches her hand and I reach for it. I remember yesterday's world-rocking handshake and it takes me a moment to push it out of my memory and compose myself. "Nice to meet you. Charlotte is my favorite name. If I ever have a baby girl, I'm planning to name her that."

What just came out of my mouth?

Babies have always ranked - let's see - *nowhere* on my list of goals for my life. I went from a handshake to a baby in milliseconds. Thank God I'll step into a boardroom momentarily and forget what's just happened. A male is walking across the lobby to claim me.

"I hope I get to meet my namesake one day!" she returns, beaming.

Sorry, Charlotte. One day after never.

I AM ESCORTED DOWN a long hallway by Chuck Holowell. I know from my cyber-stalking prep that he is a baseball fan, Red Sox nonetheless. I am at ease by the time we reach our destination, ready to crush this presentation. Chuck reaches for the wrought iron handle of the heavy boardroom door, pulling it open for me to enter.

Now I am in the castle I rule. I stride over the thickly padded carpeted floor, model-like down a runaway in the latest designer collection, into the boardroom direct to the head of the table.

Unpacking my laptop and portfolio, I gently set them on the dark wood table. I take in the energy of the room but don't yet face my suitors. The men are in cliquish crowds amongst themselves, but I know who is important and begin to make my way to greet the inquisition. I grip the hand of the man closet to me firmly while looking him directly in the eye. "Nice to see you again, Tom." He is a slightly over-weight, mostly bald man that I have three inches on in these heels. I don't mean to look down on him, but physically I do. Tom likes brief and brilliant.

Next is an attractive younger man, puffing his chest to act in charge while he probably hasn't earned it. Barely out of the womb, he is the son of another potential investor. He's a rookie I can teach a few things.

The next is a very tall, young man with dark circles. I congratulate him on his new baby. I will leverage my female assets to win him over, no doubt in need of some feminine attention.

The next in the line I recognize as the data guy. Seemingly nervous and flustered while meeting me, he doesn't even give his name or look me in the eye as his sweaty hand barely grazes mine. I've brought plenty of data and he should be an easy one to win over.

The crowd parts to make space as I pivot left to greet the next man. I squint. My eyes are not failing me, but my breath is. And my heart, which has just skipped a beat, then restarted with an erratic flutter. The translucent eyes of blue, that dimpled smile, and the hair begging my hands to tousle its strands are far too familiar.

Time stands still as I take him in. Familiar, yet different.

We're not standing toe to toe because he is sitting. I look down into the gaze of unmistakably mischievous eyes.

Ryan.

*My* Ryan.

In a wheelchair. It doesn't look like one of the wheelchairs you rent, but a manual one that appears to fit him specifically. My mind whirls trying to remember the hours we were together yesterday.

I don't have time to process this and decide at the same time if I should reveal that we have made one another's acquaintance prior. I need to think, and I can't think, because his hand is reaching toward me. Again. I stare at it awkwardly. I don't want to feel his warmth radiate through me. I don't want him to do those things to my insides.

A room full of people are watching. There is only one play here. I reach my hand forward with trepidation.

"Nice to see you, Ms. Lewis."

I exhale and realize I've been holding my breath. I barely tilt my head in a nod, the best that I can do. Letters swirl around the tip of my tongue but won't fold into words. He gently releases my hand and I force my quivering legs to carry me forward.

Each hand I shake moving around the room, away from Ryan, brings me one step closer to pulling myself together. By the time I reach my laptop, the tremble of my fingers is barely perceptible. If anyone notices, they will assume I am nervous. Which I am. Just not about the presentation. If I can just avoid looking in his direction, I can do this.

Exhaling a breath, I ready myself to speak, "Gentlemen, thank you for taking the time to be here. I appreciate the opportunity to present Paragon's offer today. I am sure you will find it worthy of your consideration."

The words flow but the room swirls. Nothing seems familiar. I've done pitches such as this near fifty times, but it's difficult to focus with nagging questions peppering me beneath the surface. What happened to Ryan? Is he injured? Paralyzed? Is it fate that he is here, deciding mine?

The voice I crave hearing again begins to speak. I turn toward its whiskey-smooth, seductive intonation in slow motion. Yes, I could get drunk on him.

I lower my eyes because I need to prepare myself to look into his. His arms outstretch on the table before him, hands tented, impossible to ignore wide shoulders and biceps pushing the boundaries of the seams of his shirt. I don't want to be thinking about the muscles of his chest, back, and biceps but it's happening. He may be the most handsome man I've ever laid eyes on. I see his lips moving but the words I hear don't align, like a foreign movie with subtitles. So far today he has hijacked my ability to form words, and now hear them as well. His face, and the aftershock of his touch, have me reeling.

"Could you tell us, Ms. Lewis, exactly why Paragon is interested in acquiring PanOptix? We have several competitive offers so you can expect a tough negotiation, if your offer is even among those we consider."

I hear the last part of the sentence clearly. A wake-up call as abrupt as the ringing alarm that jolted me awake this morning. I expected a softball. What does he mean, if they even consider my offer? The hair on the back of my neck prickles. He looks smug, even menacing, as he continues. "Perhaps, Ms. Lewis, you could share how you know that PanOptix will gain 27% market share in the next year, making it a desirable target?"

I feel my jaw drop but quickly and consciously return my mouth to a closed position. My fingers curl into a tight fist. I want to sashay across the room and plant it against his Nordic-square strong jaw. No, maybe his perfect nose instead.

He must have seen the statistic on my laptop on the plane. Did he know I would be here today? That was my ace in the hole, and he has used it before I played the final card in my deck. He has stolen my thunder, punch line and closing remarks. It would seem like common knowledge instead of my own doing. My painstaking, fifty-plus hours of research.

I'm seeing red. Ryan has shown his true colors, and I do angry much better than I do love. You do not catch me off-guard and certainly do not stand up to me on my home turf.

"Due to market conditions, as well as in-depth analysis of the company, algorithmic calculations, and predictive analytics based on leading indicators for success, we are sure that the future market valuation is in accordance with the offer put forth by Paragon. We believe a new corporation called ParaOptix will thrive in the sector. In other words, we've done our research." Looking away dismissively, I add, "Now, please, time is of the essence. Shall we?"

My parents didn't need to push me to compete. Since my first potato-sack race at kindergarten field day, I've loved the euphoria of the finish line. Tennis, swimming, running, acquiring. Winning is what I do. Today is no exception. I'll close this and get back to my real life, where I don't need Ryan Steadman or anyone else.

Cassandra Lewis never loses.

I SHOULD BE THRILLED. I just answered the few additional questions that were asked of me, thankfully none by Ryan. I pack my things slowly, to eavesdrop on the hushed conversation taking place between the partners. I steal glances of the heads nodding on the left side of the table.

I can't resist looking in Ryan's direction. His attempt to humiliate me upped my game today. After the initial anger, I enjoyed the challenge he posed. Maybe I am more masochistic than I even knew. Just the glance does things to me now, though. Things I don't like. So much in fact that I have to cross one in front of the other to stifle what I can't ignore.

Ryan huddles with the man to his left and right, looking at his computer screen. The tall, tired man leans in, one finger pointing to the screen. He mumbles something, then Ryan shakes his head in return, scowling a reply. Is he talking them out of my proposal? How dare he.

The man to his left contemplates, rubbing his thumb across the cleft in his chin. He shrugs a shoulder then nods. Tall-and-tired turns in his seat to the next man. The one I know has the power. I seize my victory with the final nod of his head. I quickly duck mine. It was all subtle, but I know how to read cues and I don't miss details. Missing the fact that Ryan might not have the use of his legs was an exception.

CECIL'S EYES are darting between the road and the rear view. It's been nearly twenty minutes, and I know he is giving me space before asking what happened. "Pardon me for saying, Ms. Lewis, but you don't seem so fine. Didn't you knock 'em dead in there?"

I should have. I flinch. Did I just think about hitting someone who might be in a wheelchair? I'm still trying to process. I remind myself he may have rocked my world briefly, but he had also tried to take me for a fool. Still, somehow, I've let him get the better of me, and now today's victory is more the sucralose sweet instead of the real thing. I can't let him get the better of me!

Ryan was a formidable foe, fighting against me. I remind myself I was the yang to his yin. We didn't want the same outcome. He was protecting the people and I was protecting the profit margin. None of this is Cecil's burden to bear. "It was a good day, Cecil. I had them eating out of the palm of my hand." All but one of them.


As I APPROACH baggage claim on the way to retrieving my car, frosted glass doors slide open before me. They reveal the crowd gathered to meet the arriving passengers. I am always reminded of the Gwyneth Paltrow movie. Destiny lies behind these sliding doors. Each time I pass through, I make up stories about those lucky enough to have someone anxiously awaiting their return. Today, an older couple is losing themselves in a kiss despite the onlookers.

Would Ryan ever meet me at the airport and kiss me like that?

I'm on home soil and he's come along.

No. No. No. And no.

I am impervious to this. To wit. Charm. Challenge. All of it. I don't want it and I certainly don't need it.

So why do I find myself frozen in place watching the couple kiss? I'm jostled by someone I've annoyed having stopped in the middle of a passenger thoroughfare. No one is waiting for me in this crowd. Not today, and probably never.

The ringing phone startles me to attention. "Cassandra Lewis."

"Ms. Lewis, seems you are luckier than our Red Sox this year."

I recognize the voice on the other end of the line. Chuck. Without his needing to say more, my lips purse smug with victory. "How so, Chuck?"

"We'd like to let you know that we are going with Paragon. Congratulations. Good work today."

"Thank you, sir," I reply, outwardly coy, but inwardly elated. "I appreciate your vote of confidence."

"Charlotte's getting the final contract out now, so you'll receive it in the morning. It will outline the T's & C's. Oh, and, just one stip-ulation."

"Stipulation?" I ask, unable to fathom what he might be referenc-ing. "What's that?"

"Paragon has to partner with another firm on the venture. We want to protect our people in the transition. I'm sure it won't be a problem. You'll get the details in the morning. Have a good evening now."

It's amazing how three little words can cause such big dread. Protect our people. "Can I ask what firm I'll be working with, Chuck?"

"Steadman and Associates."

# RYAN

*S*he wasn't supposed to fly coach. I wasn't supposed to fly commercial. Upon arrival yesterday, I pulled the trigger on the second plane I'd been contemplating for a backup in case of another episode of mechanical trouble. And then, I'd made arrangements for a charter home today.

What a pain it had been to even secure bulkhead, not able to help in the event of the emergency and all. It still beats first class, however, because those armrests are hazardous, with their width and inability to raise up and out of the way. I have people to handle the extra paperwork required, but no one could endure the boarding humiliation for me.

As if it wasn't bad enough, I'd heard a woman answering a phone call just outside of the plane on the crowded jet bridge. Rude and obnoxious sounding. Turning to see the offender, I wasn't surprised to see a gorgeous woman who obviously played by her own rules.

Damn that fateful flight. Returning home alone on a plush plane feels more like a forty-eight-hour roller coaster than a smooth plane ride. Up the first hill of self-induced exhilaration, then screaming downward into a valley. Challenging Cassandra Lewis wasn't one of my finer moments.

She may be known as Coldhearted Cassandra Lewis across Silicon Valley, but I had cracked the seemingly impenetrable tough veneer and hurt her. The expression on her face after my mocking during her presentation haunts me. I am not the man I used to be physically, but I am also not the major asshole that I once was. Usually.

The moment I knew we didn't see eye to eye on business philosophy should have been the last I thought of her. I undo her work, trying to put the pieces back together of the lives she tears apart. I have an entire staff of people doing less meaningful work, for pennies by comparison, than they once were because of people like her. Profit or bust, before all else. I should not sell out. I should not consider putting that flaw aside.

But.

Cassandra Lewis set something off in me I'd now spent years trying to get over as I fought, then learned to accept, the man I now am. I had tried to forget the thrill of the chase with a woman. When she slid into the seat next to me, she didn't know my handicap. Without that burden, I felt something I hadn't felt in a long time.

Hope.

Hope for the potential of having an equal partner in life. Smart, sexy, and willing to love me for who I am, despite everything I am no longer. If she fell for me before knowing my limitations, perhaps there might be a chance to see past them.

I can still smell her perfume, a mingling of lilac and hyacinth. I remember the waves of smooth brunette framing her face as if keeping their most prized possession safe behind them. Yes, I hung on too long when I said goodbye, having long been denied the touch of a woman who aroused me. Her eyes had shot daggers of insult straight in the center of my chest. Yes, I was pissed off that I let myself imagine the possibility only to be rejected.

Charlotte was one of my best partners in mending my wounded ego, and as with most of my trips to California, her dinner date was filled with compliments.

I thought she'd nursed me through my Cassandra hangover. I was wrong. Cassandra strode into the boardroom dark hair swinging from shoulder to delicate shoulder. Her athletic body hadn't been hidden by her tailored suit looking custom-made to hug her smooth curves. Her semi-sheer white blouse beneath the jacket left just enough to the imagination as to what was underneath. Muscular calves flexed with each step of her Barbie-like high-heel-clad foot.

Her oval face with the gently upturned nose and voluminous lips were soft features for her sharply angled personality. I'd thought she was pretty on the plane, but not in the everyone-does-a-double-take way. Until she was on in that boardroom. Then, she was soul-crushingly beautiful. She commanded the room like the lead on a Broadway stage, power suit her costume, the persuasive delivery a well-written script. She'd yielded power over all of us in the room, especially me.

I've spent nearly four years bouncing back from awkward, complicated and challenging. I'm adept at gratitude for what I can do. A break in my spine just an inch higher would have been so much worse. But, I took pleasure in the fact that she seemed shocked into silence upon the sight of me again. And, when we shook hands for the second time, anger surged as I recalled how she pulled away and stormed off the plane.

My gut and eyebrows twist into one tangled knot, an internal and external scowl all at once. I am not proud of my terrible-twos resemblance to a temper tantrum. I hadn't omitted the fact that I would be at her presentation on purpose. I was called in last minute and hadn't been prepped until after I'd arrived. I had, however, used her own information against her, mocking her on her own stage. I could have cost her the deal she deserved to win, but despite immature and selfish actions, my saboteur attempt was thwarted. I would never have forgiven myself otherwise. Still, I am an eleven out of ten on the douchebag scale.

In the prep session they likened Cassandra Lewis to a bull running the streets of Pamplona. Many are brave until they see what they are faced with, then they step aside as quickly as they can, lest they get speared in the ass.

Remembering the way her expression morphed at my words stabs me in the gut again. Men should protect and defend women. I had done neither. I'd waved the red flag in front of the bull. And now, I've got the pain to prove it.

But as I've had to learn, just keep moving forward. I've gotten over plenty and I'll get past her too. Work always helps.

I open my laptop to lose myself in an Excel spreadsheet where data is much easier to control than any other part of life. But attempting to manipulate the numbers in the twenty-four columns simple formulas have errors. Today, even the data won't compute. In frustration, I slam the laptop closed. Maybe I can escape in sleep instead.

No such luck. I jolt awake, head bobbing forward. Reality bites. I am always standing in my dreams. Thus, the sheer torture to awake. I had been dreaming of standing before her as she's carried away by more able-bodied men who all have an affinity for her. No escaping the chestnut-locked, porcelain-skinned woman, she's infiltrated both my conscious and subconscious mind.

It doesn't matter that I had blown my chance because I never really had a chance. Regardless, I owe her an apology for what I've done.

And, I had better hope she answers my call, because like it or not, our hand has been forced. The board had determined that Cassandra's firm would handle the acquisition, but not without us working hand in hand.

I DIAL her number as soon as the wheels touchdown on the runway, my palms sweaty like a damn teenager.

She answers on the third ring with a cool, "Cassandra Lewis."

Hearing her name again sends a familiar jagged pain straight to the center of my chest.

"Hey there. It's Ryan. Ryan Steadman," I try to sound casual. My introduction is greeted only with silence.

I know this tactic. "Using the pregnant pause on me?" I ask.

Still nothing. I know groveling is my only play here. "I'm calling to apologize. And congratulate you on your well-deserved victory."

"With no help from you. And I'm not at all pleased with my consolation prize of our partnership."

The words explode across her lips like Fourth of July fireworks.

I remind myself that while she is the enemy, there were two others like her that would have won if she did not. At least, perhaps, I have a chance to help her understand. She only knows the first half of the story, when she closes the deal, not the aftermath she leaves in her wake.

"I know you are upset. You deserve to be. I'd like to make it up to you."

"How did you get my number anyway?"

I let out a small laugh, because come on, it's funny. "The business card taped to your laptop."

"Do you steal information from everyone you sit next to on airplanes or am I the only lucky one?" Her tone is biting.

I hadn't considered the ramifications of revealing I had used not just one, but two pieces of information gathered without her knowledge. "I don't suppose it would be a good answer to say just the ones I find intelligent and beautiful?" She may not be the type to be wooed by a compliment, but it's the truth, and nothing else was on the tip of my tongue. She might hang up on me for the remark but too late, it's already out there.

"Not a good answer."

*Not a surprise.*

"And no need to make anything up to me. A seventy-two-million-dollar profit to Paragon is thanks enough. Well, I hope it's still seventy-two after you get your hands on it." It's quiet for a moment, then she softens, surprising me, "But thank you for the compliment anyway."

Is the tough-girl topcoat just that? If she is going to let her guard down, even just a little bit, then I will as well.

"If it's any consolation, I spent every hour since the meeting regretting my outburst. Your presentation was brilliant, despite my interference. My behavior was selfish and stupid."

She barely waits for me to finish the sentence, blurting out, "Why would you do that to me?"

*I'm a third-grader who pulled your pigtails because I liked you and you didn't like me back?*

"I guess you could say my ego might have gotten in the way of good judgment," I confess. "I think there is some line about a woman scorned, hell hath no fury? The same could be said for most men."

"Oh," she says quietly, and I know I have caught her off-guard with my admission.

"It wasn't you, Ryan. I just don't do relationships."

Relationship? At least I hadn't completely misjudged the mutual attraction. Before she knew my limitations physically, and professionally. "Well, like I said, I just wanted to apologize. And don't worry, I've made arrangements for you to work with a colleague of mine. We just need to have one meeting to brief him together, then you can be rid of me."

"Thank you for the apology."

"Take care, Cass."

"Y-You too," she stutters a bit, and I wonder why she returns the sentiment so shakily.

"Goodbye." I move the phone from my ear to end the call.

"Ryan?"

I hear my name, faint and distant, and lift the phone back to my ear. "Hi again."

"No one but my mother calls me Cass."

I'm not sure if she is informing me or scolding me. I'm not apologizing again for the implied transgression if it's the latter. "Well, I've never been one to follow the rules, I guess."

An unexpected burst of laughter spills on the other end of the line. "Well, I'm not one for rules either." She adds through her laugh, "But I bet that doesn't surprise you."

It definitely does not. "Not in the least," I confirm. "And good thing, because I don't like surprises. I am a Taurus, after all."

"Now there is a little something I can relate to. May 12$^{th}$ is my birthday. And you?"

"May 20$^{th}$," I answer.

"It seems we aren't so different after all then, are we?" she asks in a tone that implies an accusation, not friendly in the least. *What the hell?*

"Let's get that meeting scheduled. The sooner the better."

For a moment I almost that the ice queen had thawed. All business, I match her tone. "He's leaving Saturday morning for two weeks in China. I'll get it scheduled."

"Tomorrow it is, then."

"He might be booked all day. I'll give it a college try."

"Make it happen," she quips curtly, then quickly adds, "I need to go. Let me know."

The incorrigible Cassandra Lewis gives me whiplash.

# RYAN

$\mathcal{I}$'m the first to arrive at the restaurant. I always like to get settled in early to avoid any awkward moments. I'm not ready to navigate my world with anyone else. Every situation new, I'm still learning how to do it myself.

Dinner was the only option for meeting my colleague today, and Cassandra must have jumped at the chance to get rid of me so soon because she had confirmed by 9:00 a.m. through my colleague's executive assistant.

It's not a date, but it's still Friday night and I'm spending it with a woman instead of my usual company of fake people on Netflix.

I'm like a house staged for showing. I smell damn good if I do say so myself. It's an olfactive masterpiece of spice and wood. I read that; I didn't conjure it up. I wear the best money can buy: a two-goat Mongolian black cashmere sweater and the season's trendiest jeans. 7 for Mankind more like $700 for Steadman.

My twice-a-day workout regimen, and high protein and minimal carb, organic-whenever-possible diet, are both accompanied by top-notch professionals. I control what I can about my exterior. I'd also like to think I'm a pretty good human on the inside. Hard-earned, I've been winning battles in a multi-year, one-man war against the world. Still, there have been plenty of casualties.

I tap my finger on the wine menu. I used to own women. Rejection wasn't something I was used to. Before. Yes, at fourteen, I was awkward like all the boys, but as on any field, I could fake it until I made it. Learn the rules of the game, any game, play by the rules, play better than the competition, and win. Getting the girl was just another one of those. Hell, it even included balls. At thirty-four, I was learning a new game where I didn't know the rules and the competition had skills I couldn't acquire. I couldn't win at this game. I had stopped counting, but knew I'd attempted about two dozen dates.

I'd been set up by my brother's fiancé with a friend. Public service announcement. Don't mix romance with family and friends.

Then, I tried an overpriced matchmaker who specialized in supplying women to billionaires looking for love, not money, and found two women I was hopeful to meet. Both knew the circumstances. One I believe was studying to become a full-time caretaker and thought she might practice on me. I wanted a partner, not a caregiver.

The other believed enough love could fix anything. Even despite scientific evidence. She had once grown plants in the shade that science said couldn't grow without light. While I commended her desire to tend to something, I am not a garden. Neither the right amount of water, nor talking nicely to my severed spinal cord was going to grow it into something beautiful. I was permanently broken and living in the dark. She wasn't going to coax an unwilling body into the light.

Lastly, I thought of hiding behind the online world, as foreboding as it is for even the most able-bodied and minded. I studied all the playbooks and survival guides to online dating I could get my hands on.

There was only one online service specifically for those with a disability. In the United Kingdom. A little far for a date, and I wasn't considering a move across the pond, so I did what every self-respecting single man looking for everlasting love, as the catchy tune promised, did years ago. Joined e-Harmony with that catchy little jingle promising everlasting love. After an hour and a half shelling out most of my deepest secrets in four hundred questions, I put my future in the faith of an algorithm.

I answered the survey truthfully—my height, 6'2. What else would I say? What do you do for work, what are you passionate about, your favorite Saturday night activity?

There was no checkbox alongside the standard line of questioning about any disability, and it didn't ask if I could engage in normal couples' activities such as bike rides, long walks on the beach, and sex.

It could have said "if you answered no to any of the above, please note that we will supplement your online profile with a warning label." But it didn't. Anyway, plenty of people should come with a warning label. Everyone has something hidden in the cyber realm, don't they?

I may not have shared all my secrets, but I felt justified. I was also warned of another reason for careful online disclosure. Apparently, a cult-like group of men and women comb online dating profiles looking to satisfy a disability fetish. Yes, it is a real thing. And no, I didn't want a woman in my life if this was how I got one.

My inbox started to fill. Skipping the icebreaker and answering five more of fifty-seven questions, I did as real men should do and led. I sent messages to the matches received. Admittedly, I picked the woman with the prettiest picture first, who also happened to be only five-foot-one inch tall.

Several email conversations escalated to one all-night-long phone call after which we agreed to meet. I kept looking for the right time to tell her but never could work it into the conversation, "Hey, by the way, I am a paraplegic. It's the best of the worst; only a T12 complete. Mountain score one. Me, zero."

I didn't want to spoil the connection we had forged discussing philosophy and our parents. I hoped it was enough to overcome the obstacle. I was wrong. She felt deceived. I was devastated.

From that point forward, I explained everything in the first email.

Six women still agreed to a first date. Five showed up. I'd faced plenty of humiliation the few years prior, but the embarrassment of sitting at the table drinking a bottle of wine alone for forty minutes burned hot.

Two ghosted me after the first date.

One second date. As it turned out, she had her own reveal. It was clear she would look past anything for a deep wallet. I'd have disdain for gold-digging without the handicap, but no woman was going to Anna Nicole Smith me.

The last—and worst—of the dates were those that agreed out of pity. Nothing worse; I am still a man who wants respect. Pity orphans, the poor, elderly without family. Anyone else deserving. But do not pity me. I'd reached my lifetime quota with Melanie.

Spending the last eight months alone was a solid choice. Better than to risk more rejection.

WINE. I was ordering wine. To douse the useless emotion of self-pity. By now, I should be used to the cruel and unusual punishment of memories pulling me under like a tsunami tidal wave.

A throat clears with a masculine growl. I look up from the wine list as the maître d' delivers my non-date to me at the table. I am reminded that I can't do ordinary things. Like stand up and greet her. Of course, she might smack me anyway. That thought helps the corners of my mouth curl upward. I see her eyes dart to my cheek. The side with the dimple. Leverage all my assets.

She isn't as tall as I remember. Yesterday, she was wearing those take-me-now shoes with the sexy red bottom. No uniform of power suit and powerful presence tonight, she is like a Snapchat filter-softened picture. Tonight, she looks delicate. Feminine. Warm.

The classic day-to-night black dress she is wearing clings to her breasts and waist. It buttons up the front, circles of gold. I quickly count eight in total and ignore the fact that my fingers twitch with the possibility of undoing them.

The waist is cinched with an accompanying belt, the small buckle at her navel featuring the well-known intersecting letter "G" logo. Her hips are as athletic as I remember, but the dress pulled taut in the middle reminds me of the perfectly traceable shape of a woman.

The maître d' reaches to pull the chair out for her. She sidesteps him, her own hand on the back of its high-backed leather.

"I got it, thanks," she says dismissively.

I would have insisted if I could, but since I'm unable, I appreciate her fierce independence instead. She'd probably jump smack dab in the middle of the mud puddle before letting a man put a coat over it for her.

She sits quickly, then does allow the maître d' to assist her with moving the chair closer toward the table. What a handful of contradiction Cassandra Lewis presents.

We finally make eye contact, the iris so dark there is no delineation between it and the slim black line that encircles the color, nearly onyx. Flashes of brightness, the color of amber, dance like little rays of star bursts.

Like the wine I am about to order, she is complex.

"Nice to see you again, Ms. Lewis." I greet her with a wry smile.

"I prefer to be called Cass."

"Well then, nice to see you again, Cass." I emphasize the Cass. I am a quick study.

She resigns herself with a sigh like she's lost a battle with herself, "It's nice to see you again too."

I'm not convinced it is the truth. It's just one dinner and then she can be rid of me.

Unless.

No.

Hope isn't a guest tonight at this dinner.

"Where's your colleague?" she asks, tilting her head to the empty chair.

"He's usually late," I offer.

She looks past the waiting chair, taking in our surroundings for the first time.

Four booths line the wall to her left and my right. Each is made private by cabaret-style curtains of the same color draped ceiling to floor, mini stages hiding the scenes playing out behind them. Tall-backed, tufted faux leather in the lightest fawn cradles the players inside in a semi-circle. A tiny crystal chandelier casts a soft downward glow.

I watch her swivel side to side, taking in the rest of the restaurant. The curtains seem to absorb the sound of voices, because they are all around us, but in a low, hushed hum. The only attention-garnering sounds are the clink of silverware against plates and water being poured into glasses.

"Hmm."

She makes the little noise as she covers her face with the wine list.

"What?" I ask, wondering if she might be thinking the same thing that I am.

"Everyone here seems to be on a date."

*Everyone but us.*

"I don't even remember what that's like," she mutters barely audible behind the leather-bound book.

Now it's my turn to make the same sound, "Hmm." Not surprising, I suppose, considering what she had said yesterday about not doing relationships. A date is a little essential in getting to one.

"Well, I know it's not a date, but can I pick the wine?" I ask.

"As long as I can pick the dessert."

"Deal," I return with a smile.

"Did I hear deal? Is our work here done?" Mike has made his appearance, sliding into the open chair. "I suppose I should apologize for being late."

"I suppose you should, Sanders. At least to the lady. Mike, Cassandra. Cassandra, Mike."

Cassandra and Mike shake hands as looks around the restaurant, "Are we crashing date night? I suppose it is Friday. I guess when I told my admin only the best, she took it literally. Solo il meglio," he says in a mock-Italian accent.

"It means only the best in Italian," I add for Cassandra's benefit.

Her eyebrow cocks slightly, and if I didn't know better, I'd think I scored a brownie point. I'd learned some Italian when I had a lot of time on my hands.

"Why is there no wine on this table yet?" Mike asks with an air of impatience.

"We were just getting to that," Cassandra offers.

"Red or white?" I ask.

"Yes," she answers with a blink of her long eyelashes. What are the odds she isn't as high maintenance as I think she is?

Timely, the waiter appears.

"We'll take a 2009 Amarone, whatever you've got, please," Mike orders.

"Apparently I'm not picking the wine," I say, closing the menu and handing it to the waiter.

"Well, you've taught me well," Mike says, pointing his thumb in my direction. "This man knows his wine."

"Let me guess, 2009 is the best vintage?" Cassandra asks.

"Solo il meglio," he confirms. "Now, about that deal."

CASSANDRA and I throw numbers and figures around. Where I lack, she seems to have the answers. And vice versa. Mike looks between us as if watching a tennis match. We cover the deal structure and financials, then pause. He lifts his glass as if to toast. Which is perfect, because it helps me avoid getting to the tough part. The people she is willing to cast aside. It's going to cost her to take care of them, and she isn't going to like it.

"To a deal done well. You sure you two haven't worked together before? Why do you need me?"

He isn't off base. We did complete and complement oen another just now.

"I just thought it would be better if you handled this one, Mike. Semiconductor is your specialty, not mine."

"But yours is people, Steadman, and I thought—"

I interrupt him. "It would be best, Mike. It should be a short and sweet one. We have to close this out before the holiday."

"Whoa, whoa, whoa. You know I am out the door tomorrow, right? Two weeks in China? And then, I am taking my first vacation in a year and a half. My wife has threatened divorce if I even crack open a laptop during those two weeks." He pauses. "Sorry, Steadman, I'm more scared of telling her no than I am you."

He leans back in his chair as if to take himself physically out of the mix, and puts both hands up in the air. "I'm out, man."

I duck my head slightly and peer at him with harsh eyes. "Mike, I need a favor on this one."

He downs the last of his glass of wine. "Can't do it. And in fact, now that we have that handled, I'm missing my kid's basketball game right now, so if our work here is done, I'm going to bounce."

Before I can protest, he is standing with his coat on his arm, turned to Cassandra. "Nice to make your acquaintance, Cassandra," he says with a nod toward me. "I'm leaving you in capable hands. In fact, solo il meglio. This guy is one of the good ones."

While I appreciate the vote of confidence, I don't miss Cassandra's mouth hanging slightly agape with the announcement that she isn't getting rid of me quite as easily as she'd thought.

Mike disappears into the crowd and she turns to me, lips pressed tightly into a straight line. She relaxes with a sigh, "Well, how'd that work out for me?"

"That was an unexpected surprise. And yes, I recall you don't like surprises. I'm sorry."

*Maybe fate should be the one apologizing, not me.*

"Well, I still want dessert, so I guess at least for tonight, you are stuck with me a little longer."


SHE WASN'T KIDDING when she said she was staying through dessert, because she has ordered not one, but two of them. She swirls the sugar candied stick in her cappuccino while looking around the restaurant again.

"It's really beautiful in here. Especially the flowers."

She sounds whimsical, once again not something I'd expect from the brash businesswoman. One French-manicured fingertip traces the pink-tinged tip of the white rose floating in the metal rectangular bowl in the center of our table. Two candles share the space, bobbing as she displaces the water with her touch of the flower. Their flames flicker with the motion, reflecting off the metal like little shooting stars. My mom taught us to wish on each one we saw streaking across the sky. Too bad I've given up on wishes.

"Do you have a favorite?" I ask, pointing to the flower.

"Flower? Really? That seems like a question for a date." Her face contorts into a face that implies she is revolted by the thought.

"Did your mother ever tell you that if you keep your face like that it might stay that way? I seem to bring out the smirk in you."

The semi-perma smirk she has worn all night rolls into laughter. Her shoulders shrug, "Okay, you win. Depends on the season. Winter, lily of the valley. Spring, peony hands down. Summer, sweet pea. And fall, the dahlia."

A moment ago, I wasn't expecting an answer at all. Now I have four, "It's never simple, is it?"

"I bet wanted to add three more words to that sentence. Thank you for not."

"Are you referring to with a woman or with Cassandra Lewis as the three words?" I ask coyly.

She answers my question with one of her own, "So, you're an Italian-speaking amateur sommelier and mind reader also?"

"You forgot to add flower purveyor. I wish it wasn't rude to take my phone out for notes. Just in case I ever need to apologize again."

By the unwarranted, scathing look she hurls across the table I have a feeling it would take more than flowers.

"I guess you weren't planning on sharing." I wouldn't dream of getting in the way of her spoon the way she's been enjoying the dessert.

"If you had tried to steal a bite, I'd have stabbed you with my fork." She tosses tendrils of her sleek brown locks over her shoulders with a childlike laugh.

"You're eating with a spoon."

"I'd still find a way to maim you."

*Somehow, I don't think this is far from the truth.*

I realize how quiet everything around us has become. I thought it was my focus on her, but when I look around, we are the lone two guests for the evening. The bustling of servers attending to crowded tables of patrons has quieted.

As if she notices at the same time, she waves her spoon in the air with her final bite. "I guess it's a good thing I'm done with my two desserts. I think they might want us out of here."

"I think you might be right." We still have a deal to get done after we leave here, we will need to see each other again whether she likes it or not. "Are we going to be able to make this work?"

She contemplates for several seconds, picking at the cuticle on her thumb before finally catching my gaze again. Her dark eyes scan my face, what she's looking for I am not sure.

With an air of hesitancy, she finally asks, "Do we really have a choice?" She picks her spoon up again, holding it vertically before me. "But beware, I'm bringing the spoon to our next meeting."

My lips don't comply with my brain's request to stifle a smile. This woman who wields a veneer of steel amongst the wealthy, cutthroat and merciless industry of tycoons has let lighthearted surface for several moments tonight.

She cracks through the last bite of burnt sugar topping the crème brûlée. "I just love this dessert." Licking her lips as she swallows the last bite she adds, "It's like a soft, creamy surprise hidden underneath the hard, burned sugar."

My lips curl once more into the smile that Cassandra seems to put on my face often. *You don't say.*

# CASSANDRA

*A* real live doorman, looking the part with a top hat and long black velvet jacket, greets me by name when I halt to a stop in front of the building. The number 222, the address Ryan provided, is elegantly etched into the glass of the double doors of the entrance. Since I leave again on Monday, we agreed to meet for a short time today, even though it's Saturday. We need to tie off on what we will each handle over the coming two weeks.

The doorman introduces himself as Marty, escorting me inside a building I am sure was recently decrepit. Block by block, the 1920 – 1930's masterpieces are being renovated and renewed with offices, residential and retail space. Inside, accents of gold shimmer.

The late Saturday sunshine spills through a stained-glass window perched above the wide-framed double doors. The gold and glass rival any Catholic church I've been in. Refurbished woodwork has moldings and buttresses traipsing across the two-story ceiling from the front of the building to rooms down the hallway beyond the elevator bank.

"Pretty spectacular, isn't it?" Marty asks, allowing me time to look around before stretching his arm in the direction of the room in front of me. "Mr. Steadman's done a great job with it. You can wait in here and I'll let him know you've arrived."

I step into what is obviously a library, being it is filled with books and all. It also has a floor-to-ceiling fieldstone fireplace with two very sittable chairs in front of it. They look like two strutting peacocks, bright blue, with a colorful spotted pattern, and wide horseshoe-shape backs resemble fanning feathers.

I drag my pointer finger along a row of classic titles I haven't seen since high school. Moby Dick, Of Mice and Men, Little Women, Wuthering Heights. Great Expectations. I'm sure the books are imposters, not originals, but still, it's an expansive collection. Books line the entire wall, with a tall ladder that one could climb to reach those higher. Looks like an insurance nightmare, but it sure is a nice decoration. Who dusts up there?

The elevator dings in the hallway and I turn on my heel toward the sound. Ryan emerges and stops before me. Just like the airplane, the boardroom, and last night when I entered the restaurant, his presence makes it a little harder to breathe. And speak. And my heart to beat without an arrythmia. Haven't my lungs and heart possessed their skills since birth? It's rather annoying.

"Thanks for coming here today. I see you found the library. How do you like it? Are you much of a reader?"

"I like it. Very much. Makes me want to curl up with a book in one of those chairs, but no, um, I don't read often. For work yes, fun, not so much."

Pointing at the wall of books, he asks, "If you were picking a classic, do you have a favorite?"

I don't. Feel to judge my lack of cultural prowess. I answer his question with a question, "What would you guess would be my favorite?"

He throws his head back with a laugh. "That's an easy one. Pride and Prejudice. Have you at least seen the movie?"

Lips sealed into a straight line, I shake my head side to side slowly.

"Two-hundred years later, so many relevant life lessons. Let's start with this one. You can't hide in a library forever."

Now it's my turn to laugh. "You got me. I'd rather hang out with the books than get to work."

"Well, I'd rather hang out watching football than work, too, but that's for later."

He proceeds to the elevator, and I follow. He presses the button for the third floor and looks up at me. "You know our rivals are playing later?"

"No, I didn't know."

"So, you don't read, and you don't do football? What *do* you do, Cassandra Lewis?" he asks.

"Oh, my favorite question with my favorite answer. I *work*, Ryan. That's what I do."

"There is more to life than work, Ms. Lewis," Ryan says as we exit the elevator and turn left down the hallway to a wall covered in frosted glass.

Irritated, I suggest, "You can save the public service announcement, Mr. Steadman. How about we do what I do best and get to work?"

Ryan reaches his palm forward and places it flat on a black surface on the wall. The door opens automatically into an open space. It still has the new office smell, the coat of gray-beige paint fresh and unmarred.

This office has all the markings of open-office trendy. Exposed pipes painted black on the high ceiling, exposed brick on the exterior wall.

Futuristic technology is infused among the five farmhouse-type tables which form a semicircle in front of the floor-to-ceiling windows. I take in the breathtaking view of the river below. It feels like we are soaring over the city abuzz with cars starting and stopping at the lights below.

Ryan grabs a remote from the table and presses a button. A screen drifts down from the ceiling. I unpack the papers from my bag and spread them across the table, ready to get started.

We work the facts and figures side by side, and like Mike had said at dinner, we are good together. I sneak a sideways glance at him. His pen scribbles across the paper, arrows pointing here and there. His lips purse, the pen against the bottom one as he's thinking. I wish I didn't notice that I'm jealous of the pen. This should not be a thing. His elevator PSA was a perfect strike three. He used my yoga line against me, stole data from the airplane and could have cost me the deal, and basically called me boring.

If only his smell next to me wasn't so damn intoxicating.

It's not as if I have to escape a magnetic pull or avoid drowning in quicksand. I have options! I stand and move away from him, proving he's no kryptonite. I need a new perspective on the numbers anyway. Moving closer to the screen also gets me closer to the window, where I admire the view again.

"If you like that view, I've got an even better one for you," he says, my eyes drifting away from the window and back to meet his gaze. Today in a navy v-neck sweater, his eyes chameleon to take on a deeper blue like the river outside. Their mischievous twinkle hasn't changed, however.

"Like the penthouse view?" I rebut facetiously.

"Yes, like that one," he says completely straight faced but I see the amusement in his eyes.

"Well, I guess a tour is in order then," I say, starting to pack up the papers we have finished working on, thinking I am being funny. I stuff them in my purse and hang it over my shoulder. "Let's go," I say flippantly.

Methodically, he stacks the papers in front of him and neatly aligns them. He hands them up to me, and serious as a heart attack, says, "Let's go."

I STILL THINK he is messing with me when we enter the elevator. He presses the same black surface with his palm but doesn't press a button. He looks up at me with a smirk. "You thought I was kidding, didn't you?"

50

It's best I just nod rather than speak.

I step off the elevator. Not into a hallway as I expected, but I presume into his house. Like the middle of it. I know my brows rise, as much as they can with Botox, and I narrow my eyes so he gauge my reaction. Wow forms silently on my lips.

I walk forward to the wall straight before me, all glass, and framing a breathtaking view of the Detroit skyline nestled snuggly along the river's edge. A waterfront panorama of art deco, post-modern spires, and Victorian architecture rises up from the riverbank into the expanse of today's clear blue, each claiming its space and place in history next to one another.

On the other side of the river, the smaller skyline of Canada seems to wave to its neighbor, and I marvel at the fact that I can see two countries in this one spectacular image.

I tear myself away from the view because the inviting smells wafting from the kitchen are overwhelmingly delicious. Several people scurry about the kitchen, which is the size of my entire first floor. My head swivels left, finding a long table set with high-end metal and ceramic serving dishes.

"Party today?" I question.

"Just a few people for the football game."

I nod in acknowledgment but am eager to take in the rest of the surroundings. I'm not sure what I was expecting, but I thought it would be more obvious that it was suited for a wheelchair.

Beyond the party- prepped table, what looks to be a living room cozies up and stretches around a corner. Modern cozy is my best description, but I think that's an oxymoron. Gray walls and dark woods feel contemporary, but the oversized couches beckon, and two large love sacs sit in the corner with post meal calorie coma written all over them.

There are few knick-knacks, nautical in theme. Large ropes, depth maps, and four oversized compasses hang on the wall beside me. I point toward them, "It's good to know those are available in case I get lost in here."

He laughs at me from the kitchen where he pauses from chatting with the others. "If you are with me you will always be found."

Well, that was an unlikely response.

"I'm good with geography," he adds, as if needing to explain.

*Like you can find your way around a woman's body?*

I walk forward to the kitchen where everything seems automated, with no handles on the oven, refrigerator, or dishwasher. I feel like I am in the Jetsons cartoon and I've flown into the future somehow.

Ryan must notice that I am taken aback because he asks, "Do you cook?"

"Um," I hesitate, because I feel like the proper answer is yes, but the real one is hell no.

"Do you pour a mean wine?"

He reads between the lines.

"No, but I'm pretty good with a nice one."

"Well, in that case, let's have you take your pick."

Thirty-ish floors ago I was getting this deal done and back to my life. There is a problem, however. What I glimpse past the kitchen is irresistible. I can barely see the outline of rows of bottles. Lots and lots of them.

Lights pop to life, albeit dim, behind a smoky gray glass door with a decorative espresso-colored wooden frame. The door magically floats open and I follow Ryan inside as the door closes, capturing us in an eerie silence.

We are surrounded by a plethora of pink, white, and red wine from all over the globe. Each region is labeled with a world map etched in gold. I run my fingers over an engraved nameplate that says Rosado – Spain, then walk to another reading Shiraz – New Zealand.

The white is held in a futuristic refrigerator behind glass looking all industrial and badass. On each wall is a keypad, vending machine style, for making a selection of those that are too high for me to acquire.

"See anything you like?"

*You? Oh, and the wine.*

"Suggestions?" I question. "Choosing from what—" I hesitate to do quick math, and make an educated guess, "like three-hundred bottles is a little daunting!"

"Seven hundred sixty-one as soon as you pick one. Try the wall straight ahead. E61."

I press the keypad and a motorized arm rises up the wall nearly to the top.

"I'm top shelf-worthy?" I ask with a flutter of my eyelashes and know damn well it crosses the line to flirting.

"I owe you. It's an apology of sorts. And, only the best to celebrate your victory."

Oh, that. And, reality check. My victory won't be as sweet when he tears it apart.

The noise of the arm pulling the bottle forward distracts me. A small metal cage splays open then closes around the bottle protectively. It slides down a vertical rod, stopping just in front of me. The cage opens again, and the bottle is waiting in front of me. I return to the doorway cradling the bottle to my chest. I spin around the room one last time, taking it all in. "I'm never coming out of here."

"You are going to be awfully drunk," he says with a smile as delicious as I know this wine will be.

*Without even a sip, I might already be on my way.*

TWO GLASSES and a wine opener that looks like it could perform some type of surgery are already arranged on the counter when we emerge.

"Thanks, Jacqueline," Ryan says with a wink in the direction of an apron-clad woman reaching into the oven. "I'd introduce you properly if you didn't have your hands full. This is Cassandra."

She looks over and smiles a large, friendly smile in my direction. "Nice to meet you."

Ryan easily removes the cork from the bottle and pours a full glass, sliding it toward me. He starts to move away from the counter, but I remain in place. "I'm not drinking alone!" I remark. The revelation hits me. It would be impossible for him to carry wine. I reach for the bottle and fill his glass half-way without a word. He takes it from the counter, lifts it to meet mine, and we clink glasses then take a sip. Its scent and taste are heavenly.

"Want a tour of the other floors?"

*Of course, there are floors. Not a floor.*

"Um, sure?" It sounds like a question, but I've never been so sure. *How exactly did curiosity kill the cat?*

WE MAKE our way back into the elevator. I am still in awe of the fact that it spills into his house. When the doors at floor five open directly into another room, I shouldn't be surprised. It's a gym, big enough for the building, but with only one of each item and nothing to be used standing, clearly it's for his personal use.

"No workout required today. I just wanted you to see the view. It's a little different through each window on each floor. Kind of like life; you get a different perspective depending on how you are looking at things."

I bypass the equipment and head straight to the wall of glass which slides open before me. I step outside, barely noticing the cold. The balcony must jut ten feet out from the building. "Oh my God!" I squeal in delight. The view from upstairs had buildings stacked beside one another, but from this lower vantage point, what you see is the river. "It's like you are floating on the water! Can I just stand out here and pretend to swim and call it a workout?"

"Not sure if the fake river swim will cover you for the Tim Horton's sprinkle donut calories. But if you really want to swim, you probably want to skip the cold and dirty river and use the indoor pool. Whatever you like, though," he says, joking.

He had me at donut. I'm stunned he remembered what I'd told him at dinner.

I'M STARTLED by another person's presence. "Hey, Ryan." A male voice from afar.

"Balcony," Ryan returns loudly, gruff alpha-male tone.

A hand is reaching toward mine, "Hi, I'm Chris."

He is a sculpted version of a man to say the least. At least, I think he's a man. It's unfair to the clothes trying to contain his muscles. If I make him mad, I'm positive they'll rip open while he turns green before my eyes like the Hulk.

"Cassandra. Nice to meet you."

"Thought I'd get here a little before the game to make sure we are all set for Monday."

"Cool," Ryan returns.

"You are a football fan?" Chris asks me with a suspicious smile.

"Only when it's Northwestern," I quip.

"They have a football team?" This time he flashes a crooked, teasing smile then turns back to Ryan. "Feisty and likes football. Just your type, Steadman."

"No, it's not like th—" Ryan jumps in to correct Chris, but he's already disappeared, leaving the possibility lingering. "Sorry about that, Cassandra."

I shrug and start to walk inside where I see Chris put his palm against another black screen. He enters a series of numbers on a keypad. A series of clicks and beeps follow, then quiet, with the windowless door opening. What could be so secretive it would require that level of security? My imagination gets the best of me and I think of Christian Gray's red room.

Daydream interrupted, Ryan asks, "Ready for more?"


"More wine or another stop?" Ryan asks as we return to the elevator.

"I'll pass on the wine." I need to keep my wits about me. "But I'll take you up on another stop. Then I should really get going."

"I'd like you meet a few people. Can you stay for the game? Our rivals should be a good matchup." He presses an unmarked button at the top of the column of elevator buttons.

I contemplate the offer. On one hand I want to get the hell away from him, but on the other hand I am more than intrigued by what I've learned about him today, and what I still want to know. My list of questions is accumulating. Was he hurt in an accident? Suffer an illness? Born unable to walk? What's behind that door? How does he occupy so many floors of this building? Family money? New money?

And now, at quick glance upon the elevator doors sliding open, I have practical questions too. How do trees grow up here? How haven't the leaves changed color in the November cold and shortened days? I net it out in my head. I am going to need to stick around for longer than I had been expecting to get all the answers I need. I compromise with myself. "Maybe until halftime."

My jaw dropped the moment the doors opened, and I've made no effort to close my gaping mouth. We're on the rooftop. I've always seen the buildings with greenery on the top and thought it looked cool, but I had no idea it could be like this. I can't hide my wonder, wandering around and looking up at the trees. Yes, trees. Their trunks are spaced six feet apart as not to block the skyline view, but their leaves reach toward each other, tangling into a canopy of arches. A shorter hedgerow traverses between the trees, perfectly squared at ninety-degree angles.

Old-fashioned light bulbs sway in the breeze, strung across half the expanse. A gas fire pit like I've only seen at hotels. It's a European courtyard meet Central Park with its magical ambiance.

I stumble toward the hot tub, which is more the size of a small pool, but the steam gives it away.

"You like it?" he asks, rhetorically of course. "Go long," he says, catching me off-guard.

Again. "What?"

He raises a football in his left arm, ready to throw.

"Oh! That kind of long," I exclaim, backing closer to the edge of the rooftop.

It rolls through the air to me in a perfect spiral. I catch it into my chest with a thud.

"Nice catch," he says, eyes twinkling with a grin.

"Thanks. But the throw—" I release the ball. I throw like a girl, but luckily, it's not that far and he reaches up, grabbing the ball from the air.

"Come here," he says. "Want a tip for the perfect spiral?"

I saunter toward him. Why did I just acquiesce to his bossy command? "I'm not sure. Is it going to cost me?"

"Perhaps," he says as he spins the ball around, positioning the laces on top. I see a date written in the black ink of a Sharpie. 10-18, and the numbers beneath it, 49-7. His eyes catch mine when I look up from seeing it. "Game ball. Forty-two of the forty-nine points were mine. Still pissed about their seven."

"Hold onto the past much?"

He bristles.

As soon as the words leave my lips, regret hits me like one of the linemen that probably tackled him while racking up those points. I'm invasive-cancer evil. What if it was football that landed him in the wheelchair?

"I'm sorry." How do I make it up to him? Do I ask about the game on the ball? The position he played?

Are the memories painful or has he made peace?

"No worries, Cass," he offers softly, but a rumble of guilt still rattles around my insides. Only for a moment though, because in the next moment I am distracted by the warmth of his hand capturing my small one in his as he guides it to the back of the ball. "See this line? Put your pinky right there." He delicately moves my finger into position, his hand still resting on top of mine on the ball. "Got it?" I swallow hard and nod as his eyes penetrate me.

Blowing out a breath, I cross the distance of the rooftop patio again, holding the ball tightly in position. I cock my right arm and release the ball. The perfect spiral travels well past Ryan and lands just inside the glass wall encircling us. I hide my surprised expression behind both hands, then pull them away. "Oh my God, I almost just lost your game ball!"

I retrieve the ball, tossing it gently back to him.

"I was more worried about you killing someone if it went over the edge, but you have quite the arm, Lewis."

*Being called Lewis is so much better than princess.*

I lean against the railing, underneath one of the green archways. I look away from the view and back to him. "So, the roof, the penthouse, the gym and the offices. Was it hard to commandeer so many floors of this building?"

A sly smile forms as he looks up at me. "You forgot the ground-level coffee shop. Ellie and Jay brew an excellent espresso." He looks off into the distance like he might be formulating what to say next. Then he looks back at me. "I had first dibs on the space. I own the building."

I know I gulp before, "Oh. I suppose so then," sputters out. "So, the library? That's yours too?"

He nods. "Yes, those are my books."

"Why the lobby instead of on one of your floors?"

"I wanted to offer them to the others. Books are better shared."

A valiant act of show? Or less of a jerk than I judged? "How nice of you, Ryan," slides out, with sarcasm its sidekick. I guess my subconscious decided it was the former not the latter. "It sounds like you barely need to leave the building."

His eyebrows dip downward into a deep v shape, and for the second time, guilt pummels me. What if that was exactly his intention?

# RYAN

*N*ailed it. Like JFK did Marilyn. If only she knew what an understatement she had just stumbled on. I didn't intend to tell her I owned the building, but it presented itself, and I feel a little glib that I left her wondering about the how and why.

It's a story for another day, should there be another day.

On the flip side, I'm a little pissed she didn't believe I share the library with the others out of the goodness of my heart. Though, I guess I've given her enough cause to doubt it. And what happens next isn't going to change her mind either.

WE RETURN TO THE PENTHOUSE, and I watch Cassandra's eyes widen when she sees the spread that looks like today's hometown haul. I've flown in the best red shells and pink tails Boston has to offer. It's a crying shame the aphrodisiac powers of the dozens all these oysters will go to waste.

As Cassandra's eyes settle on the stacked tower of two dozen pink-frosting sprinkled donuts, her face brightens, eyes wide. She exclaims excitedly, high-pitched and girlish, "Oh my gosh! I'm having three of these for dessert, after the oysters. Is that gross? Donuts and oysters? That sounds gross. Oh well!"

She shrugs it off and then, like she owns the place, strides back to the bottle of wine where we have left it. Lifting the bottle into the air, she says, "Good thing everything pairs with wine!"

She pours a fresh glass for each of us and returns, smiling broadly. I look at her from head to toe as we each take a sip. I wasn't wrong to tell Charlotte to look out for Armani and attitude.

With her Stella, Gucci, and Louboutins, she looks the part of success. But while she might wear high-end, high-brow as a veil, underneath it seems to be a childlike innocence. It's too bad I am about to wreck our play date, because I intend for her to leave feeling plenty guilty.

WITH THE PUSH OF A BUTTON, the pre-game show comes to life on the wall extending the length of my living room. It affords the experience of being as close to a football sideline as I've come in a long while. Carefully crafted sound comes from every corner of the room as if you are surrounded by the cheering crowd. It's better than any bar and almost as good as being in the stadium.

My game-watching crowd begins to arrive. It isn't long before Cassandra is happily mingling. Not surprisingly, the woman knows how to work a room.

While in the kitchen, I overhear her ask Georgia Taylor what she does for work. "I used to run a tech company but now I'm with Steadman and Associates," she tells Cassandra, and I have to smile when she adds with a laugh, "Ryan is the only great boss I've had other than myself."

In the living room, I hear Mack McCallister with his untamed accent, all Irish and angsty even though he's now sober, tell my barista Jay, "Don't know where I'd be if Steadman hadn't dragged my sorry-ass drunk self from the street. Who knew losing a job could bring a man to his knees?" I didn't miss that Cassandra was leaning toward the conversation to eavesdrop.

I watch as she makes her way to the kitchen and quietly asks the name of first the woman, then the man who are shuffling pans and dishes from the countertops to the sink and cupboards. She shakes her head perplexed when I hear them answer.

Cassandra and I make eye contact. Rather, her eyes are daggers boring holes into my face. She hikes her purse up onto her shoulder and straightens. Her eyes dart to the bottle of wine still on the counter. She pushes the cork into the bottle and stuffs it into her purse before she stomps the five steps to me, crossed arms in a pissed-off posture.

"What the hell is going on here?" she bends toward me and seethes in a whisper.

"What do you mean?" My calm demeanor seems to ratchet up her intensity.

She asks again, more firmly, "I mean, what is going on here? Who are these people?"

"Friends."

*How do I explain they are so much more? I save them. They save me.*

"Like hell they are. Did you hire these people and pay them to tell me how wonderful you are? Was this a setup?"

*Not exactly where I thought she was going.*

"I can't be bought with good wine and food and—" her arm flails toward the donuts, then she walks over, removes the top one from the stack and takes a bite as if there was no way she was leaving here without a taste. I hold back a smile because I'm sure to incur additional torture if I tell her about the crumbs on the left side of her lower lip, all full and pouty.

"And, those people..." She's trying to whisper and it comes out like a hiss. "There is no way that every one of these people has some story about your sainthood. Not some story. The same story. They aren't real. They can't be." Her arm waves wildly again, like swatting an invisible fly, toward the kitchen. "Those people won't even tell me their real names. They said they were Bonnie and Clyde."

I can't hold back my lips curving upwards. I had told Mark and Shelley just yesterday how nice it was they didn't mind getting their hands dirty. We were talking about one of the real-estate deals, but since they had a football specialty menu, they insisted on cooking today; it just happened they were on duty in the kitchen.

Her head spins left, right, then left again.

Mine tilts to follow along, questioning what the hell she's doing.

Snarky, with a tone of disdain, she says, "Where are the cameras? I'm getting punk'd or something, right?"

"Let's be clear. I didn't put *anyone* up to *anything*," I stake my ground, steady with the simple truth. I was a misfit and discarded. I knew how it felt to be exiled from everything one knows. So yes, I bankroll these people because I understand their challenges. Challenges people like she and others imposed. I did what I could, and they were grateful.

"Was today all for show? For the deal? Did you bring me here to see how you've had to build your own little world with your own little people so I would feel guilty?"

*Yes, Cassandra. I did. But not for me.*

"Did you think that would make me cave to your demands? I did my research, and I thought your life was hard. But you seem to have it all."

She points at the Patek Philippe on my wrist. A gift from a client. I have other ways of spending my own money.

"Do you have millions? Billions? Money six ways from Sunday, a building, *and* a houseful of friends?"

She puts air quotes around the last word then continues her whisper-yell scathingly, "No one calls me Cass, Ryan. You know why? Because they call me other things. Phone a friend if you haven't heard. This deal is done. You aren't getting what you want. No one sets me up."

With a turn on the heel of whatever designer boot she is wearing, she stomps to the exit, repeatedly stabbing at the button even as the private elevator door opens nearly instantaneously.

Chris passes Cassandra as she exits, heading toward me with an empty plate. "What the hell just happened?"

"I'm not sure, really. Apparently, you all said too many good things about me."

He looks at me like I am speaking a foreign language, then offers, "Maybe she just doesn't believe there are any good guys left." He shrugs it off, nonchalant, grabs another handful of crab claws, then looks back at me. "You want to take it out on me later?"

I appreciate his offer. "You know I do."

"Working out girl problems is new ground for us. Hope I'm up for it."

"It's not a girl problem, Chris. Just a business one."

"Like hell it is, Steadman."

*Too bad for me, Chris knows me better than I know myself.*


GAME-FACE HOSTING post Cassandra's departure became tiring by the fourth quarter. At least my team got the job done. I'm pissed at myself. And drunk. Cassandra went for the jugular and the low blow in a one-two punch. Her accusation wasn't entirely wrong. I had built my own world and I had bought people. And, yes, I hoped it would bide well for my negotiation if she could put faces to names when I propose what I am going to.

I knew it was a risk and I deserved punishment, but still, she was a little harsh. As is her work. I should have known better. Not only did she warn me, but her reputation preceded her.

Regardless of today's outcome with one coldhearted woman, I am proud of what I've made of myself, a long way from the death spiral I once faced.

There is no shame making sunshine so the cast-asides can hide in the shadows. Once revered CEOs tarnished by failure just need a little ego care and feeding, and time to rebound, once cast aside. I buy them time for the rest of the world to forget, and for them to lick their wounds from the tumble of hero to zero.

I take the guts of their former companies and incubate new ones, growing a whole family of companies on several floors of this building. Some have stayed and some have moved on, but all remain friends, and most feel indebted. It's not loyalty I asked for, but I am honored to have earned it.

AT LEAST I'VE had enough practice to know what will help when I hit another bottom. I arrive to the gym and shake my head vigorously to clear my buzz from overconsumption. Too much wine. Too much Cassandra.

Chris strides through the door right beside me. He isn't just my trainer. He's a friend. And my partner in researching some potentially new business opportunities that could mean a whole lot more to me and others than money ever could.

Now that we are away from the crowd, he stands back to assess what he is dealing with. He looks at me sideways through eyes narrowed to slits, "How bad is it?"

"Go hard," I reply.

"On it." With a couple of swipes to his phone, the sound of bass reverberates throughout the gym.

Two sets into the warm-up, I drop the weight to the rubber mat on the floor with a therapeutic groan. I see Chris' head cock side to side as he's thinking. He disappears into a closet and comes back. A set of gloves for me and target mitt for him. Perfect.

I pour out everything pent up from the day in my fists flying and being swallowed by his mitt until a wave of nausea sweeps over me. I wish the puke tinging the back of my teeth was from the drinking, but it coincides with waves of memories. I retreat and breathe in shallow, ragged gasps.

"That was intense, Steadman. What's up? Talk to me."

A scream from deep within has me pounding the gloves into my own legs. It's not like it hurts. I can't talk to him except through my fists.

"Okay, let's go." Chris starts bouncing, squatting low in front of me. "Hit me. Best shot. Go!" He is in my face and loud.

I punch forward. Right. Left. Left.

The first workout in rehab. A semblance of the body I was before a five-week hospital stay.

Jab right. Jab right. Pound the left fist into Chris' mitt.

There was no physical pain since I couldn't feel a God damn thing, but the pain was from Melanie on the sidelines. I had a life. We had a wedding planned.

Left. Left. Left.

"That's good, Ryan," Chris yells over the loud thud of my punches.

Wrong thing to say, Chris. I barrage him with a series of uncontrolled hits. I hear Melanie's voice in his words, sickening, "That's good, Ryan! Good job! You've got this, baby." Melanie visiting rehab after my first week is the most painful memory of all. Her own little cheering section in the corner of my ring where I took on opponent after opponent in an infinite number of grueling rounds. Maybe I would declare victory. Maybe I'd get knocked out. Maybe I'd just forfeit.

She brought her best cheerleader. It wasn't meant to be condescending, but it shook me to the core. Baby was always her nickname for me, but the word was the death of the man I used to be by a million papercuts. I was relegated to feeling helpless as a baby. I couldn't piss, couldn't bathe myself, didn't know if I'd ever have sex again. Everything a man is supposed to be, I wasn't. The only thing I was was weak and fallible.

Chris steps back for a break but quickly moves back into position. "Give it to me!" he belts.

Guttural groans from my core accompany my angry fists.

The final blow. Melanie's face when I was learning to transfer from my chair to another. I could see her reflection in the large wall mirror of the facility. Biting her always perfectly manicured nails. When I stumbled through my first several attempts the combination of pity and disgust was unmistakable. She turned away to stop watching.

I place one more blow to Chris' mitt. A strong left hook sends him careening backwards. He catches himself with a stagger but almost goes down.

"Damn, Steadman!" he says, pacing to catch his breath. "Uncle! Only a woman could get under your skin like that."

I throw the gloves to the ground and wipe my brow with the back of my arm. He tosses me a towel and a water bottle. He thinks I am pissed about Cassandra, not Melanie.

"That wasn't about who you think."

"You could have had me fooled."

Both of our breathing is still coming in pants.

"That was about my ex. My fiancée."

"Oh, man. I didn't know."

"I know. It wasn't worth mentioning."

His eyebrows rise in disbelief.

"I'm just pissed. I lost it all. I used to be a dick and take women for granted. More than most I know, but this seems like harsh karma. I'd give anything just to have another fight with a woman. I'd take the worst day I ever had. The worst sex. I'd take it. I want another chance. The good and the bad. All of it. I need another chance."

"I can't imagine you'd be this jacked if it went well today with Cassandra. I saw the way she looked at you. There was something there. I wouldn't rule her out yet. Give it time."

*Sorry Chris, but patience isn't going to fix this problem.*

Chris squats low in front of me. Our torsos match, but I envy the size and strength of his legs. Mine used to rival his. Until I watched the atrophy wither them down to slim and unmanly remnants. His strong muscles are another reminder of what I've lost. I know it's not his fault, but I'd kick him in his pretty face if I could.

"You're alive, and tomorrow's another day to fight. At least you've got something to fight for. I know you've got some fight left in you because you damn near knocked me on my ass. It's not like before, Ryan. You've got this."

He's right. I've got this. This isn't depression that feels like a lead cloak pulling me to the bottom of a life-starved ocean. This won't throw me back into an agoraphobic state.

My thoughts won't tumbleweed, avalanche, or any other litany of catastrophic metaphors into the dark place I've already been and crawled out of.

Not even a woman as desirable as Cassandra Lewis could induce another death spiral, because I've already faced death and kicked its ass. Still hurts tonight though. As much as when I awoke after the accident to my own private hell.

# CASSANDRA

"Cecil, you are a sight for sore eyes."

He tips his hat and gives me a little bow as he opens the door for me. I'm genuinely happy to see him again, needing all the pick me up I can get to get through the next two days."

"Nice to see you, Ms. Lewis. Looks like you need yourself some California."

He's right. I do need to see sunshine. I do need a view of the ocean. What I don't need, however, is to be in the same room with Ryan Steadman. I don't even want to be in the same state.

I notice his cane as he moves for the handle of my suitcase. "Oh no, Cecil, what happened?" I take the suitcase toward the trunk myself and he follows, with much less of a limp than previously.

"I'm good, Ms. Lewis." With gentle insistence, he reaches for my bag and loads it into the trunk. I let him, not wanting to hurt his pride.

"The sun is shining. In the sky and on me. I'm a lucky man. Turns out, I got that old knee replaced. Two weeks ago, I was like an old dog. Now I'm getting back to spring chicken." He belts out a laugh, music to my ears. "I'm not supposed to be back to work yet, but I couldn't let anyone else take care of you."

"Oh, Cecil, you didn't have to do that for me. But that's fantastic! I thought you were going to wait a few more years."

"Well, Ms. Lewis, I got a little Hail Mary thrown my way. I've got another client that, turns out, has a heart bigger than gold. My pride told me no, but my pain told me to take him up on his offer."

"That's great, Cecil. I'm really happy for you."

"I got a new knee since I saw you, but how about you? You get anything new? Maybe a puppy or kitten or a fish or something? You know it's good to have something to love, Miss Cassandra."

He sounds like my mother. "Haven't I mentioned I don't do fur or feathers?"

His hearty laugh fills the vehicle, my ears, and my heart.

"I don't want you to be lonely. I know you're married to your work but there's more to life than that. I'm just sayin'."

Now he sounds like Ryan. And that's just annoying. But now that I am thinking about him, I can't help but wonder what the next few days will bring. I close my eyes and pull a long breath in, remembering the last inhale of lily of the valley fragrance that filled my foyer this morning. I'd been smelling the sweetness of the near bush sized bouquet since the Sunday after the football fiasco. Oh, Ryan, if only flowers could buy you forgiveness. I am not that easy.

All those people with stories of how Ryan had pulled them from the wreckage of their lives. It's never bothered me before that others hardly sing *my* praises. Until now. Maybe I can fake it 'til I make it. Starting with a gift for Cecil.

I glance at my watch. Plenty of time. "Cecil, you know how you always ask me if there is something that I need?"

"Yes, ma'am."

"You are a little late with the question today." I say it with a wide smile, so he infers I am not harboring any real hard feelings. "I have something I need."

"Yes, ma'am. Sending my biggest sorry to the backseat. I didn't mean to delay asking. Anything you need, Ms. Lewis?"

"I need a lunch date," I offer, noticing how my chest feels. Full. Happy. Different. "I know you aren't supposed to be working so I hope you don't try to use that as an excuse." I offer a wink along with my smile.

"Maybe I didn't go to that college up the road," he says referring to Stanford, which is just miles from where we are, "but I know you aren't the kind of woman who takes no for an answer."

"Smart man, Cecil. So, I guess that's a yes?"

"Yes, ma'am. It'd be my honor to accompany you to lunch."


THE NEXT MORNING, I armor up for battle with four shots of espresso. My confidence is fueled by the caffeine, Cecil's morning compliments, and a new Caroline Herrera suit. I almost bought Armani but wouldn't give whoever "they" were the satisfaction. I didn't need to suit up with attitude though. I have plenty stored up.

I stride through the lobby to an awaiting Charlotte, who looks up with the first echo of my high-heeled step toward her. Her lips turn up to greet me. "Guurrrl," she drawls, "those shoulders look like wings today! You're a carbon-copy of Nike. You know her, right? Goddess of Victory?" Something about her strikes me as working below her paygrade potential.

"Good morning, Charlotte," I deliver smoothly, though I feel jittery inside. Might have overdone the caffeine this time.

She leans in, like she is going to gift me with another little secret between us girls. "They are expecting you. They say they're prepared for you to try to do what you do best: in, out, and clean."

Truth. That was the plan. Those are my words and I own it. "When you say they, might you be referring to R—"

"Good morning, Cassandra," a man's booming voice startles me. He's been stealth-like in his approach. Maybe if I wasn't distracted. It pisses me off he's interrupted before I got my answer.

"A moment, Mr. Edwards?" Charlotte looks directly at the man I don't know, who looks more than eager to acquiesce, eyeing Charlotte like a glass of champagne he'd like to swallow.

Charlotte crooks her finger for me to lean in, then whispers her request, "Go easy on the one in the wheelchair. He's one of the good guys."

Seriously? I'm two thousand miles from Detroit, and yet, here we go again.

I STAND before the boardroom doors, as I had last time. Before my life got complicated.

One Jimmy Choo-clad foot in front of the other, I pep-talk myself. I can do this again. Just like last time.

A jackhammer seems to have filled the spot where my heart was beating quietly just moments ago. I need to sit before I implode. My damn legs have been replaced with two rippling noodles. I steady myself on the wood trim of the first leather chair I come to, pulling it out to sit down quickly.

How will I avoid the magnetic pull of his eyes when I look up? I look across the table and scan my eyes from face to face until I reach the man right next to me. He's not here. Ryan isn't in the room. Hadn't Charlotte just told me that he was? I hate what happens to my body next. A crushing feeling rocks me to the core. Disappointment that tells me that I already miss the coldhearted Cass that I used to be.

# RYAN

*C*assandra's eye-catching pumps, in a shade of red that matches the one on her upturned lips, carry her toward the private room where we are all gathered for dinner. I'm reminded of the text from Charlotte this morning that Nike was on her way to the boardroom. White faux-marble columns adorned with gold urns overflowing boughs of holiday greens line the walkway, perfect for her victory parade of one.

Everyone mingling together at the bar, she has no exit strategy to escape me. This morning, I had feigned another meeting requiring my urgent assistance and left the room as soon as Edwards had gone to gather Cassandra. She hadn't accepted my apology, even with the copious bouquet of flowers I'd sent over that had gone unacknowledged. I wasn't proud of being a three-time douche and I wasn't about to extend the streak. I would let the deal stand as is. For now.

Cassandra greets each man, intentionally starting on her right to leave me for last. When her black-as-midnight eyes peer into mine, daggers of onyx pierce me, "Ryan. We missed you this morning."

*Like hell she did.*

I swirl whiskey over the ice cube in my glass and don't dignify her stab with a reply.

We are greeted by a hotel staff member who wants to escort us to our table. I see Cassandra eyeing the drink I have to ditch. She has a stare down with the inanimate object. She doesn't pick it up for me, but we catch each other's gaze, her wearing an expression that looks something like compassion.

*It's an insignificant drink. I am used to worse.*

SILVER LINING to the pre-dinner drink tête-à-tête is the barbs I expected from Cassandra over dinner were contained. Dare I say it was highly civilized. We are all enjoying one last round.

Edwards leans into the circle and looks over each shoulder as if he's going to give us something secretive like an insider trading stock tip, "I made a little deal with our waitress. She's going to let us up to the roof for a night cap. She said there is no better view of the Golden Gate bridge anywhere in the city. Plus, I ordered us up some cigars. Cassandra, it's your victory to celebrate. Let's go."

I hate to say I knew it, but a big-haired blonde with even bigger boobs inserts herself into our circle. She repeats the motion of looking over each shoulder before her hands cup her mouth. "Are we ready? I've got the Cuban contraband."

She turns her back to us, motioning us to follow. Like moths to a flame, we all move with her. Then, as if she has a realization, she stops abruptly, leaving a near chain-reaction pileup of bodies in her wake. Her eyes fixate on mine. Her lips twist sideways into some imitation of a cartoon character. "Stairs only," she says aloud much to my humiliation.

I inwardly cringe. Outward, I shake my head. "No worries. I'll meet you at the bar afterward."

*Where I'll be alone.*

Golf course by day, crass storytelling with cigars and cocktails by night is the language of business I used to speak fluently but can no longer. There are worse things for sure, but it still leaves a mark.

The crowd follows the fake DD'ed pied piper and I begin to move toward the bar I remembered seeing off the lobby.

"Hey," I hear a voice behind me call out. Her voice. I stop moving and swivel toward it. "Want company?"

"Well, you wouldn't be my first choice, but hey, sure. You're better than drinking alone."

*I'm such an asshole.*

Her expression breaks me. I close my eyes and shake my head. "I'm sorry. Defense is my default. "I'd love you to join me."

"Apology accepted. And while I am at it, thank you for the beautiful flowers. I'm sorry too. That they left you out."

A turning point. Apology accepted. Grateful, I offer her my dimpled smile and a compliment, "Careful or you'll get a new nickname. They might start calling you compassionate Cass."

"Not sure I like the sound of that," she counters, amused. "I've got a rep to uphold." But then her eyes roll upward, and she bites her bottom lip, pondering. "On second thought, anything other than princess will do."


As we grab a table near the bar, I'm feeling a little victorious myself. I'm with the most beautiful woman in the crowded space, even if she is just doing me a favor being by my side.

My phone buzzes on the table, interrupting our conversation. It's a text from Charlotte asking if I can chat.

Cassandra's eyes dart to the phone, peering across the small, round table. "You can say yes," she says, lifting her wine for a sip.

"She wouldn't ask if it wasn't important."

"I admit, I'm being self-serving," she confesses without hesitation. "Charlotte might have details about the deal. And if she knows I am here, she can't say things that *they* said about me. Charlotte told me *they* said I wear Armani and an attitude."

I cringe inwardly.

Her half smile reveals she isn't angry, but I am. At myself. There is no they, of course. Just me. And I am an ass.

I reach for the phone, really hoping Charlotte doesn't have bad news. I press the call button and put the phone to my ear. She answers on the first ring.

I listen as she confirms what I feared. I tell her no problem and end the call.

"Um, hi, disappointment, nice to meet you," Cassandra says after I hang up.

"That transparent?" I try to satisfy the scorch with my drink, but it fails.

"I could call you scotch."

I look at her quizzically. "Like the drink?" I ask lifting my glass.

"Nope. Like the tape," she says with a grin I can only describe as impish.

I can't help but laugh at her joke, and the disappointment dissipates. You can't laugh and be miserable in the same moment.

"You barely reacted to all of us ditching you, but Charlotte ditching you is worse how?"

I start to ask but she offers, "I could hear. She was sorry but couldn't make it. Make what? What's so important?"

"A wedding."

"Not yours, I hope."

It's impossible not to laugh again. "No, not mine. My brother's."

"When is it? Can't you get another date?"

*I don't exactly have women lining up in droves.*

"This Saturday. She was only going to pretend she was my date anyway. It's just—" I trail off. I'll sound pathetic. Hell, I am.

"What?" She leaves the pregnant pause hanging while she takes a drink. I'm not getting out of here without telling her. I know her playbook.

"There is a little pressure from my family. It was just going to be a hell of a lot easier to have a fake date than no date at all. Sidestep the questions if you know what I mean."

A smile of understanding spreads cheek to cheek. "Do I ever. Pretty sure my mother had a Spanish tutor for her inquisition skills. What kind of pressure are we talking? Navy Seal, diamond-forming, volcanic, other?"

"Yes," I answer, "All of the above."

Cassandra blows out a little whistle of acknowledgment, then slides her tongue across her bottom lip thoughtfully. "You said this Saturday, right?"

I nod, wondering where she is going with this.

"I'm in. I'll be your fake date. My mother nearly begged me to come home for Thanksgiving, and I gave in. That pressure thing I mentioned. She said we need to sit down and talk about something. I think I know what that something might be. I'll probably only be three steps in the door before she starts asking about the special man in my life. Not to worry, I have my answer rehearsed."

"What will you tell her?"

"Not just *a* special man, Mom. Seven. One to sleep with each day of the week."

*Keep making me laugh, and I might sign up for any day ending in "y".*

"All I need is a good reason to leave on Friday or Saturday, and she will flip when she hears my excuse is a date. This is a win-win. You and I may have our differences, but there is no way that free food and drinks at a wedding far from Boston with you wouldn't be much preferred over eating leftover casseroles with peas and carrots from Uncle Tom and Aunt Carol."

She stops abruptly and I hope she isn't reconsidering, because I am pretty damn delighted with this twist of fate.

"Wait. It is far from Boston, right?"

"Chicago," I answer the question and actually consider crossing my fingers for luck under the table.

"Well, count me in then. I'm your girl."

*An idea I could get used to.*

I am letting my mind run away. I remind myself, there is no running here. For the rest of my life. It would do me well to remember this fact.

"Thank you. I can't tell you how much this means to me. And my family. But no pressure. At least not any of the aforementioned variety."

"Now that we have that settled, I'm tired. Mind if I call it a night?"

Considering she closed the sentence with a yawn she tried to hide, and we are both on east coast time, I am happy to comply. "I have a driver. Let me call him for us. If that is okay with you."

"That'd be great. I have a great one here too, but I know he's off work tonight."


CASSANDRA HEADS to the restroom while I wait in the spacious lobby. Charlotte texts another sincere apology to which I am happy to reply.

ME: No worries. You may be irreplaceable...but you have been replaced!

Charlotte: wait, what? u have another date?

ME: well, another fake one anyway

Three smiling emojis.

Charlotte: YEAH! Who is the lucky lady???

ME: Nike

Charlotte: How the Sam's chickens? Maybe we should call her Aphrodite instead? Put down the weapons, Ares. Your little war is over.

ME: Didn't falling for her get him bound by brass chains for a year?

Charlotte: Can we agree you've already done your time? Declare victory already! If anyone deserves it, it's u, Ry!


SHE ADDS three more smiling emojis, this time the big ones showing teeth. The smile on my face probably matches those damn goofy little yellow ones. It's been a good night, and my chariot awaits.

If Cassandra is turned off by the time it takes or how I look getting into a car all I have to lose is a fake date. And, I bought this damn Audi SUV myself just for this occasion, since I have a few matching ones at home.

Normally I wouldn't have to manage getting the wheelchair in, but I won't let Cecil touch it tonight, having just had knee surgery. I was happy to provide a friend with the surgery he needed, and I've paid some bills he doesn't even know about. He shouldn't be working, but when I arrived today, he had wanted to show off the new knee and insisted on returning for me tonight.

Imagine my surprise when he rounds the car and stops dead in his tracks, and says with a Cheshire Cat-like smile, "Well, don't you look mighty fine this good evening, Ms. Lewis."

"You two know each other?" I ask, looking between the two of them.

"Not that suprisin', Mr. Ryan. Miss Charlotte and I share more than our southern accent. You two have more in common than you might think." He says this with a wink while looking at Cassandra and then back to me. "But don't worry, I'll never share your secrets. I have one of my own, though."

Cassandra and I look at each other. I shrug.

"I can't pick a favorite between the two of you. You're both my favorites." Cecil tips his hat with a wink, belly shaking full-on Santa Clause-style with his laugh.

Between Cassandra's unexpected actions tonight and Cecil's declaration, I find myself hopeful that maybe this deal won't be as difficult as I once imagined. And, if I am lucky, I might enjoy the wedding I'd been dreading. I'll end today with hope. Tomorrow, though, might be an entirely different story.

# RYAN

*I*'m looking into the full-length mirror to fix the bowtie of my tuxedo. The reflection isn't too disappointing. What will be, however, is if Cassandra is a no-show. Waking up yesterday knowing I didn't have to endure this coming-out party of sorts alone eased the nerves. This morning, however, was a buzz kill.

I check my phone again for the time and for a text. The last one from her said she had cold feet. Isn't that supposed to be reserved for the people *in* the wedding, not those *attending* the wedding? I appreciate her sharing her fear, but can spending the evening with me be more intimidating than the eight-figure deals she puts together regularly?

*Apparently, yes.*

I reminded her how much it would mean to have her here for the wedding of my brother. My younger brother. I should be the one going first. On the mountain that day and down the aisle. I'll forgive him for getting married first. I've forgiven him for worse.

I am happy for him, but it still stings. I push away the fear that threatens to burn me in a private inferno. I can barely get a fake date; what if I never have the chance to marry a wife? What if no one will ever love me again?

Close. Down. The. Pity. Party. Steadman.

It's noon and I've heard nothing from her. She was supposed to leave at 7:00 a.m. on the first flight out of Boston. Maybe she didn't want to wake me by texting so early. Maybe I am making up B.S. excuses. Now, it's five hours to show time. At least it's snowing like a bitch. I'll have a reason for her no-show that everyone will believe.

IT'S TIME. Time for me to be seen by friends and family, most of whom I haven't seen since the accident. I hope Matt and Samantha are the focus, as they should be. Luckily, the new trend has the groomsmen waiting in the front of the church and not making the trip down the aisle with the bridesmaids. Dodged that bullet. No way in hell would I have wanted the sympathetic smiles and whispers from the crowd. The downside is that I can't see beyond the first couple of rows from my position, so I don't have a clue if Cassandra is here in this church.

Brotherly love helps me focus on the nuptials at hand, but it's not easy. As the ring is placed on Samantha's finger, I remember Melanie pointing to hers. Dainty, and bare, she said, "You know how good a ring from you is going to look right there?"

She had tamed the womanizing bad boy in me. I thought my future was planned. The day before we left for the ski trip, I got down on one knee. In the crowd gathered for the ice festival, it was easy to hide her mom, dad, and sister. With scripted timing, the sculptor put the final touches, the last "e" of Marry Me into the block of ice he had shaped into a six-foot-tall diamond. She said yes. The crowd cheered.

Even if I do get the chance to propose again, it can never be on one knee.

THE CROWD IS ESCORTED from the church and I still haven't seen Cassandra. The bridal party stays behind for pictures. Pictures have been a highly negotiated event for me, a post-accident first. I've avoided any to date but felt forced to succumb for Matt and Samantha. What choice did I really have?

WE ARE ABOUT to make our grand entrance into the Carnegie Ballroom. Not only do I have to be the center of attention when we join the celebration, but there is the obligatory best-man toast. Knowing all eyes will be on me overwhelms me with a feeling of dread.

Matt clasps my shoulder with a squeeze. "We've got this, man." Not the first time I've heard those words from him. They aren't any more reassuring this time. I know I am lucky to have a "we" for many matters, but a lot I must handle alone. It's exhausting to consider doorways, spacing, flooring, curbs, and carrying everything, every day, alone. For instance, while the rest of the bridal party was drinking before the wedding, I snuck in a practice run from this door to the head table. At least I've got the next sixty seconds covered.

The hotel manager pulls open the tall double doors to reveal the audience of clapping guests. I'll stare straight ahead, suited up with a fake, plastered smile.

Actually, a genuine smile won't be nearly as difficult as I thought.

I insisted Cassandra sit with me. And there she is, standing in the spot next to mine at the head table. Her silver dress sparkles in the light cast from the chandelier above. The capped sleeves show off her feminine neckline. She has pulled back the strands of dark hair usually framing her face, and I see her for the very first time.

Exquisite.

Angelic.

Beautiful.

Devastatingly so.

*God, woman. Ying and yang, war and peace, black and white. Cold-hearted and compassionate. You'll be my undoing.*

I SURVIVE the proverbial walk of shame, and reach her. She bends to hug me. Her closeness soothes every nerve that's been standing on end for the last eighteen hours. Her lips find my cheek, close to my ear. A raw shiver travels down my spine. I swear I feel it where I know I shouldn't be able to.

When I've composed myself enough to speak, I say, "I'm so glad you are here. How close did you come to standing me up?"

*Irrelevant. Unnecessary. Why the hell did I let that slide out?*

She wrinkles her nose and I have my answer. "I'm here now," she says with a cock of her head toward something that diverts her attention.

Matt is over my left shoulder shoving his hand toward Cassandra. "Pardon the interruption, but I have to meet the woman of the hour."

"I hope it's more than an hour," Cassandra retorts jovially. "And I think your beautiful bride is the woman of the hour, actually."

Matt responds with a laugh, "Nice." He has met his match. These two will get along just fine.

I jump in, "Matt, Cassandra. Cassandra, Matt."

Samantha arrives on the scene, draped over Matt's shoulder. "This must be Cassandra. I am so glad you could make it. So's Ryan, in case he didn't let on."

"Do not give away all of my secrets, Samantha," I say facetiously through my smile.

"It's girl code, Ryan. Sorry about your luck."

Cassandra jumps in for the rescue, "Thank you for having me. Everything is beautiful. I'm looking forward to the evening."

*Are you, Cassandra? If only your words were real.*

The wedding planner is beckoning the newlyweds to the dance floor. "Sorry, we have to run. Hopefully we can catch up at brunch tomorrow."

"I don't think I can make that. Early flight, but hopefully soon. Nice to meet you."

I try not to frown though I think I fail. She is getting out of here as soon as she can. Wishing things were different isn't going to change them, however. Just like all the wishing in the world can't change the fact that I'll never be able to sweep a bride across the dance floor like Matt is doing with Samantha right now. This just gets better.

Cassandra's hand is on my forearm. "I'm only leaving early because I have to be in New York first thing Monday, and I couldn't get any other flight. It's the biggest travel weekend of the year."

Relief washes over me, and I remind myself not to jump to conclusions to protect myself. Depending on how the evening goes, I might be able to let her in another secret even Matt and Samantha don't know. A private plane is available anytime. And as for the dancing thing, Chris and I haven't ruled that out altogether either. Though I'd give up every cent I have in a heartbeat to have the use of my legs, whoever said money can't buy love or happiness might not have had access to as much as I do.

# CASSANDRA

*R*yan Steadman in a tuxedo. Apparently not all of me got the memo that this was a fake date because I feel things where I don't want to. I watch him—as he watches me. We don't hate each other anymore, but what if we are more alike than we know? What if we're both desperate for a second chance at love but are too afraid of walking that sliver of a line between love and fear? It's a tightrope with no safety net.

OVER TOASTS and kisses with the clanging of forks on glasses, I try to ignore all the love in the air, but it's almost impossible. I can't resist a sideways glance of him sitting next to me though. His jawline forms a distinguishable "L" shape with its strong build and his olive skin sports a sexy evening shadow. His dark hair curls up just the tiniest bit, unruly, in one curl at the nape of his neck. The profile of his full lips that tilt slightly upward in a permanent smile taunt me.

I close my eyes. If I can't see him maybe I can pretend he isn't making me consider possibilities I don't want to be considering. No such luck, his divine scent, a masculine blend of leather and spice, make me want to put my lips against his neck. I want to taste him, but a kiss is a dangerous sip.

Sipping my much safer champagne instead, I drink to the fact that this wedding is only mere hours to make it through.

I got this.

Tomorrow morning, I take the first flight out. It was the only one available, and I'm not disappointed to be making my getaway sooner rather than later.

Small talk will be easy enough tonight because his family is busy with a wedding. Tomorrow would have been another story. A smaller post wedding event would have me being asked questions and the center of attention as Ryan's date.

If nothing else this evening, I'm going to satisfy my curiosity of what happened to Ryan, because someone here knows and it's only a matter of time before I discretely ask someone.

WE ARE BEING APPROACHED by a man and a woman I know are Mr. and Mrs. Steadman because Ryan is an amalgamation of the couple. His dark hair and blue eyes match the man's, the high forehead and chiseled cheekbones clone the female's.

She wears a nearly-black but still navy floor length dress with sheer long sleeves and a chiffon skirt that juts out around her, swishing as she walks, like she is bobbing on a surface as she floats towards us. It's appropriate, because Ryan speaks of her as if she walks on water.

"You must be Cassandra," says the male half of the couple, thrusting a hand toward me. "I'm Nick. Pleased to meet you."

His mother, anxiously awaiting her turn, wraps her arms around me in a hug. "I'm Jane."

Not Dick and Jane but Nick and Jane. The names I can work with, the hug not so much. Hugging strangers is something I usually resist, but in this case, I know it's a good idea to make an exception. My body manages to comply against my brain's wishes.

Ryan looks up from his conversation with one of his fellow

groomsmen. And none too soon, as I didn't want to handle this all alone. I've met very few parents for as old as I am. At least this is without the added pressure of a real meet-the-parents scenario.

"Mom, Dad, looks like you've met Cassandra. Sorry I am late to the introduction."

"That's okay, we were just getting acquainted," his dad says, a familiar intonation in his voice. Ryan speaks just like him. "Hey, there's always Christmas. You are both invited if you can make it. That would give us a lot of time."

Hello to a Christmas invite in two sentences? *Holy hell.*

Jane looks at Ryan. "Honey, everyone is saying how good it is to see you again."

My chest aches. I accused him of building his own world with his own people. What if that was exactly what he had done? New people who only knew his new normal.

Ryan's eyes dart to me and don't move from mine. I hear the happiness in his voice when he answers, "It's great to be here, Mom."


WE SPEND the next several hours moving from table to table together. We are only separated when I take the dance floor with all the single ladies. I didn't catch the bouquet, though a little teeny-tiny part of me wanted to.

Every conversation I collect a story, each one a piece of Ryan's life. I might not be able to form a whole puzzle, but by the end I've gathered enough to put together the border. I need more details from him to fill in the picture. Of all that I had learned about his childhood, the trouble Matt and Ryan caused as teenagers, and his favorite investments for the coming year, no one had slipped in a detail about the accident.

Thankfully, the evening is winding down. We are making our way from the ballroom toward the elevator. The crowd has died down to only a few.

"Phew. You have a lot of family and friends, Ryan. I hope you don't plan to test me on any names because that was a whirlwind."

"It was good to..." he trails off, regret trickling into the final words he doesn't say. He pulls it together though, "I haven't seen most of these people in a long time. It made it a lot easier with you by my side, Cassandra. I can't thank you enough. I hope it wasn't too torturous."

Before I can answer, Matt's voice booms with a tinge of drunk. "Hey, brother, how 'bout a nightcap?" He slumps over Ryan, arm around his shoulder. "You gotta go. You never leave your wingman."

Ryan's jaw jumps, clenching tightly. He shrugs Matt off his shoulder, but his lips still curl up.

Matt looks to me, "I get it. I'm just not as beautiful as she is." He winks in my direction.

Samantha finally chimes in, "Ryan, as always the voice of reason, thank you for the ix-ney on the par-tay. Matthew John, take me to bed or lose me forever!" She throws herself backwards, forcing him to catch her. He dips her, then kisses her, and slides an arm underneath her legs, scooping her into his arms.

I reach for the extra remnants of white fabric hanging to the ground and tuck the bridal gown around Samantha under his arm.

Ryan watches the charade longingly. My chest clutches again, the unfamiliar ache in its center. Compassion should come with a warning label.

"Thanks, Cassandra. It was nice to meet you! Hope to see you at Christmas!" Samantha waves as Matt carries her away.

I follow Ryan, and several others, into the elevator and stand behind him. He presses the number twenty-four button. The top floor and my lucky number. I look up at the numbers indicating the floors but feel him looking up at me. He might assume one of the other elevator inhabitants has pressed the button to my floor. He will have assumed wrong. I'm feeling daring, considering I've rocked the evening as a fake date. And, I'm not going to bed without filling in some of the insides of the border.

The elevator door opens, and another man and woman get off along with the two of us. They turn left and we turn right. I follow him around the next corner where he stops abruptly. "Is this your floor?" he asks up to me.

"No."

Confident he wouldn't tell me no to joining him, his eyes squint, with half of a smile forming on his lips, crooked. And cute. "Suit yourself."

I will, thank you. Following him to the end of the hallway, through first one set of doors, and then another, he inserts the key. "Ladies first."

I realize for the first time that opening doors poses a challenge for him. I remember his house. Everything automatically sensing and opening. Pocket doors that slide into the walls. I push open the door.

There is a foyer. In a hotel room. And real hardwood floors. I walk down the long hallway to an expansive living room. A long deep mocha-colored velvet couch with a gracefully curved back is a feminine flirt to the two chairs sitting across from it, all masculine, leather with large, round nail-head trim.

"Well, this is nice," I say trying to sound nonchalant. I sit down on the couch and remove my shoes from my aching feet. I pad barefoot across the room to a switch on the wall, which I press, and watch orange flames dance to life in the fireplace. I let my feet wander across the soft gray sheepskin rug spread across the floor in front of it.

I assume the bedroom is through the closed doors to my right. Double doors. Big spaces and wide doors. One way around anything challenges. Why not a handicap room? I think I know the answer. Pride.

I realize that Ryan hasn't followed me while I've gone exploring and made myself at home. I make my way back to the hallway where he has stopped in front of a full-length mirror affixed to the wall. He is removing his cummerbund. Lustrous blue eyes meet my black ones in the mirror.

"You were very gracious to do this. And, I couldn't have had a more beautiful date."

I feel the tinge of heat the compliment draws on my cheeks. I say, "Thank you. It was my pleasure."

"Did you feel any Navy SEAL, diamond-in-the-making, volcano-on-the-verge-of-eruption pressure?" he asks.

"Happy to report none of the above."

Crooking his arm, he removes the cufflink from the left, then the right sleeve.

He pulls the left side of the bowtie, and the white satin falls onto his chest. His fingers find the first black stud and push it backward through the hole it was filling. Losing the constriction from his shirt, he takes an unencumbered breath.

That makes one of us.

My breath hitches at the hint of skin revealed.

It's jumbled and foreign, but I feel something.

Desire.

A knowing that my touch and lips would soothe the pain he's had to endure.

I've fallen for the beautiful yet broken man before me who's found a way into my heart. A heart I thought was steel and cold.

I was mistaken.

It's glass.

With the potential to shatter into a million little pieces.

# RYAN

*U*nexpected. A woman so gracious with my family tonight I almost forgot her being here was only a favor.

Unpredictable. She invited herself into my room.

Untamed. Starless-night-black eyes are looking into mine daring me to take her.

I may be out of practice, but I know the wanton look. It's torturous. I can almost feel the long strands of brunette tickle the skin of my chest, and the warmth and fullness of her breasts filling my hands. I can taste her full pink lips. I've waited and wanted a woman for so long it is soul crushing.

But this is one hell of a risk. Am I willing to take it?

I feel as vulnerable as a gladiator in a ring about to be torn apart by a lion. Rejection will deconstruct me.

I remember the moment everything changed. The one they say happens when you face life or death. I chose to fight for my life. That was the first time. It wasn't the last.

Right now, I have another choice to make. Take a chance and fight for love or risk the regret of the chance not taken. We never know what will happen after we fall.

Until it's too late.

Just like that fateful day.

Just like now.

Can I do this?

I reach up, slide my palm over her dark silken locks, and press it to her cheek. She circles to my front, leans downward, and I take her head in my hands, find her lips, and give her all that I have to offer.

My lips crash against hers, teeming with need. Languishing against their softness, her tongue shoves into my mouth first, impatient. Wanting. Perhaps more than my own. Our kiss is relentless. Consuming. Silent adorations imploring redemption, an upspoken plea for acceptance of our tattered selves. In our kiss, we find more than what the world has taken from each of us.

She moans with a ragged exhale. I inhale it. I inhale her. Her desire for me. Passion that arises when hate moves to love. I fist my hands in her hair and pull her head backward slightly, just enough to trace her bottom lip with my tongue. She gasps. I pull back farther, to memorize her features close-up. Her eyes open wide and gaze into mine. Penetrating. Without words, I beg for her to see beyond my broken.

Her palms find my face, eyes fluttering closed again. She cups my face, her touch warm and soft. Her lips brush against mine. Gentle and tender, this whisper of a kiss offers me her answer.

As Cassandra rests her forehead against mine, my lips find her jawline. Delicately, I explore. She lifts her head for me to make my way down the slender, feminine line of her long neck, smelling as delicious as she tastes.

Hearing my long and audible inhale, she laughs. I feel it in the sensitive skin beneath my lips, "If you like what you smell, it's lily of the valley. Someone got me a little addicted to having it around all the time."

A smile forms on my lips, before working their way back to her jawline.

"I'm not sure I'm ready to come up for air," I growl into her mouth when I find her lips again. She shudders, then stands, her own hands sliding up and down her upper arms. In the mirror I can see the goosebumps that have exploded across her skin. It's been a long time since I've done that to a woman, and I want more.

I MOVE across the room to a table with a decanter and two glasses. Pouring caramel-colored liquid courage into the glass, I contemplate my next move. I down it. Cassandra appears next to me, "Did my kiss drive you to drinking?"

*Not the kiss, Cassandra, but what I am going to do next.*

"You never drink it neat."

She has been paying attention. She puts one round ice cube in my glass before dropping another in her own. "Sorry about the fingers. I liked the room before, but knowing it came furnished with perfect ice cubes is the icing on the cake, so to speak."

I don't tell her there are benefits to having had to learn to pay attention to details. I ordered in advance. I'd learned the hard way overindulging would never drown my sorrows, but one or two eased the ache. I'm stone-cold sober. And glad for it. I wouldn't have wanted alcohol to have marred the best first kiss I'd ever experienced.

I hadn't finished a drink all night because I was too prideful to let Cassandra carry mine in public. Here, before I know it, she has swept both off the table and is already walking toward the couch.

Facing another moment of truth, I transfer onto it. I search her face for a reaction such as wide eyes, a grimace, or anything resembling Melanie's discomfort. Relief washes over me when I find none. I relax into the couch.

Cassandra sets the glasses on the coasters she has already put onto the table in front of the couch, pulls up her dress and curls in next to me, legs tucked beneath her. I watch as her long lashes make each blink last for seconds.

She passes a glass to me. I swirl the whiskey over the ice. This is not going to be easy. "I'm surprised you haven't asked what happened to me."

"I figured you would tell me when you were ready." She answers quickly like she didn't have to consider her answer, adding a casual shrug that says it wasn't burning a hole in her pocket. Then her expression turns serious. "I want to know. Because I want to know all of you. I just didn't think that was the most important part."

*You are not who you show the world, Cassandra Lewis.*

I blow out a long breath, preparing to start at the beginning. Cassandra sets her hand on my leg, a gesture I am sure she means to offer comfort. I look to where it rests, unable to feel her touch, her help useless. As if she understands, she reaches for my hand and pulls it to rest on hers instead.

"I don't remember what happened. I've just pieced a version of others' stories together to make my own. Fair warning, it might somewhat fictional, and it's definitely not an autobiography. But it's all I got." I force half of a laugh out to lighten things up as much as I can.

Her face is solemn and attentive, but at least I don't sense pity. Yet.

"When I was waking up, my first memory was the leaden feeling of my chest. I needed a full breath of air but couldn't pull one in. It was like sucking air through a straw. My eyes had trouble adjusting to the brightness, each blink cutting through a hazy fog. There was this weird sound, and I felt my chest fill with air. I was aware I hadn't done it. I tried to turn toward the sound but couldn't move a muscle. I could sense, and swear even smell, the close proximity of metal."

"Were you in pain when you woke up? Did it hurt?" she asks with a look of genuine concern.

"Like hell. Two-ton truck meet a million baseball bats to my core, eerily stopping at my waist."

For each piece of the story I can tell her, there is a backstory I just can't. I don't tell her the physical pain couldn't touch the pain recovery did to my pride. It will never fully recover, because I'll never fully be a real man again.

"The ventilator wasn't because of my back, but the punctured lungs. Yep, not one but two. From broken ribs. Six in fact. Over-achieving on both of those."

I try to raise the corners of my lips, but they get stuck just above flat. I take a sip and let the cold whiskey soothe me. Cassandra is gripping my hand on her leg tightly, like she might if we were watching a horror movie.

"This sucks, Ryan."

I appreciate that she doesn't say she is sorry because she has called it as it is. I don't want her to apologize for something she didn't do. I lift our entangled hands and brush my lips across the top of her knuckles. "Hang on tight; I'm just getting started." I drain my drink and, without asking, she stands to refill the glass. It will be my last. It's not worth the hangover, since I know that no amount will take the pain away. She returns, removing any space between us, inching closer than before. In any other situation, how much I want her would have landed us horizontally by now.

*If only.*

"My mother was there. She was at the side of my bed at the first sign of life. She looked older than I remembered, and I knew it was my fault. She didn't have to say a word because her eyes said everything I needed to know. It wasn't good. When I was finally out of the woods, so to speak, then the fun really began."

Arms moving to encircle my neck she says, "I can't imagine. Any of this."

Her hands retreat suddenly, leaving a void. She sits straight up. "Wait! You haven't told me what the accident was. Are you saying you woke up and didn't remember and couldn't talk to ask what had happened to you?"

I nod. "I should have started there. I'm sorry. That's just not where the story started for me."

"Oh my God, Ryan. That had to be terrifying."

"It was. And I still didn't even know that I would never walk again. My SCI, spinal cord injury, is a T12 complete. It happened in a ski accident. I went over a jump and landed wrong. It was just bad luck."

And negligence, but we'd get to that part. I also leave out the part that I was following Matt, cursing his stupidity, and scared he was the one that would end up dead. I'm glad I don't remember the nearly ten-foot free-fall onto a ledge of rock. "I was lucky to be alive, as they say, but there were times I wished I wasn't. First, I fought hard to live, then I would have fought to die. I did all the stages of grief and I did them all hard."

If she knew how low the low was, she would either respect the hell out of me or think I was the world's biggest pussy. I lost my job, my home, my body, and my fiancée. My whole world. I'd prefer to think she would choose the former.

"Four months between the hospital and rehab, and they set me free in the world to figure it out. I was living with Matt in Chicago, before, and running the branch of Dad's finance firm. I had to move back to Detroit and in with my parents. That might have been the worst of all. They were great, but what self-respecting man wants to move home at thirty? Not this one."

"So, it's been four years?"

"It will be. January 14th. Hell of an anniversary to celebrate. I'll share the silver lining, such that it is. One of those ambulance-chasing lawyers came to the hospital.

He was persistent and I was in no state to fight him off. Neither was my family. He knew about some shady things going down at the resort where we had skied.

We never should have been skiing where we were, but it wasn't closed off. To top it off, they had rookie medical personnel who hadn't been trained enough to deal with my injury.

No one is sure that I would be where I am if they had done the proper stabilization. The resort paid up. The company that employed the paramedics paid up. More went down at the hospital. They paid too."

I didn't think I had any kind of future so when my dad told me about a business venture in Detroit, what the hell did I have to lose? At that point I wasn't even sure I wasn't going to take my own life.

Cassandra closes her eyes and pushes her lips into a fine line. I place my palm on her cheek. "Hey. It's okay. The story has a happy-enough ending."

She opens her eyes again. At least there are no tears.

"I gambled every penny of the settlement with two of Dad's friends that were close with the mayor of Detroit and the man who would become the tipping point of the downtown turnaround. They needed an investor. It paid off. Fast. Detroit was on the precipice of revitalization and needed residential housing pronto. They thanked me with the gift of my building. Decrepit as it was. Renovating it was Dad's grand scheme to get my sorry ass back to something productive. Metaphoric, I know. Renovate a building. Renovate my life." I pause, thinking about how that worked out.

Each floor yields a pretty penny. Plenty of costs, but plenty of profit. More importantly, plenty of space I held onto for rehabbing the professionals recovering from their own fall.

This part of the story isn't too hard to tell. I continue, "The two brothers threw more work at me than I could keep up with. I could do it at home since I wasn't getting out much."

The back story I don't share is how much of an understatement this was. The world I knew didn't work any longer, so I made the building into a new one I never had to leave. And I didn't. That part Dad hadn't anticipated.

"They did twenty-two M&As that year. I did the financials for all of them with a hotshot Harvard MBA who got four degrees when he was like twelve. I kept myself busy day and night. Hard to have time for self-pity when you are working sixteen hours a day and sleeping the rest." I lift my glass in a mock toast to the men who pulled me through my wreckage. It was also how I learned the dark side of the business. We put plenty of people out of a job before I decided we didn't have to. "As hard as I did grief, I've done acceptance harder, Cass."

She visibly relaxes, shoulders falling several inches, and I realize how tense she was, hanging on my words.

"I'm grateful to be alive. Just a couple of inches and it could have been worse. I have a wicked scar some girls might think is cool, and a lifetime of good parking spots." I know it's not funny, but humor has always helped me get by.

"In all seriousness, I've got full use of my arms and torso, and I'll never give up hope of walking again. I can't fix everything broken but Chris and I have a few things up our sleeves. I'm also funding some crazy-ass research around the globe. And, the best part of having money is supporting good causes. My family knows I have money, but no clue how much. They think I'm in a hotel room just like theirs."

I draw a long sip over my tongue, give her a cocky wink and add, just because I can, "I don't fly commercial, either."

"And I don't fly coach. Yet here we are." Her retort matches my insinuation. Our meeting was fate. My fingers slide behind her head, grazing the back of her neck and pulling her face into mine.

There will be time for me to slowly worship her later, but right here and now I need to feel every inch of bare flesh as quickly as possible. Her uncovered shoulders provoke my fingers to trace them. Energy courses through my chest and I feel everywhere. Alive. Free.

Her desperate hands hold my head in place against her lips, parting mine with her tongue, pushing into my mouth and swirling against mine. Hungrily, needly, we taste each other, and I let her deepen the kiss, her lips finding mine so greedily it's as if she will never relent. This is an unspoken apology for all that I had lost. This kiss says I am sorry I can't fix you, but I can kiss away some of the pain.

*Never let go, Cassandra.*

*Never let go.*

My hands slide down the silver satin covering her back to her hips. I cup each buttock in my hands, digging into the flesh, and holding her against me. For too long, I've been denied the chance to feel a woman in my hands and hold her in my arms. This is sacred. And I took it for granted. Before.

Looking for permission in my eyes, Cassandra reaches for the button of my shirt. Instead of granting it, I capture her hand and bring her knuckles to my lips again. While there is nothing I'd like more than to have this woman out of that dress, I can't go there yet. If she learns what the future might hold, ours might end before it begins. I'm probably unfair and selfish. Cassandra should learn the truth sooner than later, and will.

But not tonight.

I am not sure I can handle the truth because the truth might set me free.

Of her.

# CASSANDRA

*T*hank God I took this flight. I'm on a plane and not playing fake girlfriend at brunch. I'm being carried far away from Chicago with a busy week ahead in New York City.

Last night ending in a make-out session was not at all what I had been expecting from my fake date. It was better. Like, times a million. Somewhere between the respect I had for all that he makes look easy and I know isn't, irresistible charm he exhibited with friends and family, and him sharing the horrific accident that changed his life forever, I got lost in Ryan. Then found in his kiss. Holy hell, that kiss. No. Those kisses.

I should have walked away.

*But you didn't my brain reminds me.*

Thankfully, he didn't let me take his shirt off. There is no telling how much crazier in the head I would be this morning if there was even one less article of clothing involved. It was nothing, right? There is no reason to worry he will feel dejected, rejected, cast off, rebuffed, spurned, scorned, and, or abandoned after just a couple of kisses, no matter how amazing. Right?

Kisses do not a relationship make. And, as amazing as they were, I don't do relationships and don't intend to start. Nada will change my mind. Nothing. Nunca will it happen. Never. Spanish seems to capture this better than English.

I'll go to New York, be plenty distracted by work, and not freak out. Yep, I've got this. "Good luck with that, Cassandra," I mutter. Yes, out loud.

*Now I am talking to myself.*

*Awesome.*

*Using words like awesome that went out in the eighties.*

*More awesome.*

"What was that, dear? I'm sorry, I'm afraid that I don't hear as well as I used to. Hear, or anything else these days." The elderly woman in the first-class seat next to mine tosses her head back with near-neck-breaking force. She slaps her thigh, laughing at her own joke.

"I'm sorry, I was talking to me, myself, and I," I confess.

"Well, I hope you told yourself something good! No use wasting time on nonsensical chit-chat!"

"Why, thank you for the advice; I need all that I can get. It was definitely nonsensical chit-chat." I can't even say the words without smiling.

"Oh dear, I've learned a few things along the way. I'm old as God's dog! Don't you worry, you've got time."

Smiling broadly, I find myself captivated by the woman's persona. Her wrinkles emanate wisdom and grace, two things I could use a healthy dose of.

Unexpected to even myself, I do something I didn't do on a plane ride before Ryan. I introduce myself to the stranger, "My name's Cassandra. And yours?"

"Barbara, but my friends call me Barbie, so you call me that too. I've been blessed with eighty-two years, and that sounds like a long time, right?"

I nod vigorously.

She snaps her fingers loudly, her thin veiny skin shaking back and forth with the motion. "Life is short. Don't get all lost in that pretty little head of yours and forget to live it!"

The flight attendant sets a glass of bubbly liquid in front of Barbie and a coffee in front of me. Barbie lays her hand on her forearm then lifts her glass, "My friend Cassandra needs one of these, please and thank you!"

It's not yet nine in the morning but I determine Barbie isn't one to be reckoned with.

When my matching flute is delivered, Barbie holds hers poised mid-air. She waggles a finger for me to lean in closer and I comply. "You already know plenty, my dear. Like never pass on the champagne. Any time is a good time to celebrate life. Let's toast to the new you. Getting better by the hour. Each hour you spend with me!" She cackles, raspy like a witch. Not the ugly green faced one from the Wizard of Oz, but more like Glinda the good witch, of course.

My smile reaches farther up my cheeks while I raise my glass to meet hers and say, "To wisdom by the glass." The clink of our toast echoes through the cabin.

"I'm no sage," Barbie continues after taking a graceful sip of her bubbly, "but if I had to guess, you are a woman who likes to be in control." She winks. "It takes a recovering control freak to know one. But it's all so silly, dear, because you see, it's always bigger than us. You can only control two things. Love. And forgiveness."

She crooks her light lavender colored nail at me to lean in as if she is going to let me in on another secret. "You can control whom you love, and whom you let love you. Love others and let them love you back. Hell, just love everyone the best you can. They'll love you back the best they can. And then, my dear, you have something so much better than control."

I contemplate what she has said, something akin to love thy neighbor? I think I get it.

She leans her head back into the seat, closing her eyes like she is remembering something. She sighs, and shares another nugget, "Holding back won't keep you safe. It will just keep you lonely. Yes, people are people. They will screw up and they will break your heart. Everyone is doing the best they can. It only hurts you if you don't let it go. Forgive them, grab the Elmer's glue, and put your heart back together."

"Oh Barbie," I exclaim, "you make it sound so easy!"

"All it takes is practice, my dear Cassandra. Practice, and a practice. Want to know the best-kept secret? It's exercise, church, and my shrink all in one."

When she put it like that, how could I not want to know? "Please, do tell."

"Yoga, my dear. Lots of yoga."

Not the answer I was expecting. I remember the conversation with Sebastian, then subsequently Ryan, who said he loved yoga. I make another mental note to ask him about it. How could Ryan do yoga?

"That seems to keep coming up," I muse with a smile.

"Really, dear?" She leans back with a quizzical expression. "Well, that's another little something I've learned."

"What?" I question.

"If you keep hearing the same message, it's probably time to listen."

BARBIE SAID it was time for her happy hour, her definition of which was a nap. She slept peacefully until the plane bumped down on the tarmac. She patted my arm, turning in her seat to address me again with advice, "One last thing for you, my dear—let boys be boys! Get that luggage down for you, open doors, and let them lead dancing. Whenever possible. It's exhausting to fight the natural order, darling!"

She stops to pause, then shrugs. "If only I had learned that lesson earlier!" She throws her hands up in the air feigning exasperation, but her smile doesn't recede. Grabbing my shoulders, she plants a wet kiss on each cheek. I surprise myself enjoying this bit of affection. Sad my time with Barbie is ending, I promise myself I will try yoga. I tell her what a pleasure it was to meet her, knowing I've taken her words to heart.

· · ·

Ah, the sights and sounds of New York delight my senses once again. Still early, my room wouldn't be yet ready, and I have to eat before I settle in to work, right? I'm going to push the discipline to the wayside. It's Christmas in New York!

I walk up 6th Avenue and round the last corner to arrive at Rockefeller Center, gasp at the serene scene that unfolds before me.

Oversized gold and silver ornaments adorn the luscious greens of the small garden holding space between two tall buildings. People circling around the ice rink below and the magical tree that floats over it all is Christmas come to life. I've seen it before, but today the details seem more vivid and beautiful. I marvel at the couples skating while holding hands, and the kids and grownups alike wobbling around like newly birthed fawns.

I offer to snap a picture for a family who huddles together, smiling happily, in the middle of the famous icons. And then it hits me. I've always been content to experience the sights and sounds of the world alone. Today, I am not. As much as I want to resist the fact, I know this would be better shared. Removing my phone from my pocket, I take a selfie in front of the tree and text Ryan: wish u could see this with me.


When I finally make my way to my room, I drop my luggage just beyond the door and head excitedly to my bed. A perfectly wrapped package sits in the center of the white bedding. Black, shiny wrapping paper is tied with a bow of gold ribbon that curls for miles over the package's edge. A handwritten notecard leans against the package.


Cass –

You were the perfect wedding date, fake or otherwise. I hope you will understand the sentiment of this thank you gift. If not, call me and I will explain.

Ryan

P.S. I am hoping you might not understand because I'd love to hear your voice

I CAREFULLY TEAR the wrapping paper from the box, savoring the experience. Lifting its lid slowly, I part the tissue paper that cradles its contents. I hook my fingers through the narrow straps of a gray tank top sporting the LuLu Lemon logo. I set it on the bed next to me and dig into the box again. A dusty-blue and black jacket. Black pants of the tight variety. Black pants that hang more loosely. A long-sleeve patterned shirt.

Before I know it, I am dialing the phone. One ring in I want to hang up. Why am I calling him?

"Hey Cass, how's New York?"

*Too late.*

"Looks fun by the picture."

*Yep, sent that too.*

"You probably know I am calling to say thank you for the amazing clothing collection. But yes, I'll take you up on the explanation."

*The perfect excuse to hear your voice again.*

"Yoga clothes. I am hoping you try. I think you will love it. And it's good for you. I think you could use some stress relief."

*I think I know what else might be a good stress reliver.*

Sarcasm dripping, I return, "What are you worried about? Heart attacks, ulcers, other self-imposed ailments? Of course, I remember what you said. You are lucky I love the outfits. And maybe. That's all I will promise."

I think I can hear him smiling through the phone.

"I was hoping you might have forgotten that part." It was my first strike, "If you let me know when you want to go, I will join you."

I am very curious about his doing yoga. But I shouldn't encourage anything that is a date. No dates. Dates lead to relationships. "We'll see," I say, noticing the hollowness I feel when I do. What the hell is that about?

"Maybe it is, then. I didn't want you to have to drag a mat home from NYC, but there will be one with your name on it waiting for you."

"Where?"

"I'll text you."

"Sounds good."

"Have a great trip, Cass."

"Thanks again, for the clothes." I bite my bottom lip as the words come out,

"And last night."

"The pleasure was all mine."


I HANG up and shake my head, Barbie's words playing on repeat in my head. It's futile to argue with the universe. I'll be going to yoga. And I'll be seeing Ryan again.

# RYAN

*W*ell, damn. The yoga studio is warm, with a great little fireplace, but Cassandra Lewis just walked through the door and raised the temperature ten degrees. The woman rocks a ponytail like Hendrix rocked a Fender.

Outwardly, she looks like she has the world by the balls, her air of confidence bordering on arrogant, but I see trepidation behind her eyes. I wonder if she will let on that she is nervous.

She needs yoga more than anyone I know. Plus, Alexandra is an important person in my life, and I need her approval of a woman more than I need my own mother's.

Cassandra squeezes between several others making their way through the lobby. She's probably going to be pissed that I am here, especially because I used my inside sources to find out she was coming to class. It's not that difficult when you check in online.

I'm still watching her from across the lobby when Lynn hands the mat tied with a ribbon over the counter to her. I love the smile that forms as she hugs it into her chest like her newest prized possession.

Then she turns and freezes when she sees me.

She shakes her head with pursed lips, and for a moment I think she might give me the middle finger. She stomps in my direction. I hear her bare feet against the wood floor and shield myself with raised arms.

"I should have known this was a setup! What are you doing here?"

I peek through my armor of flesh with one eye, then withdraw my arms. I'm saved by Alexandra as she approaches Cassandra from behind.

"I thought we were skipping class for wine or Starbuck's tonight," she says hands raised, questioning.

"I changed my mind." I'm still looking directly at Cassandra, and now Alexandra is looking at her too.

"Well, if you're standing me up for her, I guess I'll let you off the hook," she says with a hand toward Cassandra. "Hi, I'm Alexandra. And you must be Cassandra."

"I am. And I would be happy to skip class and be your wine or coffee date," she says, giving a sarcastic smile.

"I hear it's your first class."

"Yep. And I hear yoga is like exercise, a psychiatrist, and church all in one," Cassandra quips amusingly.

Alexandra laughs lightheartedly. "I hope it lives up to the hype. And I hope that doesn't mean you'll spend the whole class praying to get the heck out of here."

We all share a laugh, then make our way down the hallway to the studio. Alexandra has saved us spots in the back, as she always does for me. Cassandra is fiddling with the hem of her shirt. The one I'd given her as a gift. "Nervous?"

"Damn straight I am," she answers, peering around the room. "I wasn't expecting an ambush. I thought I'd be making a fool of myself in front of only strangers."

I share her consternation. It's a whole different ballgame for me to have her here too. "Did you cheat and YouTube some practice videos?"

"Damn straight I did," she says with a curt nod. "I thought I might be okay until I saw those quotes on the wall out there. What the hell does 'Yoga is the journey of the self, through the self, to the self,' mean anyway?"

She is referring to the art on the wall just outside the studio. "You can ask Alexandra. Don't overthink class. Actually, don't think at all."

"Oh, that's funny, Ryan," she muses sarcastically. "You might as well tell me not to breathe."

"Actually, breathing is the one and only thing you have to do for the next sixty minutes. Everything else is just a bonus."

"Easy for you to say."

"You've got this, Cass. Don't worry, no one else will be looking at you."

*Other than me.* I don't tell her that I am the one they will be staring at. I understand their curiosity and am used to it.


IN THIS CASE, I can be thankful she is self-absorbed. I never caught Cassandra even casting a glance in my direction. Of course, she rocked the class. Even if she was only competing against herself, I saw her push into the deepest version of each pose.

As soon as we closed the class with the word Namaste, she threw herself backwards onto the mat with a sigh. "Ouch, Ryan, that was crazy-hard! Except the ending. I loved that. Minus the name. Who came up with corpse pose? At least we could just lie there doing nothing! I almost laughed out loud when Alexandra said my breath just had to be more powerful than the voices in my head. Like that's possible." She rolls her eyes.

I break into a smile, "I'm glad you survived."

"Then she told us just to leave something behind on the mat and push ourselves into a new version of ourselves for a do-over. Sure, just do it. Like the slogan. As if it's just that easy." She snaps her fingers loudly in the quiet room.

"Class isn't supposed to be stressful, Cass. I brought you here to lower your stress, not raise it." I try to calm her with the reassurance.

"Don't worry, I'll get there. I'm coming back. I'm gonna kick yoga ass." Her brows wag as she says and she throws a hip to the side.

I knew she'd be hooked, even if it is for all the wrong reasons.

"By the way, you're buying me dinner for your stalking me here."

Did she just ask what I think she did? Who am I to refuse that invite? "Sure thing, Cass."

WE STROLL THE QUAINT STREET, making our way to a sushi restaurant a few doors down from the studio. Twinkling white lights wrap historic, ornate light posts, each with a large snowflake at the top. A light dusting of snow sparkles like diamonds, paving our way.

She releases a long, yearning sigh. I look up to see her biting her bottom lip, a clear sign she's holding something inside.

"You want to let me in on what's going on in that head of yours?"

We've reached our destination and cross from the chilly air to the bustling ambiance of the warm restaurant.

"It's going to take a little wine," she says hesitantly.

I am pleased she sounds like she might be willing to share something with me, "I've got all night."

THE SILVER TRAY of perfectly presented sushi is delivered. Cassandra deftly secures a piece with her chopsticks. She sighs, disappointment palpable.

"Walking here, it's snowy and beautiful and I should think it's romantic and I want to. But see, Ryan, I don't do romance. And I don't want a relationship. Because fool me once, love, shame on you. Fool me twice, shame on me."

I'm trying to listen, but she is talking with her hand, squeezing the sushi between the two wooden sticks, and my eyes are following it. There's a chance it's going to end up flying in my direction and I want to be prepared.

She pops the sushi into her mouth, thankfully, so I can finally focus on where this story is going.

I fear never having a second chance at love.

She has sworn one off for herself. Who the hell broke her heart? I'll kill the bastard.

"I believe this roll was called Mr. Nice Guy," she says, picking up another piece of the roll. "My dad was anything but."

*Well that wasn't what I was expecting to hear.*

"My dad lived in his own world. A world that didn't include me, or my mother. He was either working, or doing who knows what, or maybe who, or... who knows. He wasn't around much.

He traveled a lot for work, but when she knew he was in town, my mom always cooked a full meal and sat our three places at the table. It was so sad to always have the empty plate with us, a flagrant reminder he was missing.

When we finished eating, she would make him a plate, cover it perfectly with Saran wrap, and put it in the refrigerator. Every morning, making my lunch, I would see it still there, waiting."

She gulps, as if trying to swallow the rest of the memory, then looks down at the napkin in her lap, smoothing it across her legs.

"I came home from school one day and she was in a crumpled heap on the kitchen floor. She was covered in food and surrounded by shards of glass. I could never forget that day because there was a deep dent in the very middle of the kitchen floor I always had to step over. It was surreal to see her so broken."

I want to reach for her or kiss her or something, anything, but she has given me no indication that we will pick up where we left off Saturday night. I don't want to cross any line that might push her away, so I just listen.

"I didn't know what to do. My father wasn't there, so I felt like I should do something to help her, but? I was twelve and ill-equipped to deal with my own drama, let alone hers. She picked herself up, told me she was sorry, and to go do my homework. I came out of my room two hours later. I was starving. The mess was gone, and her makeup was back to perfect. Like it never happened. We went out to dinner that night and never said another word about it. Needless to say, I don't do leftovers."

I press my lips into a tight, thin line, because her last comment started to draw an inappropriate smile I had to resist.

She half-laughs at herself, but then the tears brim. "Damn it. How did you do this to me? I can't tell you the last time I cried. Why'd I tell you that?"

*Because you aren't the hard woman you show the world after all.*

# CASSANDRA

aterworks, really? How did I let this happen? I had no
intention of sharing this little walk down memory
lane with Ryan. Well, at least I don't need him to dry my tears
because I've got it covered. I wipe mine quickly with my third fingers
and refill my lungs with a deep breath. I may have let Ryan Steadman
own my lips at the wedding, but I don't have to let him own my heart.

But damn it if his hands aren't reaching for mine, gently replacing
my own as his thumbs wipe my tears. I want to push him away, but
something holds me back.

"Ugh." I force myself to laugh. "Thank you. I don't know what that
was about."

*Sure, I don't. He's swimming across my moat fully armed to tear down
every wall I've every erected to protect myself from heartbreak.*

"Thanks for telling me. I was about to go hunt down some past
boyfriend who broke your heart."

I take a long drink of water. "Oh, that happened too, I'm embar-
rassed to admit. Can I save that story for another day?"

I don't want to share how I had let my guard down, starting to
want to share ordinary moments and the news of the day. I even
began looking forward to returning home after another week of

travel. I called his phone from New York after a long, stressful day, and feeling beat-up and lonely, looked forward to hearing his familiar and soothing voice. His was not the voice that had answered, but a cackling and drunk-sounding female one.

The one hundred and forty-two times he called afterward went unanswered. Not one reply to the eighty-nine texts or forty-seven emails. I watched the little red numbers rise across the bottom my phone screen like watching your winnings accumulate on a slot machine after three little symbols match up. I only had myself to blame.

He tried expensive gifts. Then he tried thoughtful ones. He sent flowers by the dozen. Involving my parents proved to be a futile effort. Surely, none of them thought I would settle for second place. Lesson learned, I had successfully shut down any possibility of future suitors. I'm so lost in my head I barely hear Ryan.

Thankfully, Ryan answers my question with, "Sure."

That story can remain safely tucked away in my head and heart for now. "Just never buy me a watch and tell me it's about time to forgive you!"

He wrinkles up his nose in disgust, "Not a chance of that happening."

"Can I ask you something instead?" I have a burning question and it gets me off the subject of the four-letter word I prefer to avoid.

"Of course. And sure."

"How did you start doing yoga?"

"A woman on an airplane."

Funny, I could say the same. Thank you, Barbie. But this is his story.

"She said she had just seen a book about a guy who was a paraplegic yoga teacher. She said it was inspiring and wondered if I had read it. Because, of course, I read every book on the subject of paraplegia." He laughs.

I don't.

"It's okay to laugh about this stuff, Cass. Really. You know that laughter is the best medicine thing? Anyway, I told her no, but I would check it out. I picked it up and it sounded like something I wanted to try. I took the book to the studio and dropped it off at the desk and asked for a teacher to call me if they were willing to help me out. That's how I met Lynn."

"The woman at the front desk?"

"Yep. And Alexandra. She was the one who called. We've gotten pretty close. She's like my second mom. Gives me plenty of rules to follow and some wisdom thrown in for good measure."

"What do you like about yoga?"

"At first it was that I felt like half of me wasn't so damn dead-feeling. I'd lost the connection to so much of my body, and it gave it back to me. I was only doing it privately with Alexandra. Then, when I got better at some of the core and arm stuff, it was the strength I felt.

She forced me to come to a class, but she does a lot more floorwork than other classes when I am there. Every class, when she instructed us to leave something behind on the mat I didn't need, I did. That mat's taken a lot of pain, anger, envy, and a whole bunch of other crap that made space for something better.

Now I go for the energy in the room. You can't get it practicing alone. You don't have to do all of the poses to get that. You just have to breathe and be open to taking it in. I always leave feeling like I've caught some sort of a buzz, without the calories or consequences of any vices." He pops another piece of sushi in his mouth like it's an exclamation point.

"Oh," I say quietly then add, "I want that too." I contemplate how far I am from the Zen and peace that I know is the promise of yoga, but hell, I've got to start somewhere.

"Come home with me, Cassandra."

I stiffen in my seat. I don't to reject Ryan, but really? I'm not sure that's a good idea. He pins me in his gaze, tempting me to deny him. His body might not be that of an alpha male, but the determination and insistence in his glare say his spirit is.

I search his eyes for a reason to say no.

Will I hurt you?

Will you break me?

I think of Barbie's words again. *Holding back won't keep you safe. It will just keep you lonely.*

The pain from broken love eclipses lonely. Lonely you choose, heartbroken is chosen for you. Yes, I can live with lonely, but I won't survive another crushing blow to the heart. There isn't enough Elmer's in the world, Barbie.

I look away because I don't want to see his expression when I tell him, "I'm sorry, Ryan, but I can't."

He squeezes my hand. "I don't mean to make this awkward, but I wasn't inviting you home for, um—" He looks at me sideways, out of the corner of his eyes, like he is stealing time to deliver the blow more easily.

I know where he is going with this and spare him, covering my eyes with my hands. "Oh my God. I'm such a—"

His forefinger against my lips stops me from finishing the sentence.

"Do not mistake me for a fool, Ms. Lewis." He brings my hand to his mouth, like he did after the wedding. I push away the thought of how his lips felt against mine. His taste. And touch. "There is nothing I'd like to show you better than my bedroom, but I wouldn't be so brazen. But I do have something else I'd like to share."


I FOLLOW Ryan into an underground parking garage. I marvel at the fact that he drives like a normal person. I notice it's the same SUV model Audi that Cecil drove in California. Walking to the elevator, we pass four other Audis in various colors parked in a row. No handicapped signs on parking spots. In fact, no other cars even occupy this level. I wonder, but don't ask.

When we step into the elevator, Ryan presses the palm to the black screen and then the number five. The next moment the doors open into the gym he had showed me the last time I was here. If I thought the view by daylight was worthy, it didn't hold a candle to the one at night.

I peek through the glass on one side to see the holiday-decorated red and green lights of the tall Renaissance Center, then walk to the other side of the room. Colorful lights of the towering Christmas illuminate tiny skaters moving in an orderly fashion around the perimeter of the circular ice rink. I can see each snow-covered peak of the tiny glass houses of the Christmas marketplace, and the orange glow of several fires warming the crowds that surround them. It's a breathtaking scene below.

I've lost Ryan in the process of getting lost in the city. I look around but realize that he must have entered the space I saw Chris disappear into the last time I had been here. Speak of the devil, the door opens and Chris' head pokes through. "Hey, want to come in?"

"Sure," I answer hesitantly, remembering my fear of what might be behind the door, some sort of Ryan's version of a red room. Now that I've gotten to know him better, I bet there would be a whole floor, not a room. I almost laugh out loud.

Once I step through the door, I almost wish it was a red room. At least I would have known what I was looking at, having been educated by the movie after all.

Instead, it looks like a physical therapy center, but other contraptions and machines fill the space as well. Shaped plastic pieces look like braces of various shapes and sizes. Mini engines are lined up on the floor along one wall. I'm not sure how to begin to take in what stands before me. Especially because it's Ryan.

I have to look up, I swear a full foot.

"You're short," Ryan says, smile licentious.

"You are not." I know my mouth agape isn't a flattering look but there isn't a thing I can do about it right now.

"Six foot two. And such a different view of the world from up here."

I'm trying to wrap my head around this, but what I really want is to wrap my arms around him. I work to hold back tears. They will not spill a second time tonight in sadness. This time, it's because I am overwhelmed. And moved. And not just because I am seeing the Ryan that was. Or could be. Or is. It's also because of the pictures on the wall behind him, the wall to my right, and the wall to my left. I'm surrounded by thousands of smiling faces.

"My inspiration," Ryan says as he moves – walking - several steps closer to the left, the wall closest to us.

"*Our* inspiration," Chris chimes in with a light laugh.

Ryan is walking with the help of some sort of futuristic-looking black-and-silver exoskeleton bracing his middle, hips, and legs. I'd seen videos when searching paraplegia online but it was different to see in real life.

"Along with Ironman," Chris laughs again, "And I am not kidding about that."

Ryan points to the picture in the top right frame on the wall. "Max. He's six. In Guatemala. He wants to play soccer." He moves his pointer finger to the next picture. "Daisy. Twelve. She wants to learn to swim." The next one, "Alejandro. He is twenty. His family had a sorghum farm in Tamaulipas, Mexico, but they can no longer rent machines to harvest. There is too much fear the equipment would be stolen or damaged by gangs. He just wants to be able to work to provide for his family."

Ryan has a story for every picture. Each picture was a child or young adult. In a wheelchair. Many only had one leg. I followed him, and Chris, the distance of the first wall, listening to at least forty memorized stories.

Chris moves protectively with Ryan, the way a mother does on a playground, preparing for the next obstacle that could break her child.

I continue to make my way around the room and take in each picture. I stop and look over my shoulder. "Do you know all of these stories?"

"Between the two of us, yes," Chris answers, then adds, "I've met a lot of them. You have no idea how happy I was when Ryan came along and gave me the chance to build the foundation I always dreamed of running. You have no idea," he repeats trailing off.

He has made his way to me. He points to a boy wearing a large smile and two prosthetic legs. He is probably about five years old.

Chris is in the picture too, on one knee, arm slung around the boy's shoulder. "That's last year. In Angola. He barely learned to walk before he lost both legs in an IED blast. Other kids carried him around for years, but he had started to get too heavy. He was getting left out of everything. It's not hard to help, with the right resources. He's got a whole set to grow into too. And doctors we trained to help."

"Those are the easier ones," Ryan says, "the SCIs are tougher to help."

Frustration is evident in Ryan's voice. It does something funny, and terrible, to the center of my chest, a gnawing feeling that spreads to my stomach.

"But we're trying," Chris rushes to add, adamant. "We've got plenty of fight left. And time—and people—on our side, Steadman."

"Chris was a collegiate cheerleader. Can you tell?"

I think Ryan is serious. I assumed his muscles were from some other kind of sport. I really need to stop judging.

"Comes in handy with this one," Chris laughs, pointing his thumb in Ryan's direction. Then he looks directly at me. "Come here, Cassandra."

It's a command, not a request. I walk to him. He takes my shoulders and positions me to stand before Ryan. I look up into his eyes. As I did the first time I met him, sitting next to one another in row ten. Entrancing eyes. With their mischievous twinkle. Cloudy-at-sunrise soft blue. The dark line where his eyelashes meet the lids. My breath hitches beneath their penetrating gaze.

"I can't take another minute of you two looking at each other the way you are. Kiss the girl like you mean it, Steadman."

He bends forward, and I push up onto my toes to reach him. Warm breath. Deliriously soft lips. His tongue pushes slowly, and deeply into my mouth. I drag mine against it, and let his lips possess me.

I reach my arms up to slide around his neck, slick with sweat from the exertion of his holding his body upright. It's the same kiss, but feels different with him tall and strong and standing. My hands walk down to his shoulders, and over the curve of his biceps, then land on his chest, muscles rippling beneath my fingertips.

It's not enough.

I want to feel all of him.

Our lips finally part, retreating to their separate spaces from having become one. I tenderly let my fingertips slide down the curve of his, letting the stubble rake my palm. I look at him with respect and admiration I've never felt for another human.

Chris has been right next to Ryan just in case, but had turned his back for us to have a facsimile of privacy. Swept away, I had forgotten we had an audience. Now, I feel the flush of embarrassment.

"Nothing to see—or hear—here," Chris says with a laugh, covering his eyes then ears with his hands. "I just want to see this guy get the girl. He deserves it." He slaps Ryan on the shoulder.

*He deserves better than me. But he's shown me I can be better than I am. I want to be the woman he deserves.*

"Ready to call it a night?" Chris asks.

Ryan nods. I guess he is.

Me? I'm not even close.

# RYAN

*I*'m going to dance at my wedding. I'm going to have a wedding. Somehow, someway. Damn hope has crept in again and I don't have enough sense, willpower, or strength to kick its ass to the curb. Standing before a woman again tonight—not to mention Cassandra's kiss—has left me feeling invincible.

This new-found confidence has me feeling cocky. Cassandra follows me into the elevator, and I press my palm to the screen to choose the floor.

We exit the elevator to the penthouse and she still hasn't spoken. "You haven't said a word since our kiss."

*I wouldn't mind having stunned her speechless with the kiss.*

"I've been thinking."

"Well then, a penny for your thoughts?" I stop moving forward and she stops before me. I look up into her eyes. *I'd even pay a cool million or two to know what was going on inside that head of hers.*

She leans back against the kitchen counter, arms crossed over her chest protectively. "I can't come up with a single reason to run away."

She almost sounds pissed.

"I want to. But I can't."

Definitely a biting tone that says angry. And I haven't even done anything this time.

"I want to believe you would cheat on me so I have an excuse to not fall for you, but I don't think you would. I want to believe that knowing you hasn't made me better, but I would be lying to myself."

She takes a step in my direction, releasing her arms to her sides.

"I want to think I could walk away and not look back, but you've already made your mark."

She stands before me and reaches her hands out. I take them and pull her to sitting on my lap, cradling her in my arms.

"I want to know everything about you, Ryan. Especially what the hell magic you worked on me to get me to break my rule of no PDA. I just made out with you and Chris wasn't even a foot away!"

I wonder what other rules I don't know. I love that this woman would keep me on my toes. I love knowing there will be more kisses with her tippy-toed and my leaning down to kiss her like a man should. But for now, I'll take her in my arms with me here. Her neck is perfectly positioned for me to place kisses up and down its exposed side. I lick my lips, tasting the salt on her skin from yoga.

"Why did you just say you wanted to believe I would cheat on you? Is that the story you wouldn't tell me earlier?"

In case she might have missed it, I don't exactly have a line of people waiting in the wings. But even if I did, that would never happen.

"Yes, Ryan. It's a story. I let my guard down for love. Once. Ask me how that worked out."

"It got you here," is my reply.

She contemplates my words for a moment. "It did," she says softly. "I guess that's a new way of looking at things."

"There's almost always another way to see things." I brush a tendril of hair that has escaped her ponytail from her cheek, tucking it behind her left ear. "Just a wild guess, you didn't give him a chance to make it up to you, did you?"

She shakes her head from side to side, "I'm pretty sure in his case there was no other way to see things."

In fairness, she hasn't been forced to learn this as I have. It's likely she also hasn't had to learn to forgive the hard way. The very hard way. Hopefully, I'll get to share that lesson as well. Before I do something where I might need it. Again. But for now, I can take one of her reasons for love being a four-lettered word off the table, "I don't make promises lightly, Cassandra, but one thing I can promise is that won't happen with me."

"I don't have any clothes. Or a toothbrush."

I guess she was satisfied with my statement. She catches me off-guard yet again. Maybe with a little luck, I'll have her in my arms in my bed.

"Well, I can cover one of those two," my voice comes out in a desire-filled rasp. I pull her in for another kiss, anticipating what's to come.

"May I shower?"

"Of course. Follow me."

Before, I would have invited myself to join her, but I am not ready to go there yet. I lead her to the guest bathroom, and press a sequence of buttons to turn on the water from the various jets. "If you want to change those, just press these buttons." I move forward and grab a towel from the heated rack and hand it to her.

"I might steal this," she says cuddling the towel to her cheek then, hanging it over the top of the door out of my reach.

Reaching for her tennis shoe, she removes it, along with her sock, and sets her foot back down on the tile. "Come on! Heated towels and floors. I might never leave."

*You don't ever have to.*

She slides her pants downward, with nothing beneath them, then steps gracefully out of each leg. Unzipping, then removing the jacket I'd given her, she reaches behind her back, crosses her arms in front and removes her bra over her head.

My breath lodges somewhere between my lungs and throat, stuck and unwavering, taken away with the sight of her naked before me. Dangerously taunting curves and full breasts beg my hands to trace and caress them. My eyes move to the cleanly shaven area between her legs, hoping that what comes next is her.

"I've never seen anyone more beautiful, Cass. Flawless. I can't wait to get to know every inch of you."

Her head ducks with the compliment, and again I feel in awe of the fact that she owns a boardroom with the air of a queen, but in this bathroom she's the humble peasant. "Get in the shower," I direct her, because her nipples are puckered with the hint of cold in the air and I don't want to leave her exposed.

She complies and I watch as she steps inside. She leans her head back into the spray of water, sexily raining down from overhead. Beads of water begin to stream over her body from the top down. I follow their pattern as they dance over her slightly turned up nose, full lips, and long neck. Then, the outline of her breasts, smooth stomach, and lean muscles of her thighs. I'm jealous of the water touching all of her naked perfection. The sight should be cause for arousal if there ever was one. Water steaming the clear glass allows me to reach for myself unnoticed. Sadly, my wanting isn't enough.

I leave a toothbrush and toothpaste on the counter, bring her my robe and hang it on the drying rack, then shower as quickly as I can. Thankfully, she enjoys a long one herself, and I am waiting in bed by the time she is done. The fireplace and small lamp next to my bed will provide the perfect illumination.

When I hear the pad of her feet, I call for her, "In here, Cass."

She crosses the threshold making a mockery of how I look in my robe. Mermaid-like, her wet hair hangs straight, and would cover her breasts if they weren't already covered. She is naturally beautiful, and I might prefer her without makeup.

Check that.

I have no preference. She is beautiful with makeup and without, in leggings or a business suite, inside and out.

I'll take her any way I can have her.

# CASSANDRA

*I*'ve always wanted a bedroom with a fireplace. A contemporary white marble surround, no less than one hundred inches wide, has orange flickering embers dancing inside of its black casing. The soft light emanating from the nightstand will be kind. No makeup and wet hair have me feeling more vulnerable than a girl would like.

Ryan's pristine white bed looks heavenly. He, tucked beneath the sheets, looks even more so. What some would call a torso, I call chiseled perfection. Sculpted shoulders and protruding pectoral muscles are exposed, peeking from the blankets, perched on the pillows like a gilded bust of a warrior.

I walk around to the far side of the bed. I let the robe slide over my shoulders to the floor. Ryan's eyes shamelessly roam over my body. I'd never just stood naked, still like a model posing to be painted, before tonight. Now, I've done it twice.

The bed is low profile, and king sized, so I traverse the space toward him on my hands and knees. I place my lips in a lingering kiss on his shoulder as if letting him know I have arrived. I lie back on the pillow and let the bedding surround me, sinking into it like a cloud that envelopes me.

We roll to face one another. "Hey you," he says, reaching his arm over my waist. I feel claimed with his hand on the small of my back.

"What is the thread count on these sheets?" I should not be thinking about this, lying naked with a man, but I know if I don't ask it will be in my head whatever happens next.

"Eighteen hundred."

I feel my eyes widen. I didn't even know thread count went that high. I thought I had made it when I bought a good satin set after the breakup. I admit, "Not going to lie, I have a little bed envy."

"I'm a good sharer," he replies, with that devilish dimple tempting me.

"So you've proven. First your shower. Then your toothbrush. Now your bed."

"The toothbrush was new," he says with a laugh. Then he adds, "The bed is new to a woman too."

My heart clutches. He said it's been nearly four years since the accident. Surely, he's been with a woman since? I can't ask that now. Either way, I am not sure I want to know the answer.

Wanting to show him I want all of him, I press my index finger to his lips, which he kisses. Dragging it over the curve of his chin, the bulge of his Adam's apple, then down his neck, I stop to rest on the tracheotomy scar that fills the V-shaped space between his collar bones. I open my hand to cover the scar momentarily before my hand drifts to his heart. Under my fingertips I feel his heart pounding hard in the middle of his chest. Or perhaps it's my own I feel, matching the pace of his. Breathless, the words, "What happens now?" ghost over my lips.

He takes me.

That's what happens.

His hands and lips are everywhere. Hands clutching behind my back as I cling to his shoulders, taut muscles too big for my small, feminine hands. I squeeze the top of each, massaging, and he groans into my mouth against our kiss. My hands glide over rock-hard biceps and bulging pectoral muscles, fingertips dancing over defined abdominal muscles. I count the rise and fall over each of the six above the waistband of his pants.

My head tilts backward, his lips covering the flesh of my neck with kisses. I thrust my chest forward against his bare one. He pulls me closer and my breasts feel the tickle of the fine hair covering his chest. They ache for his touch.

Our tongues intertwine, dancing along, and darting between, one another's lips. Learning them. Memorizing them.

His tongue traces my bottom lip first, and then I feel his thumb trace behind it. My eyelids flutter open. His eyes gaze into mine, our faces close. I think I've stopped breathing because I am dizzy.

He's been denied.

I've denied myself.

He strokes my damp hair, then his palm slides down my neck, and over my collarbone. Pausing to let his fingertips tickle my shoulder, his nails, with just the right pressure, graze my upper arm. At my elbow, they dance along the sensitive crease and my toes curl. Sliding down my forearm, his fingers then trace the outline of each of my fingers then circle my palm. He curls my arm upward and slides my index finger into his mouth, then pulls it outward with gentle pressure around it. No one has ever paid this much attention to one part of my body.

My breasts are his next playground, nipples caressed, sensitive flesh on fire as he sensually massages each with just the right firmness.

Ryan's hand moves down my back to my waist, over the hourglass of my hip, then thigh. He doesn't stop until he reaches my calf, then his hand recedes. Finally—treacherously slowly!—his fingers move upward. When his hand slides between my thighs, every cell in my body is filled with the anticipation of him touching me. I bend my leg and rest it on his thigh. "Is this okay?" I whisper against his lips.

"Yes," he answers into my mouth. I've made space for him and he has reached the top of my thigh. I gasp when his fingertips find me, his touch so light I barely feel it. "Is this?"

"Oh yes," I reply, panting expectantly.

His fingers are heavenly. I've never been touched so slowly, calmly, and thoroughly. He is paying such close attention to my body's wants and needs. When my hips push forward in delight, he lingers in the spot patiently. It isn't until every inch of me has been learned that one finger slides inside.

I'm going to come quickly, because every nerve is on fire and his thumb and fingers together are beautifully overwhelming. "Yes, Ryan," I gasp breathlessly, my hips pushing forward and retreating, moving with the motion of him inside me. His finger finds a spot I've never felt and I still and let sensation wash over me. "Right there," I gasp again. "Yes," is one long syllable. My hand involuntarily moves to his hip, bracing me against him while pleasure washes over me.

"Come for me," Ryan demands against my lips.

I do.

For him.

For us.

Everything I usually hold back, push aside, and press down, I let escape in the sounds of my release. I allow myself to feel it all. Everywhere.

He holds me. I'm still breathing. At least I think I am. Contentment settles equally in my chest and between my legs. "Thank you," I whisper.

For a moment, I can't wait for seconds, but then guilt washes over me. Most likely, I will never be able to return the favor.

# RYAN

*C*assandra just absolved over three years of desire and deprivation that collided, then melted, into her first orgasm. It was long and hard. Willing to let me linger and explore all of her, she seemed eager for my touch. Starved for it even. It pleased me to please her, reigniting what I've defended against for so long.

Lying on my back, she is cradled in the crook of my right arm, cheek pressed to my chest. I feel the exhale of each breath warm on my skin. Her hand rests upon my heart. She feels so damn good in my arms.

I stayed half clothed, and her hands have respectfully stayed above my waist. I am thankful. This is uncharted territory I want to navigate carefully. I want to control what I can, including my fear and doubt.

Unhurriedly, her fingertips drift across the skin of my abdomen, moving downward.

"Ryan, can you still feel me?" she asks when she reaches my navel.

"Yes," I answer solemnly, contemplating the sadness I will feel when the warmth of her touch turns cold.

"Tell me where it stops."

She moves so slowly I hate the anticipation of her reaching the area where feeling fades to numbness.

"There," I finally say when she reaches a few inches lower, "but I kind of feel you everywhere right now."

She straddles the line I indicated, flattening her hand against my body. It feels too heavy to think about the future and the unknown, so I reach for her hand and pull our clasped hands into my heart.

She pulls our entwined fingers to the center of her chest, then flattens my palm just left of its center. "Before I met you, if you would have asked me where I stopped feeling, it would have been right here."

"Oh, Cass." I hold her close, breathing in the clean smell of shampoo and soap. I kiss her on the top of her head.

Her breath is slowing and deepening. She isn't going anywhere but to sleep in my arms. Her breasts push against my side with each deep inhale then retract, and I wait impatiently in between to feel them again.


A SLIVER of December gray sky peeks though the opening between the two long black velvet drapes covering the bedroom door that leads to the balcony. Morning. I've not forgotten what it's like to wake with a woman in my bed, I've just forgotten how much I love it.

Waking with Cassandra in my arms, I know I want to try again. I want to feel whatever pleasure I can, even if it's not like before. I owe it to her to try as much as I owe it to myself.

She must feel me stir because she rolls away. I have to handle a personal pressing matter, and I'll make coffee.

When I return to the bedroom, she's in the exact position as when I left, but as soon as I join her in the bed again, she inches her body next to mine.

"Am I dreaming, or do I smell coffee?" Her groggy morning voice is sexy as hell.

"Am I dreaming, or do I smell the scent of a woman in my bed?" I lean over and kiss the top of her shoulder.

"Good morning, beautiful."

She groans and wriggles her body along mine, hitching her leg over my thigh. Either Cassandra Lewis isn't a morning person, or she is really comfortable. Maybe both.

"I love this bed," her lips mumble against my side, the words salve to a bleeding heart.

"We can stay in it all day."

"Or forever," she says hastily, sounding more awake.

If she's a woman of her word, she just might unbreak me after all.

Cassandra's eyes flutter open, pushing herself up onto her elbows. She steals my cup of espresso from between my hands and draws a long sip with a, "Mmm. Thank you," before passing it back to me.

I set the cup on the nightstand.

Here. Goes. Nothing.

I gently bend Cassandra's light leg upward at the knee to rest at my waist. I explore her inner thigh watching my fingers trail downward into the valley formed by her other leg bending upward as she realizes my intent. My fingertips dance lightly over her flesh, dipping into the crevice, brushing over her momentarily then moving back up her other leg with the back of my nails. Her hips writhe with my contact against her sensitive thighs, thrusting upward then releasing into the bed.

When I finally cover all of her with the palm of my hand, fingers pointing downward, she lifts against me. Two fingers are swallowed inside of her, lost in velvety softness. She groans. I reach my free hand across my body to her and cradle her breast, tracing the outline of her nipple. She groans again and I feel her clench around my fingers.

Her hands disappear to where I cannot feel, and I wonder if my body will respond. I know I have options, but I'd still like to know what might be possible.

Then, our escapade is rudely interrupted.

My phone is ringing on the nightstand. I had it on do not disturb, so a favorite contact has called multiple times, breaking through. I ignore it, and instead move my mouth over Cassandra's nipple, feeling it come to life with the flick of my tongue.

And it's ringing again. Damn it. Or maybe I am saved by the bell. Perhaps it wasn't meant to be this morning.

"Matt. Welcome home. How was the honeymoon?"

"Wish I could say it was good to be home."

"Why are you calling instead of texting?" Not Matt's usual modus operandi.

"Samantha said I had to say thank you in person. Dude, seriously. You didn't have to do that."

He's referring to my honeymoon surprise. "I know. How was it?"

"Amazing. Beyond amazing."

I hear ruffling followed by an excited Samantha with a high pitched, "Oh my God, Ryan. You are the best!"

"You're welcome, Samantha. Glad it was amazing."

"I was not expecting that. Our villa was, ugh... I don't even have words. The private butler? Over the top?"

"Totally!" Matt screams from the background.

"We'll show you the pictures at Christmas. When are you coming? Are you bringing Cassandra? Please tell me you are bringing her. I have in-laws now; I need reinforcements! Please, Ryan?"

Samantha asks too many questions for too early and too little coffee. Plus, I was a little busy.

"I'll have to let you know, Samantha."

"Can you ask her? Like right now?"

*Like while she is in my bed?*

"I'll let you know." Eager to be free of the hard press, I say, "Tell Matt I said later."

"Later," he returns from afar.

Cassandra is propped on the pillows beside me. She reaches over me, seductively letting her breasts drag over my chest and steals my coffee again. "What'd you do?" she asks, taking another sip and leaning back into the pillow. I'm disappointed we aren't picking up where we left off, but I guess the mood is postponed.

"This is so good, by the way."

"I'll go make you one in a minute. I just wasn't sure what you liked. I might have upgraded their hotel room as a surprise."

"To a villa, with a butler. That's some surprise. That was nice of you."

*Someone should get to live the life of luxury I can pay for but can't live myself.*

"A beach vacation sounds great right about now."

So apparently, we are going to talk now.

"Or a mountains one. Or any one, actually." She sits up straight as a rail. "Let's go! I haven't been on vacation in forever. All I do is work! How about after Christmas? We can leave from Florida and go farther south, somewhere hot! Or Europe? Maybe Europe."

My right eyebrow rises, contemplating. I'm pretty sure eleven hours ago she told me she wasn't coming home with me, and now she is proposing a trip? From Florida?

"Does that mean you are coming with me for—"

My phone is ringing again. No one makes phone calls anymore, yet number two is incoming. Now I am sure it's the universe intervening.

"Christmas? Yes!" she finishes my sentence enthusiastically. She looks over at the buzzing phone back on the nightstand.

"It's Charlotte. Answer! Tell her about Cecil!"

"Good morning, Charlotte."

"Mornin'! How's my favorite Midwesterner? Deal with that twenty-million-dollar problem a.k.a. Cassandra Lewis, yet? Did she like your suck-up wear?"

Charlotte's southern drawl is whiskey to the ears, until it isn't.

Haven't had a woman in my bed in nearly four years, and today I get two phone calls with too many questions getting me in trouble. My eyes fall closed. If she heard the last conversation, she undoubtedly heard this one. "I gotta call you back, Char."

Cassandra's mouth opens, then closes, then falls open again. Like a fish. No words spill out. I picture a conversation bubble above her head filled with hashtags, ampersands, and exclamation points forming each and every expletive that I deserved to be called based on what she's just heard. Her feet are already on the floor.

"Cassandra, wait!" I feel like every guy in a movie who has to chase after a pissed-off female. Only I can't chase her. "Cassandra, don't! Wait! Come back." My words are useless.

How pissed is she? She has dragged my wheelchair to the doorway with her.

There is no good way to get from the bed to the floor and to the wheelchair across the room. I can't risk the awkwardness of her walking in on me trying. Damn it. "Cassandra!" I yell out again, more beseeching this time.

She appears in the doorway, fully dressed. That was fast.

"Please let me explain. It's not what you think you heard."

*Well, part of it, anyway.*

"They always say that."

Mental note. Find out why she said that.

"I mean it, Cass."

Eyes shoot daggers the width of the room. I've seen the look before. In my kitchen the day of the football party. I don't want to think how that ended for me.

"Do. Not. Ever. Call me Cass again."

*That's where she goes?*

"Why?"

"Apparently that's your thing, since you also called Charlene Char. So, no thank you on the nickname."

I read between the lines. She thought it was special for her. It was. It is. She is. "It's not her nickname. I was cutting it short to get her off the phone. I swear."

"I can't believe that you didn't even pick out my gift!"

I try to dodge this barb too. "I only asked her to recommend the size. I shopped myself." It was the truth.

Hands on her hips, Cassandra growls, "Two hundred seventy-eight. That's the number of times my ex tried to contact me. You know the number of times he heard from me again? Zero. Let's be clear. The only way you'll ever speak to me again is if you kidnap me."

I wait for the final blow. Charlotte saying Cassandra was an expensive problem. It doesn't come. She disappears from the doorway and all I hear is the ding of the elevator's arrival.

"Consider yourself warned, I'm not above kidnapping! Cassandra?" I call out once again, hoping maybe she changed her mind. "Damn it!" I throw myself backward into the pillow. Deafening silence follows. A reminder of the fear I faced when I woke to my new reality. The pain. The loss. The loneliness. A chill sweeps over me. I grab my phone and call her. Two rings and voicemail. I knew she wouldn't answer the call. Nor will she again. Not even a truckload of flowers is going to get me out of this one.

# RYAN

*I*'m sorry.

It's the two hundred seventy-ninth time I've said it.

I've tried to reach Cassandra harder than whoever came before me.

And, I warned her.

# CASSANDRA

he sound of my stilettos on the marble floor as I make my
way to Charlotte reminds me the heels are small and
pointed and would maim an eyeball quite nicely. An eye for an eye.
Luckily for her, I've been to a yoga class each day of the last ten days.
I'm learning to breathe before I react and have started to find something inner Zen-ish, but I am still a work in progress.

Being that she and Ryan are close enough to have her doing his
shopping, I will assume she knows exactly why I wear the scowl I do
this morning like a badge of honor. I need to get this deal done today,
and move on with my life.

Except, of course, everywhere I go and everything I do reminds
me of him. When I boarded the plane this morning my phone was
ringing, and I didn't dare answer. It would have been rude to do so
surrounded by other passengers. Then, there was Cecil, who said I
didn't look so fine today. Well, thank you, Cecil, for the newsflash. I
wonder why? He probably knows too.

Now, of course, there is the fact that I am expected to walk into
this boardroom and report on how Ryan and I have worked together
on the proposal. When in fact, we have not. Which means I must be

prepared for sabotage. Based on what I overheard, it's of the $20 million variety.

"Cassandra, it's nice to see you again." Charlotte smoothly smiles in my direction as I approach the desk.

*Wish I could say the same, Char.*

"Merry Christmas! Are you ready for the holiday? What are you asking for from Santa?"

*Santa, please make Char stop talking to me like we are friends when we are so not that.*

"You know Santa's not real, right, Char?"

*I had to. Blame the little devil with permanent residence on my shoulder.*

She tilts her head and frowns like she pities me. Oh my God. I need to be transported from this hell. I am about to be rescued, "Chuck, nice to see you again." I say it extra loudly so Charlotte notices I have the congenial words in my vocabulary, I just chose not to extend them to her.

"Good morning, Ms. Lewis."

*Pretty sure he called me Cassandra last time. Not a good sign.*

We step into the boardroom and thirty-two eyes bore into me, scorching. Maybe I shouldn't have been so eager to escape the hell that was the lobby, because I may have walked into the ultimate inferno.


I DON'T EVEN BOTHER to return the goodbye Charlotte offers as I stomp, grown-up temper tantrum-style, in the straightest beeline I can to the door. Her cheeriness echoes. "I wish you a very Merry Christmas, Cassandra! I hope you have a magical holiday!" She's a female version of Buddy the Elf. Call me Scrooge, there's no Christmas spirit for me.

I briskly brush past Cecil sliding into the backseat without a word. We ride in silence, and I purposely avoid making eye contact in the rearview mirror.

I open my laptop and start the revisions I'm forced to consider.

Damn him. In no universe is there a way I can sit in the office of my chief financial officer and tell him that I am losing $19.8 million of Paragon's profit. How those bastards could believe Ryan's revenue projections over my careful calculations is unfathomable, but that is exactly what has happened.

How could I have been such a fool? Believing he didn't have an ulterior motive? Believing he cared about me? Getting close to me was just part of his carefully crafted chess game. He was taking my pawns one at a time, readying his king to capture my heart. Checkmate.

I nearly groan out loud in frustration. My jaw is clenching twenty-four by seven, and I think I may have had a few heart palpitations somewhere around 3:14 a.m. because a butterfly-like flutter replaced the normal thump in the middle of my chest. No amount of yoga can undo my uptight, though I can't imagine what I'd be like without it!

I've been watching the tree-lined highway passing by out my window, but I notice the landscape has changed. This doesn't look like the way to the airport I am used to. I look up and lean forward to Cecil, "Is there an accident or something? Do you have to take a different route to the airport?"

"No, Ms. Lewis. I have to use a different airport."

I look at my phone. I swipe at the airline app. I turn the phone in his direction, not that I want him to take his eyes off the road to look at it. "Everything looks fine to me." It indicates an on-time departure from San Jose.

"Don't you worry now, Ms. Lewis. I'll get you where you are going."

I scoot forward, to the edge of the leather seat. I look through the front window, but no signs are visible. I pull up the map app and check our location. "Cecil! What's going on?" I have no patience for this. It's already been a long day getting annihilated, and now this? Not to mention the last time I slept well was in Ryan's bed, eleven long nights ago.

"Cecil! Please tell me," I demand with mounting frustration. At least I said please.

"You've got a nice ride today, Ms. Lewis. It'll get you where you are going."

"Boston?" Since it's already the twenty-third, I had arranged to make the long traverse on the company.

"Mmm," is Cecil's reply.

He is exiting under a green sign with an airplane symbol that says Norman Y. Mineta. What the hell? I haven't a clue what this is about. He turns right, driving along a sideroad next to a fence with several smaller planes and landing strips to our left. We reach a guard shack where Cecil rolls down his window. "Merry almost Christmas, Mr. Jackson. You get that wife of yours something nice?"

So apparently, he's been here before.

"Nah, not yet. I've got a whole day left. That's for tomorrow, Cecil."

"Well, good luck with that."

"I don't see Mr. Steadman on the manifest today." The man runs a finger down a clipboard.

Steadman? I knew he had a hand in this!

"Not today, sir. Passenger Lewis, confirmation echo, delta, roger, one, eight, one."

"Ah, yep. Got it. We've got you on number two. You have a good holiday now."

"You too," Cecil replies while the window rises to close.

When just a couple of inches are left, the shock wears off enough that I yell forward, "I'm being kidnapped!"

The gate rises and Cecil pulls beneath it. The window raised to closed, I'm too late. "I'm not getting on any airplane here, Cecil." I'm obstinate.

He keeps driving, staring straight ahead, until he turns like he's done it one thousand times. Two men in black that look the part of stereotypical bodyguards, complete with earpieces, approach the car as we roll to a stop. I am hanging onto the headrests of Cecil's car. "I'm not kidding. I don't know what's going on, but I am not going anywhere until someone tells me."

Both of the back doors open on either side of me, one suited man stationed to my left and one on my right. Cecil is already out of the front seat. I hear the trunk open behind me and peer through the window as he hands my suitcase to the man holding open the door. He makes my bag look like it weighs nothing more than a dragonfly, so I don't think making a run for it is going to go well.

Cecil stands next to the man on the left, casually chatting like they are BFF's while I contemplate my options. With a resigned sigh, I slide to my left, so I'll have one more shot at getting Cecil to talk.

I get out of the car, facing him squarely. "This isn't fair, Cecil. I deserve to know what's happening here."

"I promised Mr. Steadman I would take good care of you. I have, and now these gentlemen will. I'd never put my favorite in harm's way, Ms. Lewis. I'd only do this for my other favorite. You're in good hands with Marcus," he says with a tilt of his head to the man rounding out our little circle. He looks to the left across the car, "And Jack. And Ms. Mary on board. When you arrive, you'll be in good hands with Mr. Steadman. I gotta good feeling 'bout this. You'll be back to fine in no time. Merry Christmas to you, and enjoy your time in Florida."

"What?" I scathe. "Florida? Are you kidding me? I'm being kidnapped and taken to Florida?"

Marcus laughs at my flair for the dramatic. Rude. He has my elbow and is guiding me around the back of the car, and now *I* feel like the dragonfly, my feet barely touching the ground. We reach the long ramp; stairs obviously wouldn't work if Ryan were flying. Marcus finally releases my elbow when I'm stuck between the two metal sides behind Jack, then steps in behind me. I feel like an elected politician, or maybe a prisoner of war, or a criminal being flown to jail. I want to be none of the above. But if I must play the part, I guess it isn't totally awful that I've just been escorted onto a nicer private plane than I could have dreamed up.

I look to my left and right as I cross the threshold, right foot first. To my left, the cockpit with a male and female pilot. To my right I assume is Mary, but am about to find out.

"Welcome aboard, Ms. Lewis. Let's get you comfortable."

*You have your work cut out for you, Mary.*

Soon we are seated in the softest tan leather seats I think money can buy. Not a little money. This is the kind of plane that only a lot of money buys. It's been custom designed, I can tell, with space between the seats that will accommodate everything Ryan needs. Besides the six seats, there is a room with a desk the size of my home office and a bedroom with a full-size bed. There is also a full-size bathroom with a shower. Yes, a shower. On an airplane.

"Passenger is acquired and ready for takeoff," Jack speaks into the small microphone he pushes to his mouth.

Acquiring is what I do, not what gets done to me. And I am so not ready for takeoff. Clearly, it's not as if I have a choice at this point.

"Will let you know when the eagle has landed."

He pauses.

"You too, Mr. Steadman. And you're welcome."

Oh, I can't let this one go. I scream in Jack's direction, "You're not getting away with this, Ryan! I don't know who you think you are dragging me to Florida against my will!"

Christmas in Florida was off the table faster than Charlotte had said the words twenty-million-dollar problem. I have zero intention of spending an hour in Florida, let alone Christmas.

Jack leans forward, "He said, tell her I am sorry. It's the first time he's saying it and won't be the last."

It will be if I have anything to say about it.


ABOUT FIVE HOURS LATER, it's clear that I don't. There is a cavalry of four of the same Audi SUVs, this time black, waiting on the landing strip I can see below us through the plane window. By this point, I assume he has a fleet.

Not another word had been spoken by me to Jack, Marcus, or Mary for the duration of the trip. I stubbornly refused to accept any of their service. In retrospect, it was a stupid idea because I am starving and thirsty and I could have had him buying me all the free drinks that I wanted. Whatever the cost, it clearly wouldn't make a dent in his net worth. This was a war I was ill-equipped to battle.

I spent every minute of the flight ratcheting up my anger and plotting my revenge, but the moment I stand at the top of ramp, I soften. I'm pathetic. I need the warmth that washes over my body from the streaming sunshine overhead. I feel my shoulders release from where they'd been hunched, angry and defiant. I close my eyes and let the breeze blow across my cheeks and nose. I breathe in the scent of humid sea air.

Opening my eyes, I see Ryan sitting in his wheelchair at the end of the ramp. I start forward, and see he is holding a sign in front of his chest. In thick black magic marker, on a simple piece of white paper probably straight from a printer, it reads: HEY, BEAUTIFUL. I APOL-OGIZE. #280. AND AS MANY MORE AS NEEDED.

I bite my bottom lip so I don't crack a smile. He has gone to an awful lot of trouble for me. I knew he tried to reach me a lot, but hadn't been counting. I'm glad he had.

I stop in front of him. God he looks good in a tight white tee shirt. Now I know what it feels like in his arms too.

I almost relent.

No. I know better.

I'm not caving. Screw. Him.

"I know you are angry with me," he says pointing at the sign. "I'm not kidding when I say as many takes as it takes."

"I was mad before I was kidnapped," I seethe through my permanently clenched—now eleven days running—jaw. "Now, I'm incensed."

"At least I didn't buy you a watch or call your mother. You told me kidnapping you was my only option, so I had to take some drastic measures. I assure you; you were in good hands. I knew you weren't going to give me a chance to explain."

"I think plenty was already explained this morning. In the board-room. You should be happy. Char said I was a $20 million problem, but turns out it was only $19.8."

"Check your email," he says.

I have to step aside for the crew to exit the plane. They hug and handshake Ryan and thank him for whatever Christmas gifts he must have given them like I am invisible. It seems he is saintly kind to everyone. Everyone but me that is.

I sync my email then scroll until I see why he has told me to check my email. All I need to see is the subject line reading: Proposal Accepted. I open the message to read the confirmation. How can this be? "Dear Ms. Lewis, on further discussion post your departure, we would like to inform you that we will proceed with your final proposal as presented." I skip the rest and turn back to Ryan.

# RYAN

"Better now?"

Her eyes squint at me. I wish the sunlight was the cause, but I think she's still pissed.

"You're relentless, Ryan."

That's not really what I think I am, but I'll take it for now. She has grabbed her suitcase delivered by Marcus and is heading across the tarmac toward the waiting car, the only one left. She is stuck with me.

I'm braving another first. She puts it in the trunk and moves around to the other side of the car.

"I can't believe I was held hostage on an airplane and now in an Audi." Her arms are crossed over her chest. I've seen that before and it didn't go well for me.

"Well, I can think of worse places to be held hostage than an Embraer jet and a Q7."

Just then, her stomach growls. So loudly I can hear it across the car. I press my lips together. I'd gotten a message from the plane she was refusing any food and beverage. I would have played her for the take- everything-she-could type in the revenge game, but once again she's surprised me.

"I'm feeding you, Cass."

"I wasn't kidding when I said never to call me that again."

I deserve what she's giving me and I'm happy to take it. Just like I was happy to pay the $19.8 million myself.

"Can I tell you something?"

She doesn't answer, but I proceed anyway.

"I followed Matt over the ledge. I was afraid something would happen to him. We never left our wingman."

She turns in her seat, arms still crossed but wide eyed. I have her attention.

"Forgiveness is never the easiest thing, but sometimes it's just the right thing to do."

If I hadn't been able to forgive Matt, I'd have lost more than the use of my legs. I would have lost a brother. And if my parents weren't heartbroken enough, it would have added to their pain.

"It was the hardest thing I've ever done. People screw up. Sometimes they are ill-intentioned, and sometimes it's just an accident they hurt you. I think everyone is just doing the best they can."

"Damn you!" she bursts out.

I look at her. Tears brim. Then overflow down her cheeks. "I don't cry, and I don't talk to strangers on airplanes, and you keep saying the same things Barbie did, and now you are like Jesus with the forgiveness thing, and damn it, I always wanted someone to be waiting for me when my plane landed." Her words, and tears, are spilling out. "Everything I thought I was I might not be. I liked myself just fine before you. Even the little red devil on my shoulder. We were BFFs!"

She sniffs, and I press the button for the glove compartment to open. She reaches in for the small box of tissues. "I can't do this, Ryan. I have to be in or out. I can't straddle love and hate. I couldn't even do the splits when I was young and flexible. Now I'm old and I thought I liked my ways. Turns out," she stops and groans loudly, "I can't believe I am going to say this. Turns out you have made me want to be a better woman."

"I think I might have heard that somewhere before," I reply, admittedly a little delighted." Plenty of songs, movies, and books tell that tale as old as time. Sometimes love has a way of doing this, sometimes you're forced by something else. If you get a choice of what to pick to make you better, love is the right answer. Right now, I am not sure she knows that answer, and I need one too, "I'm not sure if I should apologize for that, or kiss you. Which do you want?"

"Yes? Neither? I don't know. I don't know what I want." She lets out a very long, very exasperated sigh.

At least now I can finally offer her an explanation." I am sorry about what you heard with Charlotte. When I told her about the deal, it was a business problem. It was the truth. It was-" I hesitate, then add, "Before."

*Before I knew you were someone I just might fall in love with.*

"Don't hold it against Charlotte. I didn't tell her how our fake date ended, but she knew I was more than a little smitten with a beautiful brunette. She's been a good friend and all she wanted to do was protect me from falling for someone who might break my heart."

She shakes her head. I think in disbelief.

"Oh, the irony. I want to be mad; I really do!"

I know I shouldn't smile, but she's so cute when she's stubborn.

"How can I be mad at her for giving you exactly what I want from you?"

I'm officially confused. "What do you want from me, Cass?"

"I want you to promise me you'll try not to break mine."

I'm pulling into the restaurant parking lot. I turn into the closest spot, twist in my seat to grab her face and pull us together. I give her my promise in a hard kiss, devouring her taste and smelling lily of the valley. I smile against her lips knowing she didn't stop using the perfume.

I soften my lips against hers, so she knows there are always two sides to balance. It's a dance and a gift to have the chance to figure out how to do it together. Some days will be hard, some will be gentle, but just as our lips join together so beautifully in both, we can get through them together.

"I promise," I finally whisper into her mouth.

She swallows hard, hopefully capturing the words that I mean to fill her soul. Her lips begin to move against mine, "They say everything is better in the morning and on a full stomach. Dinner is going to cost you, and I'm going to test that theory in the morning."

I'll trust I've filled her soul, and I'm happy to fill her belly next.

I'VE PICKED a beachfront restaurant with a view. And a patio I know I can easily navigate. I had already called ahead and made sure to have the table waiting, with one chair and two settings. The sun is an orange ball getting ready to drop into the sea, with the cast of colored characters about to take the stage. There is not a better spot around to lose yourself in the romance of the sunset.

Cassandra did run up a nice dinner tab with steak and lobster, and of course dessert. It's one I am happy to have the chance to pay.

Sated, she leans back against the cushion tied by ribbon to the white wrought iron chair. "If you thought a romantic sunset was going to get you back in my good graces, you were right." Her words, softly spoken, hang between us in the heavy night air. She gazes in thought as the stars begin to dot the horizon where the sky meets the sea.

She closes her eyes and shakes her head. "Just great," she whispers, annoyance coursing.

"What?" I ask.

"I guess I have to add making me a romantic to the list of things you've done to me."

Thrilled to hear this, I know she'll appreciate her Christmas gifts even more.

"Do I need to apologize for that egregious offense too?"

"No, Ryan, you do not," she says shaking her head in resignation. "I surrender. Take me to bed. I'm exhausted and I need to rest up for the parents. I'm going to need to do some shopping in the morning because I did not come prepared for this."

"I might have you covered, but of course. It's the least I can do."

"Yes, it is."

With that, I slide my hand around the back of her head and pull her to me. I remember her rule. There are three other tables still populated next to us. I want to show her I do respect her, even if I did kidnap her today. "How do you feel about a little PDA?"

"If we missed the most romantic kiss ever, I'd be pissed," she says with a laugh. "Rules are meant to be broken, aren't they?"

Okay, then.

I pull her lips to mine and take her. The breeze blows her hair across my face, I taste the salt in the air on her skin, and hear the waves lapping at the shore beside us. This kiss is pure magic. Magic to heal the ache of the last weeks without her. Magic to fill the void of the last few years. The magic of surrendering to forgiveness.

CASSANDRA HEADS straight for the balcony of our oceanfront room. She had nodded off in the car on the way, but she seems awake enough now.

As she heads back into the room, she cries out, "Uncle. Uncle. Uncle. I thought I had resolve but apparently not so much. Hours ago, I wanted to kill you. Now I want you to kiss me. Again."

She walks to me and sits on my lap, arms around my neck. I kiss her softly and slowly, relishing the feel of her against my mouth. When her eyes flutter open, they dart toward the bed where I've spread clothing options for the next few days.

A pair of jeans, leggings, a floral-patterned sundress with a light sweater to match, and several short- and long-sleeve t-shirts are arranged in arcs across the bed. She jumps up, slides the pair of Ray-Ban aviators on, and picks up a pair of Tory Burch leather sandals from several pairs arranged on the floor at the side of the bed. Holding one in each hand, she smiles the prettiest smile I've seen yet. "You were pretty confident I was going to be in this room, huh?"

I try to resist a smirk, but I fail.

"I'm not saying I am easily bought, but you have sucked up adequately. At least for today."

"I shopped for everything by myself. I swear. You should check the drawers too."

She walks to the long dresser supporting the television and opens the top drawer. I've filled it with a variety of undergarments.

"Thank you for realizing it would have been humiliating to do laundry at your parents' place."

"You are welcome."

She returns to my lap and snuggles in again.

"Can I ask you something, Cass?"

"Mm-hmm," she answers without protesting the nickname.

"Are we past you being my fake date?"

She answers my question with a very long kiss.


FALLING asleep with Cassandra in my arms makes the darkness more tolerable. The last few weeks had reminded me of the loneliness of each night in the hospital, and then rehab. Each night, the gravity of the situation surrounded me like a crypt.

She flinches as she falls asleep. I kiss the top of her head. "I've got you, babe." I'll try out the new nickname again tomorrow when she's not half-asleep.

"I know," she whispers sleepily. "Thank you. I wish I wasn't too tired for makeup sex." My gut wrenches into a nautical masterpiece of a knot. If she's faced her fear of becoming my girlfriend, it's time for me to face mine as well.

# CASSANDRA

My eyes spring open. No, I am not a morning person, but my mind is already full of thoughts running around like kids on a playground. Falling asleep last night, I think I made mention of sex. Maybe he was already asleep? Maybe he didn't hear me? Maybe he hopes we might try? I won't bring it up. I'll let him lead. There's an idea. I need to stop. Breathe.

"Morning, babe."

*He's never called me babe before.*

"Good morning," I try to sound nonchalant. "Have you been awake long?"

"Yes, but that's okay. I was entertained by your snoring."

I prop myself halfway to sitting on my elbows. "What? I don't snore!"

"No, you don't," he says with a laugh that makes my heart happy.

I look around and don't see a clock. "What time is it?"

"Nearly eleven."

"Oh my God!" I exclaim. "I guess I was tired! And comfortable! Do I need to get ready?"

"Well, the festivities start at three per the text from my mom." He lifts his phone toward me as if for proof.

I do quick math in my head. I need an hour. But the beach calls my name. "Do we need to check out? Go early to help cook?"

"Do you want to go to the beach?" Is he reading my mind?

"I really do."

"Let's go."

"Really?" I ask with childlike anticipation.

"Really."

My feet are on the floor. I sift through the pile of clothes he has laid atop the dresser.

"It's seventy-two degrees."

"I can't wait!" I clasp my bra and pull on a t-shirt and leggings from my new collection. I head toward the bathroom to brush my hair and teeth. Moments later, Ryan appears in the bathroom doorway, wearing only black pants and bedhead. Sexy as hell. I walk to him and grab handfuls of his untamed hair, pulling him in to kiss me.

"Uh-uh. Only one of us has morning breath," he says turning his cheek to me.

"Good thing I'm patient," I say relinquishing the grip on his hair.

I know he doesn't believe me for a second. Tapping my nails with impatience on the stone countertop, I wait as he brushes his teeth.

"Ready," he says, and I lean in. He grabs me and pulls me down quickly into his lap. I laugh in surprise then let him kiss me knowing what I said in sleep last night was only foreshadowing. Santa, I need a Christmas miracle.


HERE. Goes. Nothing.

We arrive to a not-so-humble abode situated on the intercoastal waterway. Starting to pay attention to the details that might impact Ryan, I realize upon arrival that this house hasn't been made accessible. A removeable ramp awkwardly spans the distance across the Florida-style grass to the front door.

Jane greets us just inside the door, clearly anxious for our arrival. She squeezes him long and hard then does the same to me. I hold my breath but let her. "I'm so glad you are both here!" she squeals, near giddy with delight. "Come on in!"

I look around, taking in the cozy beach-themed décor, cool tile underfoot and lanai beyond the kitchen in front of us.

Following Nick through the living area and down a hallway to the right, I drop my bag and Ryan's in a guest room. Nick deposits each of our suitcases. On my return to the kitchen I walk slowly, glancing at the pictures on the table at the end of the hallway and affixed to the wall. Samantha and Matt looking happy, at a younger age than they are currently. Nick and Jane at the beach. Matt in a football uniform. Matt in a lacrosse uniform. Matt's senior picture. Nick, Jane, Samantha and Matt with a birthday cake donning a small explosive on top. My heart palpitates. It's as if Ryan doesn't exist.

When I reach the kitchen, I'm thrilled to find Ryan alone, because I can't hold myself back from asking, "Why isn't there a single picture of you?"

"You noticed?" He looks at me, dumbfounded.

*Of course I did.*

"I asked Mom to get rid of them. Too much of a reminder."

I want to hold all of him. Right now. I can almost hear the sound of my heart ripping into two like it was as thin and flimsy as paper. I move behind him so he can't see that tears have welled. My hands on his shoulders, I bend to place a kiss on his neck in place of the words I don't have.

OVER DINNER, the conversation is easy and varied. Matt and Ryan take turns throwing each other under the bus with stories of teenage screw-ups. Nick and his sons enjoy spirited banter speculating on the upcoming market conditions in the new year. Matt and Samantha share their current work projects. Nick and Jane speak of upcoming vacations to exotic locations.

I am asked plenty of questions, but I'm a master of the simple answer, and the 'how about you' turnaround, until Matt slips in, "Cassandra, have you ever been married?"

I nearly choke on my wine. "No. Never."

"Engaged?"

"No. Never."

"Huh." Matt joins the others in a hushed silence, as if this is unbelievable. Everyone resumes eating but there is something peculiar about the conversation. As if to change the subject, Ryan says, "Mom, Cassandra would like to see some embarrassing pictures of me."

Her face lights up. "Really?" Eyebrows raised skeptically, she seems to need confirmation of what she's just heard.

Ryan gives her the validation, "Really."

As SOON AS the last dessert plate is cleared, Jane disappears. Returning, she holds a large blue plastic tote in her arms. She removes the lid and carefully lifts a smaller box from inside. She removes the rubber band holding the lid closed and begins to unearth a lifetime of memories.

For the next hour, Jane digs through the first box, then others, extracting picture after picture. In addition to the loose pictures are framed ones that have been packed away for safe keeping. Each time she lifts one, she is an announcer responsible for introducing the next act. "Ryan and Matt in their Red Flyer wagon. Aren't they cute?" She looks to the room for agreement. "Ryan's handsome senior picture!" Held outstretched, she turns the standard posed headshot to face me. "Isn't he handsome?"

The next shows Ryan in his football uniform, kneeling, and looking formidable with no smile to be found. My breath hitches. I hope it isn't obvious. It's the first time I've seen him before. I study his wide shoulders, trim waist, and sturdy-looking legs. He looks tall. Solid. Strong.

"You should see this woman throw a football!" Ryan laughs with the compliment directed at me.

"I had a good teacher," I return, happy to offer this compliment in front of his family.

Jane lifts the next picture. Ryan and Matt on a boat. "Were you boys drunk here?" she asks innocently. Ryan grimaces. Each picture has a story, usually accompanied by the easy laugh of a shared family experience.

When Jane reaches the bottom of the bin, she chokes up as she lifts, then lowers a framed picture. Swallowing hard, she manages to prevent the tears from spilling after they have crested.

Ryan places his hand on her forearm gently. "Mom, don't cry. It's okay."

He reaches for the frame, peering at it intently.

My eyes move to the faces too. Ryan holds skis, Matt a snowboard. They stand on a mountain top, goggles on top of their helmets, sun shining overhead. Their arms lock behind the back of the other. Ryan looks down upon his little brother. Both wear exceptionally happy smiles.

Silence fills the room. Ryan rolls himself to the table at the end of the hallway. We all watch as he moves the pictures already occupying the space. He nestles the picture in his hand amongst the others, back in place with his family. Exactly where he belongs.

WE ALL JOIN in the living room after dinner, forming a kumbaya-esque circle. My family has never had this fairytale scene with siblings. The tree sparkles with white lights, and red and green ornaments adorning its frosty branches. Presents spill from under the tree into the room.

Matt appears before Ryan with a guitar. He plays with the strings for a few minutes then strums. I wait expectantly for the first song, like a groupie. The notes to Silent Night drift through the air. If my heart wasn't full enough, it overflows now. I fall harder than I ever have. I memorize this moment.

When the song is over, I pat the couch next to me. Ryan moves his legs, then body, to fill the space. I lean to whisper, "You are the sexiest man I've ever laid eyes on, Ryan Steadman."

"Are we doing PDA this evening?" he growls into my ear. A spark of energy hits deep in my core.

I return an answer, "No. But I can't wait for bedtime."

"How about bedtime right now?"

"How about yes?"

THE STARS outside our window seem to be twinkling just for us. Moonlight from the full moon casts soft shadows across his profile. If I could write the description of a perfect day, I just lived it. Whatever happens next is icing on the cake. I don't know what that means. But I am willing to find out. He is lying quietly next to me. Maybe he isn't sure what this means either.

"Cass, do you ever think about your deals and the people whose lives you change?"

I'm thinking about the possibility of sex, and clearly, we are not on the same wavelength. What was the question again? A hard-to-answer question is best answered with another. "What? Why do you ask?"

"It's Christmas. Do you wonder what kind of Christmas they are having this year?"

The truth is not what Ryan wants to hear. I leave the question lingering between us until he speaks again.

"I'm not going to lie; my life isn't easy. I wish it was different. Often. But I'm still grateful to be where I am. There were eighteen other T's or C's in the spine I could have broken. Each would have been worse. I know every time I take a deep breath that there are others who can't. Seeing the sun is different for me than others. I never take it for granted because there was a time I was trapped in a broken body inside a building and I couldn't see it.

I didn't get where I am alone, so I guess any chance I get to make things easier for other people, I take. Because, why not?"

I'm really not sure where he's going with this.

"Cass, the people that get left behind when you acquire their company are good people. I'm not saying it's not important for you to make sure Paragon gets their fair share, I'm just saying don't forget to think about what fair actually means."

"Okay. I will. I'll think about it. Is there a reason we are talking about this now?"

"You know how they say that when something on you breaks the other parts compensate for it? I want you to know my heart most, because I think it's gotten a hell of a lot stronger because of the broken parts. I don't know if the rest of me will work, but I know my heart does, and it's the best part of me."

"I love you."

My words breathe into the world unexpectedly, but I feel them with certainty, "I love your heart, and the rest of you. Especially those abs that put mine to shame. I love those too." He laughs, and I join in, grateful to have the mood lightened.

He wraps me in his arms and, holding my body close from head to toe, he whispers, "Me and my abs are falling in love with you too, Cass."

His lips speak the words, then seal them with a kiss, "And even if the other parts can't show it, they are too."

"I'd like to find out if they can," I say, without any apprehension. I've just declared my love; everything else seems less daunting than that. "How about right now?"

# RYAN

*I* expected Cassandra to say she loved me less than I was expecting to try to have sex tonight. I unwrap her from my arms trying not to notice the void and cold that could be permanent if this doesn't go well. "Give me a minute," I whisper. I'll need a little privacy.

A few minutes later, and a shot to the nether region I can't feel anyway, I am ready. I've only tried this solo once but it felt pathetic. Everything I've studied, and others I've talked to, said it would be different with a woman. I guess I am about to find out.

"You know I've watched every video and read everything written in printed and digital form about this, don't you, Ryan?

I didn't. Not going to lie, it eases the pressure, and I can breathe again.

"I know what you probably just did. And I know we have plenty of options for what we are going to do. I'm not even stuck being on top for life but that wouldn't have been a deal breaker anyway."

She says all of this so casually I feel a bit foolish for how much time I've spent obsessing over this moment.

"We got this," she says as her lips brush against my earlobe drawing a shiver. Her Then her lips find my neck, "Together."

"I may have done my homework about my favorite Taurus' favorite spots too," she says, placing teasing kisses all around my neck with her lips while fingers play in the hair at the nape of my neck.

"A little self-serving, are we?" I ask playfully, remembering her birthday near mine has us sharing the sign. I've done my homework too and know every erogenous zone on a woman's body, which will be very well attended to. I'll make up for any lack with extra attention to the details.

I bite her neck gently back before I kiss up her chin to her lips. I roll onto my back and sits on her knees straddling me, "It's really too bad you remembered to buy me pajamas. I didn't really need them."

I laugh and feel the pressure of her body bounce up and down around my waist. I reach for the hem of the tank top and she lifts her arms. The silhouette of her body is beautiful in the light of the moon.

Cassandra leans forward until her breasts are firmly pushing against the naked flesh of my chest. I wrap my arms around her back while I cover her lips with mine. I slide over the curve of her hips, moving beneath my hands. I may not feel them grinding against my body, but I can imagine.

"You feel so good," I growl into her exhale as her fingers get lost in the strands of my hair.

She whispers back, against my lips, "I want you, Ryan. Whatever it means, I'm ready. And so are you." I hope that means what I think it does. She writhes over my body, and finally, I'm willing to be completely exposed. I am going to be with a woman for the first time in a very, long time.

# CASSANDRA

"**M**erry Christmas!"

It is not Ryan's voice I hear first. Am I dreaming? Had I fallen asleep with the wrong brother? No, I barely had any wine. I should just keep sleeping.

A knocking sound. Then the same voice, closer this time.

"Delivery. Stay under the covers, Cassandra. My wife will kill me if I look at another naked woman."

I'm not dreaming. I smell coffee. And meat.

"Thanks, man. Now get out."

I hear the door close.

"It's safe," Ryan says with a laugh.

I groan, but push myself up to seated, leaning into the pillows. I fist my hands and stretch, then rub the sleep from my eyes before opening them. I smile when I do.

Ryan looks so happy, boyish with his hair tousled. By me. He pushes a steaming mug in my direction. "Merry Christmas, beautiful!"

"We had sex!" I can't help it. It just blurts itself out.

"Yes, we did," he says with a chuckle that fills my entire chest. This is what bliss feels like. Coffee in bed with a gorgeous man who you have realized you love despite everything you ever thought you knew. And soon, there would be presents. And food. I lean myself back into the pillow to let it all soak in. I can't imagine a better definition of heaven.

"Breakfast is ready!" Nick's voice rings out beyond the door.

I can't even get to a bathroom without passing by people, so I will ponytail up and be thrown into the family fire. Somehow, I don't even care.

SAMANTHA and I serve the feast of stuffed French toast with plenty of meat and potatoes as sides. Neither of us helped prepare the meal, and I apologized for that, but Jane assured me that she and Nick weren't expecting, nor wanting, help in the kitchen. They like to cook together. Maybe I could learn, and Ryan and I could cook together as well. I might be getting a little ahead of myself. Love might conquer all, but I am not sure my cooking ability falls into the all category.

The conversation flows comfortably until Jane asks the simple question, "How did you all sleep last night?" I'm busy scooping fruit onto my plate but quickly realize all eyes, sans Ryan's, are on me. Matt and Samantha start laughing first, followed by Nick. Jane tries to act demurer and hides hers behind a napkin.

I'm the deepest shade of crimson, realizing what they'd heard. Ryan's hand reaches for mine and squeezes it.

Jane picks up the bowl of fruit where I have set it down. As she scoops some onto her plate, she says, "I'll have what she's having!"

My choices being laugh or cry, I choose to laugh.

"Dude, we're just glad you can still get some action!" Matt, of course, points out. I wonder, however, if it's not a relief for all of them to know.

The conversation quickly changes to New Year's plans, the wedding presents Matt and Samantha had received, and nothing has seemed to change post the revelation of hearing our prior night's escapades. The gift of them accepting me, in spite of this, is the best Christmas present I could ever hope for.

.   .   .

AFTER BRUNCH we move to the tree to unwrap the cornucopia of presents spilling from beneath its boughs. Ryan strums random Christmas songs by my side, and other than the fact it is sunny, not snowy like I'm used to on Christmas, the scene can't be more perfect.

"Cassandra, as our guest, you go first." Nick points to the center of the room and I sit cross-legged in the middle of the familial circle. He takes great pleasure in playing Santa to the family, lifting each gift and reading the tag aloud. I feel like a child again.

Removing a three-tiered green foil-wrapped red ribbon-tied package, I can see my name written on the tag in Ryan's handwriting.

Slowly tearing off the wrapping paper of the small box, I peer inside. I remove a red tissue-wrapped item and peel back the paper. It's a sturdy metal Eiffel tower ornament, in shades of rose pinks and dusted with glittery white snow. I open the next, revealing a ceramic figurine in the shape of a girl sitting cross-legged in lotus position on a yoga mat that looks like a flying carpet. I unwrap the last item in the box. This time, I pull from the tissue a crystal pair of crossed skis. I look across the room, where he catches my curiosity without stopping his strumming.

"All the places I want to take you."

Everyone looks in his direction, "Yes, I'm even going to ski again. Lots of paras do it. Why not?"

This time, I catch Nick swipe a tear.

I walk to Ryan and kiss him, PDA be damned.

Returning to the circle, I unwrap the second box and lift the lid, revealing a stack of postcards tied with a white fabric ribbon. I untie the bow and examine each picture. Beach scene featuring several yoga mats, a beautiful open-air studio sporting downward dogging students amidst palm trees, and a spectacular sunset. Tantalizing food, a zipline above a canopy of green, and several other pictures danced across the last card. It all looks luxurious and exotic. I flip the final postcard over and Ryan has written in its empty space: Can't wait to share all of this with you. We're booked for January...XOXO. I look up to him. "I can't wait! Oh my God! I love it!"

I proceed to unwrap the last box and try not to look surprised at the word on the top of the box. Cartier. I know the significance of its contents. Both its price tag, and it's meaning. It's not one, but two of their famed love bracelets, one gold, one silver. I am breathless and speechless!

"I couldn't decide which one, so I got both," Ryan says as I make my way silently to him, box in hand. He sets the guitar on the floor beside him and reaches for the outstretched box. He slides the bracelets onto my right wrist then pulls me forward by it to whisper in my ear, "Designed in 1969." I laugh through closed lips to keep the secret ours while looking into those incandescent eyes twinkling with mischief. I'm thrilled he's thinking of new possibilities, both skiing and sex.

In the middle of my profuse apology for not having brought gifts, Ryan stops me.

"Look under the tree, Cass."

I look at another package wrapped as mine was, and see my name signed along with his on the gift's tag. While I find this endearing, it's also slightly annoying. It means he had assumed I would be here with him.

"Confession time," Ryan says. "Come here, babe."

I like babe.

He lays his hand on my leg and looks across the room. "I didn't actually know if she'd be here today." He proceeds to tell his family our story. The whole story. Our first meeting where we didn't see eye to eye, then being forced to work together. The feigned wedding date to impress the family. He shared for the first time the work he was doing around the world with Chris.

Leaving out the exact number, he surprises me with the knowledge he'd financed the $19.8 million himself. Finally, he told them of the forced flight to Florida. I jump in at the end, "But I'm so happy to be here now!"

Unexpectedly, Matt offers an explanation, "There is just no

arguing with fate." He stands and walks to Ryan, lifting his coffee mug in front of him. Ryan reaches for his on the side table. A brother's sacrifice and the redemption of everything lost is celebrated in the clink of the china mugs meeting one another. I cover Ryan's hand on my leg with my own and hold on tightly.

SAMANTHA and I are alone in the kitchen, tackling the post-meal mess. As an only child, I would welcome the chance to have a sister-in-law for a friend. We are bonding our way through packaging leftovers, returning jars to their rightful places in the fridge and pantry, and dealing with dirty dishes and pans. I wait, towel in hand, to dry the pan she is washing.

"Can I ask you a serious question?" Samantha asks looking in my direction.

I'm not sure I like the tone of her question so when I answer, "Sure?" it sounds like a question.

"Don't take this the wrong way."

*Cue rapid heartbeat.*

Nothing left to scrub on the pan in the sink, I know she is stalling, probably to draw the invisible weapon about to hit me. She leans her hip into the counter, "It seems like you really like Ryan, but are you sure you are up for this?"

"Up for what?" I genuinely wonder what she is referring to.

"There's a lot to deal with. It just seems like it would be daunting for anyone, let alone someone who is used to, you know..."

*Actually, I don't. What I am used to is burying myself in work because I can't deal with relationships.*

She sighs. "I just don't want him to get hurt again is all."

*Again?*

"I'm not sure what guarantee you want from me. There are never any guarantees. I've fallen for a great man, and all I can do is my best. I'm not in this for the parking if that's what you are worried about."

Relief washes over Samantha as she laughs at the absurdity of that. I am happy for the conviction I feel defending my want to be with him, especially considering the last few weeks.

"Love him hard then, Cass. He deserves it."

Yes, he does. And I am going to be the woman he deserves by doing just that. I might be sorry, but I have to ask, "What'd you mean by hurt again?"

"Shoot," she says looking guilty. "You don't know about Melanie."

"No. What don't I know?"

Ryan appears in the kitchen. Looks like I will be waiting to hear that story. "Hey, we've got to get going, babe. There is something I have to do at home."


WE MAKE our way through goodbyes, with Samantha the last in the lineup. "It was so great to spend time with you, Cass. And you too, Ryan, but you know I really want a kickass sister-in-law! And you two seem like you belong together."

Ryan and I exchange glances. "Maybe we do," we echo in unison, sharing a laugh.

Once settled in the car, I call my parents. Mom answers the phone cheerfully, "Merry Christmas, darling!"

"Hi, Mom, Merry Christmas! You are on speaker. Ryan's here too. We just left the Steadmans'."

*And I'll be flying home in a private jet, Mom.*

Ryan chimes in, "Hello, Ms. Lewis. Nice to meet you. I look forward to meeting you in person."

"You too, Ryan. I'm jealous we had to share you this year, Cassandra." Then she adds quickly, "Happy for you, but nonetheless, jealous! We missed you!"

When I told them about my Thanksgiving date, I'd left out the minor detail that Ryan isn't like most others. I should explain soon.

"Did you two have a good time?"

I hit the mute button and turn to Ryan, "Yes, Mom, it was, um-."

He laughs at the inside joke about getting caught in the act by his whole family.

Unmute.

"Yes, Mom, it was pretty wonderful."

"I must say I am a little surprised to hear you say that, Cassandra. I know how you love small-talking with people so much." She could try to be a little less sarcastic, but not a chance.

"Mom, don't give away all of my secrets!"

"Was Santa good to you?"

"Yes, very." I touch my wrist as I lean my head back against the seat and look over at Ryan. Black hair. Blue eyes. Heart of gold. "He planned for us to go on a yoga retreat! I can't wait!"

"My Cassandra is doing yoga?" She covers her surprise as well as a small child playing hide and seek who hides in plain sight.

Ryan stifles a laugh.

"What have you done to my daughter, Ryan?"

*If she only knew.*

SAMANTHA'S DISCLOSURE is still burning a hole in my pocket when we enter Ryan's penthouse. I didn't have the heart to bring it up on the plane ride home because I didn't know what emotion it might evoke for him. We are having our second perfect day and I wouldn't want to spoil it.

When I round the corner to put my things in the bedroom I stop, frozen in place. A tree of the prettiest magnitude stands before me. It has to be sixteen feet tall and professionally decorated in mostly silver with coordinating jewel tones of blue and green. For the second time of the day, I feel like a child, full of awe and wonder.

"I can't believe you have a tree like this!" I exclaim thinking of my last few years without one at all, let alone one this magnificent.

"Well, I didn't exactly decorate it," he says looking toward its top with a broad smile.

I set my things down right where I stand and pull the box of ornaments from my bag. I hand the ornament with the skis to him. I hang the Eiffel tower by its gold thread right at his eye level. The yoga girl doesn't match the tree's sophisticated décor in the least, but I hang her next to it anyway. Ryan leans forward and adds the skis just above. "Now it's perfect," I say and lean in to kiss him, long and deep.

"What are all these presents still left?"

"I'm hoping you're game to help with that. It's my next project."

"I believe you meant *our* next project," I correct.

MINUTES LATER, on the thirtieth floor, we enter a similar, but much smaller, version of Ryan's home. The scrawnier Christmas tree is decorated with strung popcorn, cartoon-character plastic ornaments, and seemingly every sports-themed item ever made to hang on a tree, all bunched together in one spot.

The picture on the mantle shows a little boy about ten, not surprisingly in a wheelchair, with a woman leaning down next to him. He isn't smiling, but she is. There is just one gift under the tree. I pick it up and find myself overcome with emotion. The clumsily wrapped, handwritten tag says: To Mr. Ryan. From: Santa. I take it to Ryan and hand it to him. He opens it to reveal a pair of socks inside. Bicycles in every color of the rainbow adorn the socks. Ryan smiles, heartfelt.

"Tell me. Please." I'm impatient to know more.

Ryan shakes his head, "We have to go; we don't have much time left."

"I need details, Ryan! You're killing me!"

"Soon enough, Cass. Let's go."

We return to the penthouse and repeat the process four more times. When we reach the last home, there is one gift under the tree, hand wrapped. I move to set it to the side to place our last bag of gifts under the tree. I notice the tag. With my name. From Santa.

"Does a girl named Cassandra live here?" I ask Ryan.

Both his eyes and his smile match. Mischievous as ever.

"I'll answer my own question. It's for me?"

"Yes."

"Can I open it now?"

"Yes."

It's a book. Pride and Prejudice. And by the look of the somewhat tattered condition, it's an authentic early edition. A homemade bookmark with a punched hole tasseled in yarn reminds me of eighth grade. And it should. A picture of an awkwardly teenaged girl with a braces-filled smile is attached to the bookmark by puffy stickers of hearts and butterflies. Immediately below the pictures reads Maggie, age fourteen.

I flip the bookmark over, where she's written:

*Obstinate, headstrong girl is a compliment.*

My lips reach upward into a smile. Below it she has written, *I've read this three times, and Mr. Ryan and I think you will love it too. I'm happy to give my gift to you now.*

Of course, my eyes dart to his.

"Don't worry. It's been replaced." He points to the bag of presents.

By the time I make my way to him, tears slide freely down my face and I don't bother to wipe them away. I'm thankful for the gift in my hand, but more for the gift he's given my heart.

"Play Santa, Cass. We've gotta go," he says, returning my quick kiss.

"THIS WAS ALMOST the most perfect day of my life," I nearly coo with happiness as Ryan and I share the corner of his comfortable couch in front of the fire.

"Only almost?" he asks while tucking a strand of hair behind my ear. "I would give it a perfect, myself."

"You gave me amazing gifts and I didn't have anything for you. Obviously, I had no idea I would end up here."

"Oh, Cass, not true. You gave me something better than anything you could have wrapped."

*My heart?* "What?" I question.

"Watching you tonight. Your excitement at putting each and every gift underneath those trees. You will make a great mother someday."

Well, wow. That was quite a leap, a conversation for another day, far, far away.

"You have to tell me. Who are those kids? Families?"

"Patients. Sometimes families come from out of town for procedures. Their family needs a place to stay while they are here, and I happen to have a way to provide a suitable place."

*Suitable all right.*

"They were all at a party at the hospital tonight. Maggie and Shawn will be home soon, Kevin and Kendall won't until later this week, but they'll Facetime to see that Santa was there, and presents are waiting."

"What about the socks?" I ask, pointing at his feet, where he's already put them on and texted a picture to Shawn.

"Shawn wanted to give up. He was paralyzed in a car accident where his dad died. The first time he made any progress was when Chris and I came to his rehab and I rode a bike next to him. He saw if I could be in a wheelchair and do it, so could he."

"That was so nice of you."

"I was just repaying a favor."

I want to know more about the favor, but I can't wait any longer to ask about my conversation with Samantha. "I need to ask you something." I don't want to throw Sam under the bus, so I am careful. "Have you ever had your heart broken?"

"Of course. Haven't you?"

I know this question-on-question tactic. Besides, he knows it's a rhetorical one. "Of course," is all I offer.

"I was engaged once."

I know I straighten even though I try not to. I had expected a relationship but not an engagement. At least now I know why the family had gotten strange during our Christmas dinner conversation.

"I proposed the week before the accident. I ended it the month after."

Oh my God. "I'm sorry," I offer. "Why?"

"Don't be," he says, pressing a kiss to my temple. "It wasn't going to work with Melanie. She wasn't the one to help me pick up the pieces. When you fall, that's what love can do. That's why I do what I do for those kids. And the others."

"What do you mean the others?"

"The people you met here that day, Cass. Remember I told you about the many acquisitions I was involved with?"

"Yes."

"I just help them pick up the pieces. A lot of people lose when you win."

I swallow hard. I have a job to do and I do it well. I'm not sure how I am to blame for the misfortune of others caught in that crosshair. But, he's given me something to think about, and somehow, he is still here despite knowing what I do.

For now.

"Don't go anywhere," he says, moving back into the wheelchair, looking like he has an idea.

I think I should be the one telling him this. Don't go anywhere, Ryan, because you almost have me convinced I want to fight for love too. With you. Because of you. For you. And for everyone else. I settle into the couch contentedly, "I'm not going anywhere."

HE RETURNS A FEW MINUTES LATER, legs braced differently. Ensuring the wheelchair locks are secure, he reaches for my shoulders to pull himself to standing. He blows out a long exhale and grips my shoulders tightly.

I slide my arms around his back and hold him. Above the line.

"Alexa, play "Bless the Broken Road."

I know the notes to the song that starts to play.

"Are you sure you should be doing this without Chris?" I ask, fear-filled.

"Yep, I've got this part. It's taken a lot of practice. It's like my second first dance as an eighth grader. Just as stiff and just as scary."

I look up to where he towers a foot above me. I look up to him more than just physically too. What he's done with his money. What he's done with his body. What he's done to me and for me.

"I think everything that's happened to me has been for this. To get me here," I say leaning my head against his firm chest as he envelopes me.

"Yes, challenges can shape who we become, break us or push us to be better. But we can always write our own definition," he says, kissing the top of my head.

"Well, I think Jane Austen wrote my definition for me. Obstinate and headstrong."

"It's a compliment."

"I'm difficult," I concede.

"Luckily for you, I've learned to do difficult pretty well."

"I'm impatient," I confess.

"I have enough for both of us."

"I'm a better version of me than when we met, but I'm still flawed," I exhale into him.

He pushes me back, looking intense with eyebrows dipped to a deep crease. "You're flawed? Have you seen me?" He laughs from a place deep within his core. "Don't underestimate the beautiful woman you are. Do you have any idea what you've given me? You gave me hope. I didn't expect to take another vacation," he says, pointing to the tree with one finger while not letting go of me. "I didn't expect to ever dance," he says softly, shifting his weight slightly to sway with the music. "I never thought I'd have the chance to make love again. But here we are."

"I didn't expect to fall in love with you," I tell him.

"I know. That's why I figured if you could face your fear of falling, I should face mine of standing." He grips my shoulders more tightly. "You won't let me fall, will you?"

"Never!" I say, incredulous.

He bends down to plant a sweet and tender kiss on my lips. "Well, neither will I you."

# RYAN

*I*nseparable. I'm not supposed to be thinking about anything other than breathing on the yoga mat, but that's the word that is playing on repeat in my head. Our lips and our bodies have been intertwined and entangled for three entire days and I've never been so damn happy.

In child's pose, in the dark and warm studio, I'm fulfilled beyond measure. Silently, I laugh inside at Alexandra having scolded us in the lobby a few minutes ago when we kissed, breaking Cassandra's rule yet again. I'm not sure it's even a rule any longer it's been broken so many times.

Her hand skitters across the floor to find my own, like she can't bear for us to not be touching even for these few minutes. I open one closed eye and she is wide eyed and smiling at me.

She lifts the hand not holding mine and makes a fist then opens her fingers three times over. She is counting her classes, and this is her fifteenth. I'd like to think I've helped her become a better woman, but I'm a betting man so I'd have to put my money on yoga instead. I wink and her eyes fall shut, but the smile doesn't leave her face.

Alexandra enters the studio, closing the door softly behind her. She starts to address the class, "The holidays are a difficult time to be mindful. Busy begets breathing, and the next thing you know you are wrapped up in knots."

I smile, thinking about what Cassandra and I had tried last night, our first experimentation. And, while I have compassion for the others who didn't have a fantastic holiday, mine was better than I could have dreamed.

Alexandra continues, "When all else fails, find one little thing to be grateful for. Find one thing, and then another, because there is always something. Build upon it, and it gets better from there. You can't be in a state of gratitude and anger. You can't be in a state of gratitude and fear. Let gratitude claim its space as the only space."

It's been a long time coming, but I am there. I am grateful for this second chance at life. With Cassandra. Everything I thought I wouldn't have after the fall. So damn grateful.


"Now, rise up from child's pose, slowly and mindfully, to table pose," Alexandra instructs.

It's finally time for my new favorite pastime. Watching Cassandra during class. We've been here each day since Christmas, and her grace and strength in each pose is plain sexy. I sneak a peek as she wiggles her ass getting into the pose. Table pose reminds me of doggy-style. If I am creative enough, we might manage to pull that off. Maybe Chris and I will have to work on a new project. I'm not too proud to ask him for help with that.

Alexandra is talking; I should focus. "And keep breathing. Your breath doesn't have to be loud, but it does have to be louder than your thoughts."

So busted. I used to be good at this, but Cassandra has changed me too. In this case, not for the better. But I'm overdue. I had plenty of time off from thinking about sex and I'm still a man. A man who is very happy to be back in action. There is nothing as satisfying as hearing the moans of pleasure, watching the faces she makes, and feeling Cassandra's trembling body at my undoing.

*Back to the mat, Steadman.*

Good luck with that, I say to myself as Alexandra's music begins. She has chosen Ed Sheeran's "Thinking Out Loud." With the first line, I know she's picked the song for us. No, my legs don't work, and I can't sweep her off her feet, but I can love her for a very long time. I haven't said the three words yet, but I will. She's learning love and I am teaching her. As for the next time there's a business deal on the table, I hope being by my side will have some influence. I have to trust. The best kind of love, you don't look for. It finds you. Fate got us here, and love will keep us here.

The words speak of people falling love with the touch of a hand. I remember our first touch and how she had pulled away. We've come a long way from that moment.

WHAT THE HELL WAS THAT? An odd sound catches my attention. It sounded as if the door smacked into the wall. Because that is exactly what it was.

My eyes dart to the doorway, it's frame filled by a body of epic proportions. I thought Chris was a big man, but this man could kick his ass with an arm tied behind his back. Envy sweeps over me like a tidal wave for a minute. His strength looks impressive.

"Peyton, where the hell are you?"

Not so impressive is his slur. What could he be doing here? Looking for someone obviously, but, really, here at 6:00 a.m.?

Some of the people in the room are frozen mid-pose, others are scrambling to their feet. I am screwed if I need to be doing the latter.

The man staggers, one leg stepping right at an off angle as he stumbles forward with his left. Something is clearly wrong. Drugs? Drunk? I don't know, but something.

"Where are you, Peyton? You think you can leave me? I don't think so."

One staggered step further into the room and I start to think maybe we have a problem on our hands. I am sure when he gets the girl everything will be okay though. Won't it?

When he pivots on one foot, I see I've been overly optimistic. We definitely have a problem. There is no mistaking the metal object tucked into the waistband of his pants. In a split second the studio has gone from a place of peace to one of terror. The villain's shadow dances on the wall.

I'm not the only one to notice, someone cries out, "He has a gun!"

A chorus of screams follows.

"Someone call 911!"

That someone won't be me.

The flickering candles illuminating the studio are bouncing across the mats as people run for the exits. They look like shooting stars, and I make a quick wish to get out of here alive. Cassandra is crouched next to me. "We have to get out of here! Come on!"

"Everyone out!" rings in the air. Alexandra's roar. It's large and loud from someone so little.

I'm in the wheelchair and we are close to the exit.

But then. I look back at Alexandra, because what kind of man am I if I don't protect her? She is putting herself in harm's way!

No!

She marches straight toward the man, chest jutting outward. It makes her small physical frame appear larger than it is. However, she is still, literally, about half his size.

"Peyton!" The man's voice is a drunken cocktail of fierce, anxious and shrill. It evokes fear. To my core. I need to protect Cassandra. I can't leave Alexandra to fight him alone. What the hell do I do?

Gunfire rings loud, echoing and reverberating. No! Alexandra's body falls to the ground, lifeless. A trickle of red forms a river flowing from her body.

A second chorus of screams reverberate. Everyone stops moving. Hands of surrender go into the air.

Run for your life. You hear it. You never think you will be in the situation to live the words. And I can't. But even if I could, how could I leave Alexandra here alone?

Cassandra is pulling at my arm. I am looking at Alexandra. Can I get to her? I need to help her.

Where is Peyton anyway? If she is here, surely she wouldn't leave us all to die at his hands, would she?

"How could you do this to me?" The man's voice has dropped an octave. It's through clenched teeth, sheer rage on his breath. Where the hell is Peyton?

The boot of the man just crushed a woman's mid-section. His second victim let out a shrill scream of pain before slumping against the wall.

"Don't you DARE hurt them!" Alexandra is sprawled across the floor, but her voice roars out again, mother lion protective of her cub.

Thank God she is alive!

His large frame tries to spin toward Alexandra's voice, but the motion makes him stagger. He starts towards her but then he stops and shakes his head as if he is trying to clear his vision. He leans against the wall to steady himself. Cassandra jumps forward, unnoticed, toward him.

Inside my head, I scream at her to stop but it's too late. He's heard her coming and pivots to the right, arm outstretched still clutching the gun, just as she arrives by his side. Cassandra's head turns at the wrong moment, and the gun makes a startling impact with the side of her head, a loud thud echoing.

I feel her pain in every cell of my body. I think "NO!" is screaming from my core but I'm not sure, because I'm not here any longer. I can't be here where the woman I love has just fallen lifeless to the floor like a rag doll, sprawled next to Alexandra. My world is collapsing around me and I am helpless.

The hit has caused the gun to fly from the man's hand. I watch as it bounces across the floor, each rubber yoga mat like a mini trampoline. Alexandra army-crawls using one arm and covers Cassandra's body with her own.

"Kyle, I am right here. I'm not leaving you. Come with me. Let's talk about this," a new voice enters the mix. It's about damn time, Peyton.

The man we now know as Kyle drops his face in his hands and starts to cry like a baby. Then, he drops to his knees on the floor in front of the woman who must be Peyton. Where the hell was she while Kyle was hurting both of the women I should have been able to protect? If I was a man at all.

I need to get that gun.

Peyton leans over Kyle's body, crumpled before her in devastation. My eyes having adjusted in the dim lit, I can see she mouths, "Get out!"

I mouth back, "No way!" I am going nowhere with Cassandra and Alexandra's lives hanging in the balance.

I roll over to where the gun is, but I can't reach to the floor to pick it up. A boot covers it as I struggle for the needed extra inches. Kyle bends over, puts his hands on his knees to look me in the eye, and laughs, ferocious and mocking.

I raise my fist, but realize I have no leverage from this position. He towers over me. I watch as his fist raises in return. It's big and it's going to hurt like hell. I brace myself for impact by holding onto the wheelchair. My neck snaps as the crushing blow is absorbed by my cheekbone.

"Worthless," Kyle growls inches from my face, drops of his spit joining the blood I feel trickling from my jaw to my neck. It drips onto my white t-shirt, at first a gross connect-the-dots of crimson, but in seconds it merges into a tie-die effect.

Back in power with the gun, Kyle returns to Peyton but, knees buckling, falls to a heap on top of her. She is screaming, trapped beneath his limp and lifeless body. No amount of adrenaline could help me lift his dead weight off her. Just another woman I can't help.

My eyes dart back to Cassandra. She is picking herself up from the ground. Thank God she has regained consciousness! She looks at me. Her eyes squint in the light, but I see them move from my face to my shirt and back again. Fear and concern reflect in her features then dissolve. Her next expression takes a minute to form, like a Polaroid picture, a blur becoming clear pixel by pixel. Creased eyebrows. Sad eyes. Wrinkled up nose. Pouting mouth. Every feature screams pity. Now, it doesn't matter that Kyle hasn't killed me because Cassandra just has.

In a moment she is before me, covered in blood. Alexandra's blood. And then mine. She swipes at my lips with her thumbs and blood runs over her fingertips. Her lips find mine in a kiss I don't return. "Are you hurt?"

"No."

*Like hell.*

She runs to a small shelf in the corner which holds tissues. She returns with the box and pulls one out then reaches for me. I encircle her wrist and push it back.

"Ryan!" she gasps, startled. "Please be okay," is a whispered plea she leaves hanging between us.

Cassandra runs to the woman slumped awkwardly sideways and checks for a pulse. The woman's eyes open and I read her lips telling Casandra she is okay.

My eyes follow as she moves to help Peyton, who has shimmied herself free from entrapment and is curled in a fetal position like ball, rocking forward and backward. Cassandra swallows her body in a hug. Then, we are no longer alone. Guns poke through each of the doorways. Cassandra's hands fly into the air in surrender. "Hurry! In here!" She tries to stand quickly but now her knees buckle, and she collapses to the ground. Missing a yoga mat by just inches, which would have cushioned the blow, the eerie sound of her head hitting the floor sends a shiver up and down my entire spine despite it having been severed. Please God, let her be okay.

Moments later the room is overtaken with police, fire, and para-medics. Stretchers pop up, commands are yelled, and more chaos than in the gunfire seems to ensue. Beside Cassandra's lifeless frame, I watch as they make quick work of strapping her head, then body, to the wooden board. I'm desperate to see any sign of life but her eyes never open again.

Alexandra's arm, the site of her injury, is bandaged from elbow to shoulder. She cries out in pain while they work on it. I know the sound will haunt me later. They rush her body through the studio door on a stretcher. I stare at her blood left behind, still warm, pooled into a disgusting lake of red. It sends waves of nausea coursing through me.

It's clear Kyle's life hangs in the balance as they inflate and squeeze a bag to do the work his lungs should be doing. The woman slumped against the wall seems stable as they've left her with just an IV while they attended to the others.

I'm finally tended to by a female paramedic who crouches before me. "Are you okay?" she asks. I can't answer her simple question. Physically, sure. What the hell is another scar? But I am not okay. I nod anyway. She pulls gauze from the black bag on the floor beside her. "Can you apply pressure, and I'll be back in a minute?" I take the gauze and hold it firm. Another paramedic tosses a towel in her direction, which she grabs from the air one-handed. She offers it to me to wipe away the blood that seems to be everywhere, but I don't reach for it, so she sets it in my lap and disappears.

"CAN you please get me a status on the two women in the ambulances?" I ask the paramedics over the sirens that seem to be coming from every direction.

"It's another company, sir. We'll get you the info as soon as we arrive."

Technology everywhere, and two different ambulance companies can't talk to each other.

Two of the most important people in my life are in ambulances because I'm worthless and couldn't do a damn thing to protect them. Sure, just let me lie here, consumed with worry.

Why not me instead? It should have been me. I should be the one in an ambulance, shot for defending innocent people. But no, Cassandra and Alexandra were the heroes while I was useless. Pain courses through me. I know this pain and it's not my friend.

We finally halt to stillness and I hear the driver's door close. The back door opens with a rush of cold air that causes me to wince at its harshness.

"No life-threatening injuries to the women," the driver reports, and I put my head back and take a deep breath of relief. Thank you, God.

"Not sure about the perpetrator. They also said someone is married to a doctor here so I'm sure they'll get all the bells and whistles."

He closes the door a bit and I hear hushed conversation outside. It opens again and two police officers fill the space where he just stood.

"Mr. Steadman, Officer Stosman," he introduces himself gruffly. "We're glad you are okay. You'll be on my watch now. Hopefully, you can help us understand what happened this morning. After we get you fixed up of, of course."

The thing is, Stosman, there is no fixing this broken.


MINUTES LATER, I'm amid the chaos of triage, straining for a glimpse of Cassandra while listening to every word coming from a medical professional's mouth. I finally hear, "Head CT," followed by an urgent, "Move it." A doctor tilts my chin up with two fingers. Lifting the pressure bandage on my cheek, he hollers over his shoulder, "Call Banks in plastics." He slaps my shoulder while still holding my lifted chin. "They'll fix that up. You'll be fine."

*Glad you're so sure, doc, but inaccurate from my point of view.*

He leaves to attend to the woman who was slumping in the studio. His lips brush hers, and she flinches, though it doesn't appear to be from physical pain. Obviously in a drug-induced haze by the way her eyes wander listlessly, her lips move with words that I can't hear. His expression flashes stoic but the bulge of the veins in his neck coursing with blood shows the simmer of rage beneath. Whatever's just happened, the doctor is now sharing in my bad day. Hey, buddy, I doubt she told you you're worthless.

Alexandra is being wheeled past me to the operating room. "Stop!" she cries out, voice harsh. They halt with its ferocity. "Ryan!" We make eye contact. "Are you okay?"

I need everyone to stop asking me this question. Not one of them wants the truth for an answer. "Just another scar to add to my collection. I'll be here when you get out of surgery, Alexandra. You're in good hands. They'll take care of you."

*Because I couldn't.*

Her departure leaves me alone in the triage area to wait for the doctor. I'd actually prefer Stosman return to get my statement instead of having this time to wallow in my melancholy. Several other officers had been protecting our perimeter, but one has accompanied each patient to wherever they are headed. I want to be anywhere but here. I'd leave right now if I could but, of course, I need to know if Cassandra is okay, and I promised Alexandra I'd be here for her.

Just like the last time I was in a hospital, I'm left to wait. Wait to see if I'd ever walk again. Wait to see what my life would be like. After. Fun fact to spice up the morning, I didn't walk out then, and I can't now. The difference this time? I know the hell I'm returning to.

EVERYTHING AROUND ME IS WHITE. To my right. White. To my left. White. In front of me. White.

Snow?

No. I'm not cold. It's people in white coats. Surrounding me.

Breathe, Ryan. This isn't like last time. Yet everything inside my chest is seizing.

I am alive, says the heartbeat throbbing inside my head.

Another flash in front of my eyes. Blinding.

Why is there so much beeping?

The beeping confirms he is still alive. For now. Until he wakes and wishes he was dead.

My mother says it will be fine. She is horribly wrong.

I JUMP IN MY CHAIR, startled back from wherever shards of memories just took me. It feels like the four walls are closing in around the bed. The one with Cassandra in it. Not me. This time, I am the one standing guard, helpless in her fight to come back.

Her eyes flutter open. Wide. Scared. I know the pain of the light.

They fall closed again. Back to the safety of darkness. She looks peaceful again.

I should touch her. Kiss her. Hold her.

I want to.

But I can't.

I force air into aching lungs. I close my eyes and run my palms slowly over my legs, my blood-soaked pants replaced with purple-blue scrubs. I pull in another long breath. I stare ahead at Cassandra's still frame.

I can't be here alone. In fact, I can't be here at all.

I ROLL into the hallway just outside the door to escape. Her phone, given to me during what felt like hours of interrogation by three police officers, is in my trembling hand. I press home and our faces smile at me. Broad, happy smiles in front of the Christmas tree. "You deserve new memories with new pictures," she had said.

*Clearly, I don't.*

I type her birthday, 0512, on the screen then open the camera app and flip the screen towards my face.

Pulling at the tape which holds a white bandage, I lift the fabric. Frankenstein stitchwork, in nineteen short black lines, form a crescent moon curve from my cheekbone to my temple. If only they could suture up the gaping hole in my heart.

I hover over the phone icon, gathering enough nerve to search her recent calls. Christmas Day. When everything was different.

Shame and guilt paralyze me. How did Matt survive making the call to my mother after my accident?

No choice now. Ringing.

"Hi, Cass. How's my girl?"

Cheerfulness I am about to crush.

"Mrs. Lewis, it's Ryan. I'm afraid I have some bad news."

*Your daughter almost died today. I couldn't keep her from harm's way. Because, as you can see, I'm worthless.*

# CASSANDRA

"Mom?" Oh damn. That hurt.

How can the act of talking hurt my head? Oh. Thinking is worse. Don't do that. Ouch. I did it again. Did I really just see my mother? Am I at home? In Boston? I need to open my eyes again and see if I am losing it.

Do I have a hangover? Maybe that's why my head hurts like, oh, it hurts to look for words to describe the pain. I really need to rub my temples. And some water. And an Excedrin. Extra-strength, please. Did I have fun getting this hangover? Was I drinking with Ryan? Where's Ryan? Is he here too?

I try to will my eyes open again but they don't seem to like the light. Can someone kill that light, please, so I can see what the hell is going on? Maybe I should sit up and figure this all out. Yes, I should do that.

Push into the mattress, Cassandra. What is that plastic thing in my arm? It's in my way. What is that annoying beeping? My head roars in a surge of pain as I push up. Vomit hits the back of my teeth. Bad idea. Bad, bad idea. Swallow. Sink back into the mattress. Blow out a breath. Yoga-breathe. Pull air in. Yep, like that. You've got this. Swallow. Breathe. Repeat.

"Honey?"

Yep, it's Mom.

"Mom." Pretty sure she knows who she is but just in case she needed a reminder.

"Honey."

Yes, Mom, that's me. Pretty sure, anyway, because I don't think I can feel like myself and like hell at the very same time. At least I'm some facsimile of her daughter.

"I need something for this headache, Mom," I mutter, but not sure it's coherent since it sounds a little like the wah-wah-wah of the teacher from Charlie Brown in my head.

"Baby girl, you have a concussion. You need to rest."

Oh my God. I remember. Yoga. Loud-pitched screams. People running. The sound of gunfire. Alexandra lying in her own blood. Then over me. Ryan. His face. Oh my God. Where is he? Is he alive? Is she? The other woman. Peyton. Her crying careening off the walls of the studio. The body of the gigantic man—Kyle—falling to his knees in heartbreak. Then succumbing to whatever substance had turned him into a villain.

Oh my God. "Ryan?" I hear desperation and panic tinge my voice. "Ryan?"

This time I know my words are clear. I pray for him to answer and hold my breath.

"I'm here."

He's alive! Thank God!

My breath moves in and out in short bursts. I would cry of happiness, but it will hurt too much. Behind my closed eyes I see the last image of him I remember. Kissing him through his blood. Blood dripping everywhere. He was alive but his eyes were dead. NO! I want to scream. Go back to yesterday. When everything was perfect. It's too much. I can't do this. I let go and return to the darkness where I can pretend my world will be fine when I wake up from this nightmare.

·  ·  ·

MY EYES BLINK open to find darkness. They work to focus on the silhouette of shapes. The shades are drawn but I think it's nighttime too. I'm unsure how much time has passed. Turning my head left toward the green, red, and white lights, I watch as they flicker details about me that I don't understand. I bend my arm upward, until I am forced to stop by the IV. It's uncomfortable and I moan. A stirring sound to my right has me wanting to roll my head toward the sound. I swallow another bout of nausea, then slowly twist my neck in the direction, pushing through stiffness that feels as if I've been lying still for a week. Ouch.

My head still throbs, but it's the same with my eyes opened or closed so I will push through with them open. I have nagging questions begging to be answered. My eyes haven't acclimated so I can't see across the room yet. My mother is at my bedside first, but I sense Ryan's presence. I think I can make out the outline of the wheelchair, but my unclear mind could be playing tricks on me.

I try to hear through the rustling. Anything that will tell me he is here. The warmth of my mother's palm on my cheek is comforting and I feel like a child again. I need her, but I need Ryan more. Finally, he is next to me too.

"I'm going to go tell the nurse you are awake," my mother says, and I hear the door close behind her.

"Ryan."

"Cass."

It's so good to hear his voice but I wish he called me babe.

"Is there anything you need?" His words are right, but his tone is wrong. Cold. Why? What happened to him? Please, no!

"I need a kiss." I drag my tongue across sandpaper lips and force them to smile.

"I can't reach you."

Great. I've just made it worse. I'll kiss him then. I push into both elbows to lift myself to him, but the nauseous feeling is overwhelming. I can't very well kiss him if I am going to puke into his mouth. I lie back into the pillow. It's so disappointing. "I'm sorry, I can't," I whimper. "I'm sorry."

I reach over the railing of the bed for his hand. Any contact that will tell me that he is okay. That we are okay. Nothing. My hand slides from the railing onto the bed.

I should apologize for more. For being stupid and going for the gun and putting myself here. We should have gotten out of there like everyone else. Of course, who am I kidding? He would never have left Alexandra in that studio to possibly die alone.

"What happened? Please tell me."

Silence.

"Don't shut me out, Ryan." It's painful to push out words with enough power to save him. Save us. My head pounds.

The room is suddenly filled with people. A cold stethoscope finds my chest, a flashlight steals my eyesight. The questions begin. "What's your name? Birthday? What day is it? Who is the president? What city do you live in? What's the last holiday you celebrated?"

I answer them all, pausing when I remember the perfect day that was Christmas.

"Do you remember what happened?"

Yes, when I was conscious. I wish I didn't. I fear I will never forget. But not nearly as much as I fear not knowing what happened to Ryan while I lay unconscious.

"How bad is the pain in your head? Scale of one to ten?"

*Who cares about a headache and a scale of one to ten?*

*Why don't they ask about my chest pain? What kind of a scale is there for that?*

*None. Because there is no way to measure the pain I feel in my heart.*

# CASSANDRA

*I* startle awake in the night. I'm sweat soaked and gasping for air. In my nightmare, gunshots rang out. Alexandra's body crumpling to the floor plays on repeat, images on a movie screen, behind my closed eyes. Blood everywhere. So much blood. Ryan is nowhere to be found. Tears stream down my face as I scream his name in a hoarse voice. It's terrifying. What if I am waking up to the reality that I've lost him?

I don't settle back into sleep, and before I know it, yesterday's process of prodding and questioning begins anew. The doctors have deemed me fit enough to go home provided I have care there. The doctor looks past Ryan to my mother, who gleefully volunteers. I see Ryan's face fall when this happens, and I know what he is thinking.

He couldn't protect me yesterday.

He can't take care of me today.

He'll never be enough.

EVERYONE SEEMS to be moving at warp speed, a whirlwind of instructions being dispersed. It's exhausting to hold my head upright, let alone listen. Now I am expected to sit up, then stand with the dizziness that has me feeling like I'm in the middle of a category-five tornado.

I can't dress myself because I have to keep my eyes tightly closed. The light sends daggers to the center of my brain. I can't get to the bathroom without holding onto my mother. I can't read the paperwork I'm required to sign because the letters jumble out of focus and dance across the pages. A nurse finally eases me into a wheelchair so I can depart.

Oh my God, all the help I just needed. The wheelchair. A have a horrible realization. This is what it feels like to be confined to a broken body. My life was so much easier to live when I did it cold-hearted. Now, my heart has melted into a million tiny tears that cry for him. For me. For us.

We exit the hospital, Ryan and I side by side in our wheelchairs. The cold air is a bitter attack on my overactive senses. I steady myself first on the arm of my wheelchair, slowing rising. Then, I balance myself on Ryan's. Leaning forward, I place my palms on his legs wishing I could crawl into his lap and let him hold me. That is all that I need right now. His arms holding me tight and warm, his words telling me everything will be okay. I whisper, "I love you," into his ear. "I'm not giving up. We were meant to be together."

I place my lips against his, holding his cold face in my warm hands. I silently beg for him to kiss me back. His lips form words instead. "I can't do this," hangs frozen in his exhale, cold as ice. His eyes meet mine, as if to confirm I've heard him. Without their mischievous twinkle, they are the angry gray of a tumultuous ocean. I'm too exhausted to argue in my outside voice, but inside, my resolve is steadfast. He's made me softer, but I have muscle memory of who I used to be. Consider yourself warned, Ryan Steadman. Not doing this is not an option.

WE ARRIVE HOME and I curl onto the couch. My mother visits the kitchen. "Sweetie, what do you eat? I'm happy to cook you anything you like." A few more cupboards open and close. "Do you own any pans?"

Normally, I'd want to refute her help, but I don't have the strength to answer her questions let alone fight. All I can do is lie in fetal position fighting my body wanting to retch. I think it's the concussion, but it could also be the four words Ryan had spoken. I find myself glad to have the company of my mother. I hope Ryan isn't alone.

It's dark outside when I wake again. "Mom," I call from the couch. I never made it to the bedroom. I bet I have a completely organized pantry, and she's cleaned every crumb from the toaster. Not that there was much to do in an unused kitchen.

She's by my side, with a glass of water, and two pills, in an instant. "How are you feeling?"

"Nearly human. Thanks for asking. Do you mind grabbing my phone from my purse?"

She hands it to me. Not a thing to look at. I lean my head back against the cushion.

"I'm guessing that sigh means you didn't hear from Ryan?"

"You guessed right."

She settles in beside me.

"He's not as big a jerk as he seemed yesterday," I feel an obligation to defend the only side of him she's seen. "Were you surprised when you met him?"

Now it's her turn to sigh, long and heavy. "I was surprised at his being in a wheelchair, yes, but not at how he acted. Not after we spoke on the phone. I understand more than you know."

She tucks a strand of my hair behind my ear, like she would do when tucking me in at night as a child.

"What did he say? On the phone, I mean?"

"He said you were courageous and brave and that you had to try to save the lives of several people because he couldn't.

"He told you that?" I ask, incredulous.

"Yes. He didn't say so, but I know he was devastated he wasn't able to protect you in the face of danger. I know exactly how he feels."

"I don't understand. How do you know?"

"I couldn't keep you safe either."

"I'm going to need a little more to go on here, Mom."

"Oh, Cassandra. I wasn't the mother I wanted to be to you. And because of me, neither was your father the one he could have been.

"What do you mean, Mom?" I really need her to get to the punch line.

She sighs deeply. "Do you remember what you asked Santa for at least six years running?"

The memory surfaces easily, "A brother or a sister."

"You weren't the only one. We all wanted more babies. Your father and I both wanted four."

"The day you found me in the kitchen with the broken dishes was the day I had my fifth miscarriage. It was the day I knew I had to give up trying forever. I couldn't do it one more time."

"Oh, Mom. I never knew."

"I know. No one did except your father. And I pushed him away because I didn't feel worthy of his love. He gave me the space to grieve. He wasn't home because I couldn't look at him without hating myself. It was so selfish of me to do that to you, an innocent child. I've spent a lot of time, not to mention money, on therapy, working to forgive myself for what I did to you. I'm so sorry. And I'm so thankful. He never gave up fighting for our love. We are only together today because of him. You all have the best parts of him, Cass."

"I had no idea, Mom. I'm so glad you told me."

All this time, what I thought I knew was wrong.

"I hope now that you know you can forgive both of us. I'm not sure I deserve it, but your father definitely does. He would have liked to make amends decades ago, but it wasn't his story to tell and I just couldn't. I'm so sorry. I didn't think you would be able to understand, because you had never really known what it was like to be in love. Until now."

She is right. I wouldn't have understood. Nor would I have been able to forgive her. "Mom, Ryan has taught me a lot about forgiveness."

"And he's taught you a thing or two about love. I knew at Christmas. You haven't been that giddy since you got all serious on us somewhere around eight years old!" She pokes at my ribs with her index finger. "And the way you looked at him and tried to reach him today when we were leaving, I saw a side of you I wasn't sure you had in you."

"Thanks, Mom!" I hit her gently with the decorative pillow next to me.

"I'm glad that you have found a man who has helped make you your best self. How's your patience these days? Has Ryan made any progress with my beautiful daughter in that department?"

I think about it. Yes, everything is slower with Ryan, but my respect for how he makes the hard look easy is real. "Better than I think you'd expect, I'm pleased to report."

"Well, good. You never know how someone is going to react to grief. You are probably going to need it."

"I think there is something I need to do, Mom."

"That's my girl." She already has my coat in one hand and the keys in her other. "Let's go get your man."


I TRY to figure out a plan for what to do upon arrival to Ryan's. As my mom slows curbside, I've only got the next step covered.

"Good luck, honey."

I step out of the car and Marty, looking dapper as ever, opens the building door as I approach. Good thing he can attend to residents and guests as the doorman from inside the vestibule. "Hi, Marty. You are a sight for sore eyes. Is he here?" I don't know what he knows or if Ryan has told him I am not allowed to be here under any circumstances. His eyes flash an answer, and he's already walking me to the elevator. He palms the black square and tips his hat in my direction but doesn't say a word.

The elevator door opens with a ding that won't keep my arrival discrete. No need to worry, however; it's pitch-black throughout the space. I feel my way toward the bedroom stopping just once to get the spinning under control. I feel for the door handle. Locked. I jiggle it. I knock. "Ryan. I know you are in there. Will you please let me in?"

I look around for a clock, having no sense of the time. It's just after eight. He is alone and in bed, and the twisting in my gut because of both is gnawing pain.

"Ryan!" My voice is more urgent. "Please! Can we talk? Please!" I want nothing more than to feel his body next to mine. The separation by wooden door is just not acceptable. The separation by choice is even less so! My temper flares hot. It hurts my head. I need to sit down. Leaning my back against the door, still in my winter coat, I slide to the floor and stretch my legs out straight. I can't stay long, having left my mom in the car, and soon I'll be out of options.

I reach into the coat pocket for my phone and dial his number. I hear it ringing, probably from his nightstand. It goes unanswered.

"I'm not leaving without you. I don't want you to be alone."

"Which part of I want to be alone is hard for you to understand?"

His voice startles me, and I realize how desperate I was to hear it. "All of it," I answer, leaning my head against the door.

"Go home, Cassandra."

"No. I'm not leaving."

"I'm not coming out."

"I guess we have a stalemate."

"But I'm the one with the lock on my side."

"Ugh. Fine," I huff. "You win. Today. But I'm not giving up! Tomorrow is a new day. I love you, Ryan Steadman. And I am fighting for our love!"

On the way down the elevator, by the fifth floor, I come up with Plan B. When I walk past the library to leave, I snap a picture. Plan C. And, if needed, there are twenty-three more letters to go. I remember my arrival in Florida. Ryan had said, "As many as it takes." If twenty-three letters in the English language isn't enough, then I'll switch languages. No matter what, I'm in this. Whatever it takes.

# CASSANDRA

*I*'ve finally slept well and awaken to a new day with a headache that feels like a belligerent hangover instead of a javelin stabbing me from ear to ear. I check in with my heart. Yep, still broken. It's New Year's Eve, and mere days ago I expected to be kissing Ryan at midnight. I'm not giving up yet. I still have fourteen hours to try.

"CASSANDRA. You are a sight for sore eyes!"

Alexandra is propped up in bed, and except for the sling cradling her shoulder, barely looks like a hospital patient. Her shoulder-length gray hair flows gracefully over a rose-colored pillowcase I am guessing is her own. Her smile lights up the small, stark room.

Reaching her free hand around my back in a hug, she holds me close.

"How are you?" I ask.

"Missing yoga already. You'd better be going back because I'll be needing to share some of your good energy in class until I can practice again."

"Happy to let you borrow or steal anything you need. Your

teaching has already left your mark on me. I'll just be repaying the favor." When I say this, I remember what Ryan had said on Christmas. He was repaying a favor. Maybe Alexandra knows.

"Ryan's a mess, Alexandra. When you are strong enough, I'm going to need your help. I won't give up on him. I love him."

Her eyes widen, and if possible, her lips turn farther upward, "You have no idea what that means to me. You have no idea what *he* means to me."

"I wish I knew what happened to him in the studio. Do you know?"

"No. I'm not sure which one of us was unconscious longer. I've called him a dozen times and texted more. Nothing back. Yet."

"Do you know about before, Alexandra? What worked to help Ryan?"

"If only I did. All I know is that there was someone who visited him in rehab."

I think of the socks. The gift from Shawn. A man visited Ryan, and Ryan visited Shawn.

"I know he was quadriplegic. Worse off than Ryan. He had gone back to his life and lived a new one fully. I remember he told me the man even went skydiving and mountain climbing. After the accident, he still got married and had kids. Ryan knew if that man could do it, then he could too."

WE ARE INTERRUPTED by a younger version of Alexandra, in male form, who enters the room. "Morning, Mom. Hi, I'm Joe," he says, reaching his hand to me. "I was going to go and get us Starbucks. I need a change from the hospital coffee."

I should go. I need to face the fear of seeing the studio again before too much time passes, or I might never go back. Plus, I find myself wanting to do anything I can to help Alexandra. I smile at just another way that Ryan has rubbed off on me.

"I'll go. Please. It would be my pleasure. Orders, please!"

. . .

MOM STEADIES me as I face the greeting of yellow crime-scene tape strung across the yoga studio door. My daily dose of dizzy settling in, it's comforting to know she is next to me and I am not doing any of this alone. But Ryan is, and I can't let him.

Waiting in line, I see a woman sitting on a stool facing out the window toward the studio. Tears slide down her face, and I see the puffy disfigurement of eyes and lips that indicate there have been more than a few tears. I squint in her direction, focusing on her familiar features. I recognize her.

"I'll be right back," I say and head toward her.

"Peyton?" I ask, strangely knowing her name only from the gunman yelling it in the studio.

Her eyes grow wide with realization. "I'm so sorry," she says, a sob catching the words in her throat before she pushes them out around it.

"I'm Cassandra."

"Are you okay?"

"I'll be fine."

"And the man in the wheelchair? Will he? I tried to apologize to him. I saw him when we were giving our statements to the police. I told him I was sorry." She cries harder now, shoulders shaking. "He said I should be." Oh, Ryan.

"His name is Ryan. Can you tell me what happened to him when I was unconscious? I don't know."

"Kyle overdosed. He's still alive but he might not make it. He wasn't in his right mind, but it was awful what he did."

"What did he do, Peyton?" I feel impatient and needy.

"Ryan was trying to reach for the gun but couldn't."

Hardest thing to do in a wheelchair, he had told me.

"Kyle laughed at him, then called him worthless. Ryan looked like he was going to punch him, but I think he realized he couldn't reach him and pulled his fist back, but Kyle's was already on the way. He hit him in the cheek so hard it sounded like a firework exploding."

I barely hear a word after worthless. The entire room is spinning, and I have to sit down. My hands are trembling. Worthless. Worthless. Worthless. The word tumbles around inside my head. He couldn't defend me. He couldn't defend his own honor. I force myself to inhale. My mom is by my side. I hold onto her arm and stand up. I leave her with a hug. It's not her fault. "Thank you, Peyton. Take care of yourself."

I REENTER Alexandra's room a shell of the woman I was the first time.

"Whoa, what happened to you?" she asks as I make my way to her bedside.

"Peyton. I saw her at Starbucks when I was getting the coffee. She told me everything that happened."I recount the story through tears of my own rivaling those Peyton had cried.

Alexandra looks thoughtful, "Ryan's been to hell and back already. It was a bumpy road. Let's pave the way this time. We've got this. I know we do."

When she says we, it gives me an idea. Plan D. I'm already at the hospital so I can start right now. "Thank you, Alexandra. I'll see you tomorrow."

# RYAN

Oh no, she didn't. She has not commandeered Chris. He was mine first. I pay him. His loyalty should be to me.

"Sorry, man."

I pivot back to the television. Away from both of them. If she looks at my face with that face of hers that I saw the other day, I don't know what I will do. "I'm busy."

"Too busy to shave, I see." Chris stands in front of me, great wads of muscle blocking my view. "That's a pretty one," he says coming in for a closer look at my cheek. I don't know where Cassandra has gone or if she's paralyzed in place, not knowing how I will react to her being here. Ha. Paralyzed in place. I'm funny.

"What's going on, Steadman?"

"Celebrating a little NYE in NYC. Just waiting for the ball to drop. Can't wait for the new year. How about those resolutions?" I point the remote in the direction of the screen where some teenage pop band is crooning away the time until the countdown. I flip to the other channel broadcasting the holiday festivities. Lame. I know I sounded like a dick, but they are invading my space, so I don't know what the hell they expected.

"What exactly are you doing here?" I ask, finally looking back over my shoulder at Cassandra, who still hasn't moved from in front of the elevator. For God's sake, tears are streaming down her pretty little cheeks. I think I feel a little shift in my chest. Damn her.

"Plan B and Plan D," Chris informs me.

The asshole is glib. He's looking at Cassandra for confirmation. I don't like them partnering up in the least. Especially not against me. "Right, Cass?"

Yeah for me, that means there is a Plan C out there somewhere. And if I know Cassandra, and I do, there is a whole alphabet she can drive me crazy with. And wait, just wait. Did he just call her Cass? This grates on every last nerve I have.

"We have something to show you."

The sound of her voice really does soothe an ache I can't quite put my finger on.

Chris has his phone and is stabbing at buttons on both it and my remote. He looks directly at me. "You aren't spending New Year's Eve alone. We brought you a better message than Dick Clark ever could."

Okay, tough guy. I guess I don't have a choice but to listen, since I know from recent experience how pathetic I am. No chance to kick your ass, you tall son of a bitch.

I watch Cassandra walk around the couch to sit down. She staggers a bit and needs to hold on to the back of it to keep her balance. She isn't fine at all. And probably overdoing it because of me. Her eyes purposefully dart away from my cheek. I know she wants to look. Still swollen, it sports a nice rainbow of blue and dark purple that will fade to green soon.

Chris sits on the couch next to her and I feel my jaw twitch. It would be better this way. She should be with someone like Chris. I pull my eyes away from them and to the screen. I know the scene coming to life and I'm just not in the mood.

Shawn's little body fills the screen. He's at the hospital and Cassandra is meeting him for the first time. She shakes his little hand, frailer than I'd like to see. Why is he still in the hospital? He was supposed to be home by now.

"Hi, Mr. Ryan. It's me. Shawn. I heard Santa brought me presents.

197

I didn't get to open them yet. Will you come and open them with me when I get home? Oh, and Miss Cassandra said to tell you Happy New Year. She's pretty!" The way he hisses the letter "s" when he says Cassandra makes me like her name even more than I already did. He's a cute kid and I hope he's better soon.

Similar messages follow from Kevin and Kendall, neither are home yet. They haven't even had the chance to celebrate Christmas, but they both said they can't wait for the new year.

Next, Chris' voice booms on the screen. "You've got this, Alejandro!" A translator shares Chris' fervor when he chooses words to match. *No se rindan. Tu puedes.*

I translate in my head. Don't give up. You can.

They are outside a small clay-brick structure, presumably their home. Alejandro sits in his wheelchair, with a metal walker in front of him. About eight feet away are three small children, an elderly couple, and four others gathered in a semicircle. He gives a smile and a thumbs-up to the camera then grips the walker.

Rising shakily, but then steadying himself, he hesitates concentrating deeply. His chest heaves with a breath to prepare himself for what I know he is about to do. Shifting his weight from foot to foot, he moves the walker slightly forward, away from his body.

A cloud of dirt kicks up where his right foot slides cautiously in a step. He balances on it. His left foot meets it. A squeal and a cheer erupt from the waiting crowd. A young woman covers her mouth with her hands. The elderly woman blows kisses to the sky. An eternity passes but the crowd is patient. When Alejandro has made the long journey, he throws the walker to the dirt and wraps his arms around the young woman who cries tears of joy into his shoulder.

On the screen, Chris is enthusiastic, "Yes! You did it! Yes!" He walks to the couple, camera trembling. He hugs Alejandro while the camera shakes and shows only dirt. Then he pans back to Alejandro's smiling face. Alejandro says into the camera, "Voy a trabajar. Voy a trabajar. Me voy a casar. Gracias, Mr. Steadman. Muchas gracias." He's going to work and he's getting married. I couldn't be happier for Alejandro, but not everyone gets their happy ending.

"How about that for some holiday cheer?" Chris says putting his hand on my leg and I wish he wouldn't remind me.

"It was something. I wish you could have been there. The doctor couldn't have been more appreciative either. He's got three others he thinks he can help right away. You got him trained, Ryan. And the therapists who taught him to walk again. This is on you Ryan. Score one for the good guys."

Chris and Cassandra share a silent communication that says he's going to leave me alone with her. I close my eyes and shake my head. I can make this short and sweet.

He stands up. "Toast to a new year, Steadman. We've got a lot of good to do together."

I agree, we do. And I don't need Cassandra by my side to get it done.

When the door closes behind Chris I turn to Cassandra. I've rehearsed this. I just didn't think I'd be delivering it so soon. Better not to drag out the inevitable. "Cassandra. I love you. I love you but this isn't going to work. I'm not the man for you. I can't take care of you the way other men can. The way you deserve. I can't give you the life you should have."

"I know what you must be feeling, Ryan. You are not wor—"

"What? You know?" Damn it. How can she know?

"Yes. I know what Kyle said."

"It's not just what he said. It's how you looked at me. After. Just like Melanie. She couldn't pick up the pieces then and you can't now. You have no idea what it was like to see you hurt in front of my eyes. The woman I love lay there and I was helpless. I couldn't pick you up. I couldn't even pick the damn gun up off the floor. I'll never be able to protect a woman. Or kids. I am not man enough, and I will never be enough."

Cassandra inches her way next to me, so close I can feel her warmth and remember what it felt like to have her in my arms.

"You are more than enough, Ryan. I chose to go after Kyle. It was my choice, not yours. Don't push me away. Don't give up on us. These might be dark days, but you've gotten through them before."

"This is different. I don't deserve to be with anyone. Men are supposed to provide and protect. As a man, I am wor—"

She jumps up and I watch her try to focus as her body swoons. She is not fine. Because of me. She still manages to find my lips with her index finger.

"Don't you dare say it."

"We are better off alone. We both know how to do alone."

"Maybe I used to, Ryan. But I don't any longer. I don't want to do alone. I want you. Let me hold you. Let me kiss you. I love you and I know we can fix this. Please let me try."

She is unwavering in her words, but I am resigned to my fate. She is better off without me.

I move to the elevator to indicate her departure should be eminent. Stabbing at the button, the door opens.

"This isn't something love can fix, Cassandra."

"How do you know? Why won't you let me try?"

She doesn't even bother to wipe her tears as she stands in the elevator and the doors close, the curtain on my last act of love.

# CASSANDRA

*N*ew Year's resolutions:

1. Survive my first day (in ten) without Ryan
2. Have girlfriends because doing life alone sucks
3. Yoga, yoga, and more yoga
4. Get Ryan back
5. If #5 fails, drown self in shoes not sweets

UNFORTUNATELY, Alexandra was going to be hospital-bound for an extra three days due to a complication from her surgery. Thankfully, in good spirits, she arranged a get-together in her hospital room for all of us that had been involved in the incident. As in each yoga class, you get a do-over at the end of class. She was going pretend that noon on the first of January could have the same significance as its twelve-hour earlier counterpart. A New Year's midnight makeup toast.

The tiny hospital room is crowded, with all of us gathered around Alexandra's bedside. Peyton is here, and Liz, the other woman who was mildly injured in the studio, has snuck in the contraband in her large purse. In mine, I had brought four champagne flutes in mine. I might not own a set of china, but these I had covered. Removing each, setting them gently on the food tray that has been swiveled in front of Alexandra, Liz and Peyton begin to unwrap the protective white tissue paper.

"Please just let me unwrap my own glass," Alexandra pleads sounding as if she's being held prisoner against her will. She and hospitals aren't friends. "I feel useless and it's making me crazy!"

"Well, I can't do anything. Moving is excruciating." Liz has been attempting to open the bottle but is cringing with each turn of the little metal basket that holds the cork in place due to the broken ribs she sustained. Peyton jumps in to help. Wrapping an arm across her middle, Liz says, "I can't decide if I love it or hate it. I might have an excuse not to vacuum or load a dishwasher for months. There are silver linings in everything."

"This too shall pass," I offer to Liz and Alexandra, wondering what hole that cheery little pick-me-up crawled out of. They both spoke of physical pain I knew would resolve, unlike Peyton and my disasters.

"Thanks, Cassandra," Liz says, laying her hand along her forearm. "I appreciate you trying to cheer us both up."

I made a resolution, and I'm showing up here today.

Peyton pops the cork with a loud echo off the walls of the small room, then pours into the four glasses.

We are all messes, but Peyton might look the saddest of all. I hope she doesn't blame herself for this. Only Kyle is to blame, and he's still barely alive somewhere else in this hospital.

"I shouldn't drink this on pain meds," Alexandra laughs, "but I am going to."

"I shouldn't either," Liz adds, "but I am as well."

"Well, that makes three of us," I say, raising my glass.

Liz lifts her glass to meet my already raised one. "Let's get to it, ladies. Happy New Year. Auld Lang Syne."

"To A Happy New Year," we all say together in varying intonations. The chime of crystal sings out loudly in the sparsely decorated room.

"I've just toasted to Auld Lang Syne and have no idea what it means," Liz says. "I probably shouldn't admit to not knowing, but I have no clue."

Soft laughter breaks out amongst the others. I could only muster one round of cheeriness.

"We should Google it," Peyton says, phone already in hand. She reads aloud, "The song, traditionally sung to celebrate the New Year, poses the rhetorical question of whether it is right that old times be forgotten, and is generally interpreted as a call to remember long-standing friendships."

Alexandra raises her glass again. "I know it's not exactly what they mean, but to long-standing friendship among us. We need each other for this one."

I hate that she's right. I know that we do. I've never been one to need friends. Or anyone. Awesome. Thanks so much, Ryan Steadman.

"Shall we drink to forgetting the old times?" I propose, thinking about what life would be like if I could turn back the clock to when I didn't give a damn about anything but my job.

"I'm not sure I want to forget all the old times," Liz chimes in with a bit of a mischievous look, "but I'll drink to forgetting some."

Maybe that's the best we can have. Let go of the painful, keep the beautiful. I wouldn't want to forget all things Ryan.

We clink our glasses again. Our eyes lock. Silence falls. The shared experience is fresh and raw. We all want to forget what happened in that studio.

Alexandra is the first to smile, like she has moved on from the past. She raises her glass again, the sun streaming through the window reflecting a small, colorful rainbow off the glass. "We've got this, girls. To do-overs. Sometimes you have to change everything, sometimes just your perspective. We've got this. Together."

"To do-overs. Together," we echo in perfect unison, hopeful smiles spreading across our faces.

There are laughs and tears amid quiet conversation for a while longer, until everyone's ailments call for rest. With promises of seeing each other again soon, we go our separate ways.

In the car, I call Matt. Has Ryan told them what's happened? I know it's not my place to do so, but desperate times call for desperate measures. Reinforcements are required.

"Hello?"

"Hey, Matt, it's Cassandra."

"Hey, Happy New Year! We texted Ryan last night. What up with the no response? I thought it was rude but since you are calling, I guess I shouldn't have been so judgey."

I blow out a breath.

"That didn't sound good. Please tell me you have a hangover and not anything else I need to be worried about."

"I wish that was the case."

*God, how I wish.*

I tell him the whole story, leaving out what Kyle had said. I can't even say it without a vile taste in my mouth. Then I ask him, "What worked last time? To bring him back?"

"It's pretty hard to go there," he says, solemn.

*I know, Matt. You made it through. I'm living there now.*

"I know you won't want to hear this, but it was his choice. Melanie tried. My parents tried. Doctors tried. Nothing worked. It was just his choice."

"What happened with Melanie? Did she leave him?"

"No, Cassandra. He pushed her away. Said she deserved better."

*She couldn't help me pick up the pieces.* That's what he had told me. She couldn't? Or he wouldn't let her?

*When you fall, that's what love can do.*

That is what my love will do. I'm picking up every last piece. Whether he likes it or not, I'm not going anywhere.

# RYAN

*N*ew Year's resolution: Get a new phone number.

# RYAN

New Year's resolution: Get a new untraceable phone number.

# RYAN

*N*ew Year's resolution: Get a new untraceable phone number and don't give it to: Chris, my mother, my father, Matt, Samantha, Alexandra, or any other human who might know Cassandra Lewis.

# CASSANDRA

Two weeks. Too long. Too lonely. I'm forced back to real life boarding another airplane. Starting tonight, each day will be filled with new associates and revolving researchers. Working from before sunrise to after sunset, eating food from whatever plastic and paper containers will be delivered, the lines from day to night will blur, along with my eyesight from data, numbers, and more data. I might have been dreading it, if it weren't for the fact that I needed something—anything!—else to think about other than Ryan.

THIS IS a new year and a new deal. My biggest yet. If only I could stop thinking about the collateral damage thanks to Ryan. I need to think. We are coming to the end of the night. Emotions are running hot. We're on the verge of thunderous temper tantrums breaking loose. My gladiators are hurling expletives, one-upped with adjectives I haven't heard since college. They say a team storms before they perform, but my internal radar says there is no rainbow just around the corner.

Unless I make my own and salvage this.

"Take a break!" I yell out over the rumble of escalated voices competing to be heard. "Paige, I need you, please."

I whisper instructions to Paige who is thrilled to be my accomplice, and then head out the door to run my own errand.

Thirty-six minutes, and a traipse through fluffy white flakes that, of course, remind me of my sushi date with Ryan, and I am back in the conference room.

"Got it!" Paige bounces excitedly through the door. She brings her package to me and together we make quick work. The others are filtering back in from wherever they had been. Marco and Dom are in the corner having a pseudo-snowfall fight with crumpled paper, the discarded remnants of the poor work we'd been doing. Someone has procured wine. We've got this. Together.

Paige carefully holds a stack of items in front of her, proceeding to affix each picture in an arc across the whiteboard. I follow suit, adding mine below hers until we have our rainbow. The team watches us, half-perplexed, half-mesmerized, all curious and finally calm.

I turn to the harsh gaze of tired eyeballs and say quietly, "Let's not forget why we're all here."

I tell the story of each person. George Shepherd: mail clerk to CFO. Abagail Hoffmeister: the CEO's admin who only took one week off with each birth because she didn't want to let him down. Tonya Tucker, mother of eight. The list went on until each face had a name and each name had a story.

High-fiving at 2:35 a.m. we wrap it up, each having gone into crisis-management-meets-good-manners mode. Data was crunched, presentations polished, and expletives traded for endorsements of one another's work. The final printouts are composed and compiled. We all high-tail it to our hotel for what will be considered a nap by any standards.

It was a roller coaster of a day, but I am on the top of the hill. I didn't know if losing him meant I could still keep the woman I was working to become, but now I know. If only he could see me now.

# RYAN

*T*oday, I need a break from it all. I want to run, but I can't. I want to hide, but she won't let me. There's an ambush around every corner and digital assaults coming from every direction. She is unrelenting. Persistent. Incessant. Cassandra is nothing at all like Melanie.

WHAT I WANT today is just one person to remember that today is today. Not my parents or brother, nor Alexandra or Chris. Just John. I can finally start to breathe when my phone is ringing with his name scrawled across the top.

I can't place the background noise, loud and odd. "Steadman! Are you up for a little irony?"

*Is no an option?*

"Guess where I am?"

I don't think that's a real question, but it sounds windy.

"Top of a mountain. Wish you were here with me. I'm holding you to your promise. You said you were doing this."

I might have mentioned it in my text wishing him a Merry Christmas. When things were different.

"You have to try it. Wait until you feel the wind in that full head of hair of yours. I am a jealous asshole for that hair. Seriously though, it's awesome. You should see my kids. Fearless, I tell you!"

"I wonder where they got it?"

"How's the day?" John turns serious.

"Just another day in paradise." Sarcasm is just as good a friend as he is.

"Steadman. Come on. It's me, and I am calling B.S. Let me know how I can help. You know I'll do anything for you, man."

"I know, John." *But for this one I'm on my own.*

"Damn you, I know where your head just went and no, you're not. Last I checked there was a sassy brunette that would like to argue that point too. Stop sitting around brooding. You know the way out. And book your damn ski trip already."

"I'm sorry, did I miss hearing myself ask for your advice?"

"Nah, you didn't. But you know I'm right. I always am. Learned it the hard way. And speaking of that, there's a pristine, freshly groomed powder-black diamond run calling my name. You know what I say! A life of fear is a life not lived. I gotta go. Love ya, man."

I hear him yelling, "Let's go, kiddos!" before the phone disconnects. From the first day we met, and every anniversary since, he's reminded me if I'm still breathing, I'd better be dreaming. He'd stolen the line from James Dean, never mentioning he died of a broken neck when he crashed his Porsche. I'm done with dreams. For myself. But I'm grateful he's helped me remember there's nothing better than helping others live theirs.

"Looking good, Mags!"

*I probably shouldn't lie, but what do you say?*

I force a feeble, but convincing, smile. Even as weak as she is, she'll throat-punch me if I show pity on my face.

She lights up and even sits up straight. "Hi, Mr. Ryan. I would have done my hair if I knew you were coming." She points at her bald head. Pull back your arrow, Mags. Humor is, indeed, a secret weapon.

"What are you doing here?" she asks, leaning over the edge of the hospital bed. We are eye to eye.

"I was having a hard day, and I knew my friend Maggie would know how to cheer me up."

"I do! I do! Mom! Will you get my journal?"

Now it's Miriam whose weariness seems to transform to energy before my very eyes. I'm thankful for John's reminder that service fixes a sorry ass every time. My eyes follow her across the small room to its one cabinet. When she opens it, I see a stack of books I recognize.

"I see you've been reading."

"Yep. Miss Cassandra brought me those from our library. I mean, your library," she corrects.

"Your library," I say reassuringly with a wink, not missing the fact that Cassandra seems to have a hand in everything these days.

Miriam hands Maggie a leather journal, bright sunshine yellow, with a quote on the cover, embossed in black. I shake my head when I read it: *She certainly was a fearsome thing to behold. – Elizabeth Bennett*

Straight out of Pride and Prejudice. My penance for giving her the book for Christmas.

Maggie purposefully opens the cover and flips the first page toward me. I know the writing. Turning it back, she practically squeals out the words, "Thank you for being my reading buddy...and Plan C! Love, Cass."

I suppose Plan C could be worse. Based on my phone, she had to be getting close to Plan Z.

The next page is filled by whimsical handwriting which I presume is Maggie's. She reads aloud, "Moonlight drowns out all but the brightest stars. I loved the Lord of the Rings."

On the next page she has written, "I have been bent and broken, but—I hope—into a better shape. I picked that one for both of us, Mr. Ryan."

*Great Expectations. Too bad they aren't always met, dear Maggie.*

"Oh this is my other favorite!" She points to the page with her index finger and traces the words as she reads aloud, "Beware; for I am fearless, and therefore powerful. Mary Shelley, Frankenstein."

She looks straight into my eyes, as if a test. John's words echo in my ears. A life of fear is a life not lived. "I'm trying really hard to be brave, but it's hard."

*It is, Mags. It is.*

Because she is more resilient than I, she moves on, flipping to the next page. "I know what helps though."

"Oh, yeah?" I ask. "What's that?"

"Someone who loves you, so you don't have to do hard and scared all by yourself."

*Out of the mouths of babes. She's wise beyond her years. Broken will do that to a person.*

"I think Wuthering Heights is my new favorite." She turns the paper toward me again and I read aloud, "He's more myself than I am. Whatever our souls are made of, his and mine are the same." Around the written quote, in various shapes and sizes, are doodles of hearts and stars.

She closes the journal and leans back into her pillow.

"I have a lot of dreams." She sighs, as if knowing she may not have the time to live them. Then, however, her eyes flash fierce, perhaps a warning to the fates that she won't go down without a fight. Her next words are full of resilience and conviction, "I need to go to England someday and see the places in these books. And I want to read every book in our library. But mostly, I just can't wait to fall in love."

*Our fear of falling might paralyze us but fighting for love is the anti-dote. Life is for living our dreams. Dreaming might be what keeps Maggie alive.*

"Those are great dreams, Maggie," I tell her. Then for both us our sakes I add, "Never stop dreaming."

# CASSANDRA

*A*lexandra and I are gathering at Liz's house to celebrate her birthday and prepare for a fundraising event she is hosting this weekend. We have carryout containers all around us, but also a winter wonderland of sorts. We are assembling four hundred snow globes to serve as decorations at each place setting. With only five of six working arms, we don't have an extra minute to spare.

We do take a short break for Liz to blow out the three candles on the chocolate cake in front of us. I ask chidingly, "What did you wish for?"

"You know I can't tell you or it won't come true."

"I know, I know. I wasn't expecting you to answer. I'll tell you what I would wish for if it was my birthday. I would wish for my New Year's resolutions to come true."

"I thought you said yoga was a resolution," Alexandra chimes in. "At least you got that one."

"Yes. And I said I wanted girlfriends. I'm grateful to be here. Peyton and I had a great trip, minus the one missing piece, of course."

It was supposed to be me and Ryan on the trip he had gifted me for Christmas. There wasn't a minute that went by that I didn't wish he was by my side to share the surf and sun, not to mention vacation sex. But at least Peyton and I were sharing the same little private island called hell. "I really loved getting to know her better. And for that matter, I feel the same about both of you. I don't know how I did this crazy thing called life without women."

"Well, I hope you think this little project is better than knitting, but why do you think knitting circles were so popular?" Liz offers.

"And book clubs!" Alexandra chimes in. "We need each other. I love strong women coming together. Love picks up the pieces after broken."

I stop and catch my breath, "Ryan must have been quoting you, Alexandra. He told me that. When he was telling me about Melanie."

"He told you about her?" She sounds surprised.

"Yes. He said she couldn't pick up the pieces for him. And I guess I can't now, either."

"You're right, no one can. It has to be his choice, but you aren't Melanie, Cassandra. You haven't given up, have you?"

"Of course not. I still have a few letters to go." They know about all about Plan A through Plan Z. "Charlotte is helping next."

I may have barely survived my resolution to get through a day without him, but I've made it nearly a month. Not that I don't wish every day it was different. I guess that means there is only one resolution left. The one to get him back.

"I'm breaking resolution number five right now," I say as I reach for a second slice of cake. A big one.

"What might that be?" Alexandra asks, eyeing how it occupies the entire plate.

"Shoes over sweets if I don't have Ryan in my life."

They both laugh. With me, not at me.

"If it's meant to be, Cass—" Liz starts, but then cuts herself off as if she knows I don't want to hear it, and nothing she can say will make it hurt less.

"It's fine, Liz. Really, it was silly. It was only a couple of months. I shouldn't have let myself fall so hard."

Liz looks like she has wisdom to share. "It's not as if we always have the choice. Besides, there is something special about loving with reckless abandon. You seized the moment, and no matter what happens, you will be changed forever. Good thing you did it now. At your age, you can love knowing you deserve romance and happiness. It was worth taking the chance."

I contemplate her words. "You are right, Liz. But that doesn't mean it sucks any less. I don't suppose there is any chance in hell that either of you can convince him to come Saturday?"

Alexandra's face drops. The answer is obvious. "I tried, Cass, I really did. I feel like a professional nag. I can't even get him to yoga."

If a lightbulb could actually form in the air when an idea springs to life, it does over Liz's head when I see her brighten, "I might have a Hail Mary. I'll give it one last-ditch effort."

For some reason, this overwhelms me. It might be my last chance. I feel tears well and I choke them back as I envelope her in a hug, "Thank you, Liz. You have no idea what that means to me." She surprises me when she says, "I do, actually. More than you know."

# RYAN

"We'll you've looked better."

"Hello to you too, Charlotte. Never one to hold back an opinion, are we?"

"Only when I think it can make a difference."

"Wait. No. Not you too? You're frenemies and yet somehow Cassandra has you on her side? What are you, Plan R?"

"Can't say she hasn't tried. What a hard head you are. And what can I say, we all love you. Certainly, Cassandra. Maybe more than you deserve."

"Newsflash. That's exactly the problem."

"You're wrong. Let me see your phone."

Arguing will be futile, so I take it from the pocket of my suit jacket and pass it across the desk to her.

"Password," she sighs, scolding, with her southern drawl accentuating the two syllables.

I type it in and hand it back.

She scrolls. And scrolls. And scrolls. Then scrolls some more.

"My God, Ryan. There has to be damn near one thousand messages here."

*Seven hundred fourteen, including ninety-one declarations of love from Cassandra. But who's counting?*

"Are you really going to tell me that you're ignoring what all these people have been trying to tell you for the opinion of one heart-broken bastard who was on drugs? You pity the rest of us to be fools? I'm not gonna lie, I'm kind of insulted. Look at this!" She flips the phone forward shoving it in my direction.

*I've read them all, Charlotte, don't need a recap.*

Clearly, I am going to get one anyway.

"Monday from Alexandra. I miss you in class. I need your energy. I need your smile.

Tuesday. Matt says get your head out of your ass before you lose the best thing that has ever happened to you. Remember, I heard what you did to her in the bedroom. You really want to give that up?"

She cocks one eyebrow at me, then smiles salaciously. She knows better than anyone what that means to me. "I'm so happy for you. I know it's what you wanted."

She had offered. I had refused. But she knows.

"You really want to give that up?" she repeats what Matt has said. She looks back to the phone, "What else we got? From Chris. STEADMAN. In shouty caps. Beat me up. Come walk it off. We got work to do. Don't let our kids down. Don't let yourself down. Don't let me down. We've come a long way. Don't stop now."

She pauses, presumably making sure it sinks into my thick head and calloused heart. Then she asks, "Walk it off?"

"He's on a mission. We've been working on a few things."

"You can't give up on this, Ryan!"

I think about standing in front of Cassandra. How it felt to have her look up to me. Holding her dancing. How I felt like a man. Until I didn't. She can't understand. No one can understand.

"Chris is right. About the kids, Ryan. This isn't just about you. This is hurting everyone around you. Look at all of these from your mom and dad."

*She hasn't checked the calls. They call more than they text. Luckily, voicemail fills up quickly.*

"Selfish doesn't look good on you. You should stick with Armani. And lose the 'poor me' attitude."

*Armani and an attitude. Memories of Cassandra will always be everywhere.*

"Okay, we're done hurling insults around here." I roll away toward the conference room.

"You're going the wrong way," she drawls behind me. I look over my shoulder and she's pointing to the hallway straight ahead of her desk. Roosevelt boardroom today."

She probably booked it that way on purpose just to annoy me.

"See, you need me. Whether you like it or not. You need all of us!" She yells after me as I get the hell out of her lobby.

IN THE CONFERENCE ROOM, I'm joined by several key stakeholders and partners of the company that bankrolled my new lease on life.

"Sorry to call you out here on short notice, Ryan, but we have a bit of a dilemma." Hank Bradenton doesn't apologize to anyone, so this starts out on an odd note.

"We had a recent round of pitches for the Diggs-Epson deal. One of them took a very different direction, and we trust your opinion. We've got some financials for review, because we just aren't sure if it makes sense."

He has my curiosity piqued.

"Let's start with the fact that a whole team pitched this. Thirty-five years I've been in the business and it's never been but a singular affair. You know how those execs don't like to share the floor, the glory, or the payout."

I consider the ramifications—a higher cost to the firm handling the deal if more people are involved. It's all about the billable hours. Then again, it seems like a great idea. "I guess that would work out well—more brains behind the balance sheet so to speak—as long as they are willing to share the usual cut."

"We agree. But then they pitched that we keep everyone at both companies on the payroll. They showed us the numbers."

He pushes a folder across the table. I peruse the data. It looks thorough. "They also proposed that we bring in this unique cast of characters," he says, motioning toward pictures sitting on stands throughout the room. Interestingly, they are faces I recognize. I don't have reason yet to argue. "Let's take a look at the numbers, but at first glance they seem pretty solid. I'd say if they have a case for the revenue to substantiate keeping the people, I'd go for it."

"They've got some name for the new venture. Altruism and corporation something?" He looks to a younger male on his left to answer the question; by the looks of him, one of the analysts.

"Yes. Altrusion," the young man confirms.

"Yes, that was it. Can you imagine altruism and business as the foundation for this new company?"

"Actually, sir, I can. You've done it before, and it seems to have worked out for you."

We both laugh, knowing it's the very reason I'm in the room.

"I guess you are right about that." He points to another analyst. "Call Charlotte in here." He looks back to me. "You two are the best judges of character I know."

Charlotte seems to appear out of thin air, a skill she has mastered.

"Charlotte, do we go with Cassandra Lewis on this deal?"

This, I did not see coming.

"Cassandra Lewis pitched this deal?" I ask, pointing to the pictures and not hiding my surprise in the least.

Hank nods curtly, then turns to Charlotte. "Yep. She did. Charlotte, what do you say? You always do enjoy the last word."

"She's one of the good ones, Hank. She has my vote."

He taps his pen on the table, looking out the window in thought. "I trust both of you but I'm just not sure. I need to think on this a bit more."

I can't believe I am going to do what I am about to do. "Hank, I gave you my professional opinion, not my personal one. Cassandra Lewis has that unique combination few people do. She thinks with her head but acts with her heart. She is courageous and isn't going to shy away from a challenge, and she's most definitely tenacious. She will not go down without a fight, and as far as I know, she hasn't lost yet. And I mean ever. She is grace under pressure and a fixer. If anyone can make the people and profit pieces work together, it's her."

He leans back in his chair, fingers steepled in his lap, eyeing me suspiciously, "Well, that's a mighty fine endorsement. It's none of my business, but if that's all true, you might want to see if you can snap that one up. We can move forward on one condition. You get her to come on board and lead this through the transition. If you can get her to agree to that, the deal is done."

He looks upward, tapping his forefinger on his lips in thought. "Maybe you two belong together. Yes, let's get you working on it with her. Two of the best and brightest. You'd make a good team. Charlotte, you too. Ryan's told me you should be doing more around here."

I try not to look at Charlotte, but out of the corner of my eye I don't miss her chomping down on her bottom lip. She's trying to squelch the laugh dying to burst forward at the hand fate just dealt. Here we are again. Full circle.

Trying to process what has just happened, his flippant words were also those that had been etched in my heart. Maybe we belong together. Watching Charlotte's reaction to the inevitable, have distracted me from responding quickly. By the time I manage to blurt out, "I'm not sure that's a good idea," no one is listening. Hank's portfolio is closed and he's deep in conversation with another man. I'm too late. I should have kept my damn mouth shut.

WE ARRIVED A BIT LATE TODAY, with the San Francisco fog, so Marcus was kind enough to do extra duty as chauffer. Cecil is picking me up, however.

"You look good, Cecil."

It's nice to see his painful-looking limp has nearly disappeared. Glad I could fix someone else since I can't buy my own cure.

"Thank you, sir, but if you don't mind my saying, you don't look too hot yourself. You alright? Counting sheep not working for you?"

"What are you saying, I look tired?"

*Maybe if I had someone to sleep with, I wouldn't be dreaming of falling down mountains and shootings in yoga studios.*

"You could say that. But I think it's more that I haven't seen that wicked smile that says you're probably up to no good."

I smile it now. Inauthentic, but it serves the purpose.

"That's better. Now if we could get that twinkle back in those sad eyes."

"You get one out of the two. Let's call it a day."

My phone buzzes in my pocket. It's not often I get a Facebook messenger notice. It takes a second to sink in its probably Cassandra finding yet another way to reach me. I've got to give it to her. I wonder what kind of crazy is coming my way this time. Contrary to popular belief, I haven't ignored the contents of the messages. I just haven't responded to any. I won't to this one either. She should understand I'm just taking a page out of her book. And I've made it well past two hundred eighty.

"You see Ms. Lewis lately?" Cecil asks after I return to looking forward.

*Here we go again. I should have known better and asked Marcus to pick me up too.*

"No, Cecil. I have not. How about you?"

"Um-hmm," he says with a nod.

I shake me head, "Let me guess, you have a message for me."

Might as well take the bull by the horns before it spears me in the ass. I'm a sitting duck, trapped for thirty more miles.

"Yes, sir, I do."

I've never seen him look so smug, like he can't wait to torture me.

"I am supposed to tell you that she wouldn't have traded the wedding, Christmas, or yoga for all the money in the world."

*She doesn't really understand money like I do, clearly.*

"She said she thinks you two belong together." I think of the damn words Hank had said. Perhaps the universe is making sure I get this message. It's more than annoying. Even more annoying, he's not done.

"Oh, she also said to tell you she loves you. Still. And always."

We make eye contact in the rear-view mirror.

"An awful lot, it seems. I'm adding that part myself."

*If she loves me so much, why doesn't she just listen and move the hell on?*

I look at my phone still in my hand, the texts I couldn't bring myself to delete. Every night, for the last thirty in a row, she texted goodnight, xo, and two kisses. Then she added: you are more than worthy of my love.

Could she ever say it enough that I could believe it? I just don't know.

I look out the window to avoid Cecil's eyes stalking me. Are we there yet?

"That's just what she said to tell you, Mr. Ryan. But I have my own advice too, even though you didn't ask." Cecil chuckles.

I brace myself, blowing out a slow breath.

"When I met Ms. Lewis, she was working hard protecting herself from the big, bad world. She seemed tough, but she was sad. You know what she was like? One of those brown, ugly rocks. On the outside. Then you break 'em open and the inside is beautiful, all colorful and sparkling crystals. That was Miss Lewis. She was rough 'round the edges, but I knew there was something special inside. I knew she had a big heart somewhere in there, just with a lot of rock keeping it safe. After you, she's different. She's still sad about you, but she's all colorful sparkle now. She's a different kind of beautiful."

I concede, "You are right, Cecil. She is pretty damn beautiful."

"I think it might be all your fault, Mr. Ryan. You broke her open and showed all her beautiful. And when you got that kind of beautiful you better do your damnedest to keep it. My momma wouldn't be happy I said damnedest, but I think in this case she would let it slide." He laughs, deep and real.

CONSIDERING what he said for a moment, I suppose he is right. About the sad and the beautiful. It might be my fault, but reality is what it is, and not Cecil, nor her little army, can fix this. I know as time passes, she'll move past her sadness, but I hope she'll forever keep her beautiful.

# CASSANDRA

*I*'m so proud of Liz and the amazing event that she has put together. The Snow Ball is aptly named, as it's beginning to snow as the event starts. Alexandra and Peyton are here too, so despite my wanting things to be different, I am grateful the four of us have each other.

The ballroom has been transformed into a winter wonderland. White twinkling lights send shooting stars of light off the glitter and clear sequins sprinkled upon Styrofoam snowflakes nestled in a foot of fluffy fake snow. The dance floor is strung with exposed lightbulbs across it, resembling an outdoor ice rink, with stacks of mock snowballs lining the sides.

In the center of each table, five crystal snowflakes, each eight inches high, stack to form the vases holding blue delphiniums. They gracefully tower over the tables, taller than the guests so conversation can flow uninhibited beneath their canopy. Forming semi-circles on either side of the flowers, the silver base of the snow globe sits atop more fake snow. The eight hundred napkins, all in periwinkle to represent gastric cancer, won't let anyone forget the cause they are here to support.

. . .

EVERYONE IS SEATED and ready for dinner to begin. I pass the basket of bread over the empty space at the table next to me, mocking. Someone has even stolen the chair but left the setting just to further get under my skin.

As I'm lifting my fork for the first bite of salad, I feel a hand on my bare left shoulder. A throat clears. I look up to find Cecil's white-toothed grin staring back at me.

"Good evening, Ms. Lewis."

I push my chair back, looking up at him, "Oh my God, Cecil. What are you doing he—?"

It takes me a minute. "What does this mean? Does this mean? Oh my God!" I jump up, throwing my arms around his neck. "Thank you, Cecil!"

The perfect gentleman, his hat is across his chest and he bows gently in my direction, then quickly steps out of the way, his outstretched hand pointing toward the entrance.

My new high heels, compliments of resolution five, carry me to the lobby where my tall, dark, handsome, heartbreaking, and heart-broken hero is waiting for me. I run the last few steps to him.

There has been a void in my chest. My heart expands, filling in where emptiness had been. Memories of us, and love for him, flood over me.

*...the first touch on the airplane months ago, love not in my vocabulary...*

*... the scorn of a boy pulling at my pigtails...*

*...love becoming a four-letter word, until it wasn't...*

*...a first kiss that spoke words I couldn't...*

*...my body revered so beautifully...*

*...our first dance...*

*...compassion changing everything...*

*... A man who forgot how worthy he was...*

Has he found his way back? Does he remember too?

"Cassandra," he says, and I remember the whiskey-smooth of his voice. "Your friends are relentless. I didn't want you to be alone tonight."

*How about neither of us are ever alone again?*

"I still don't know if I can do this. My being here doesn't mean—"

I look at his dark hair, styled tonight, and my fingers beg, and will, mess up in moments whether he likes it or not. I interrupt, "Once, I was invited to this wedding and I wasn't sure if I was going to show up." I'm trying to tell him that I understand. I was scared too. "But, I did."

"Beautifully, I might add." I know that smile. It draws my eye to the dimple.

"Just like tonight. You are so beautiful, Cass."

*Please call me that forever. And babe, and sweetheart, and anything else. Maybe even wife or mother to your children.*

"I bet you've called me a few more adjectives over the last month." I know a few of the good ones, because Charlotte had me on speed-dial within minutes of their meeting in California.

"How about brilliant? Altrusion? Well played. When I introduced you to Georgia and Mack that day—"

I interrupt. "And Bonnie and Clyde," I say with a wink.

"You taking care of them was unexpected."

"And I wasn't expecting any of this." I feel impatient. I'm still a work in progress. I can't wait any longer. "May I kiss you, please? Please, may I kiss you?"

"That's not a good idea." His voice is firm.

Heart overruling my head, my lips find his anyway. It is the softest, most tender kiss I've ever placed on his lips. It is love.

He resists, hands planted firmly on his legs, lips not moving against mine. I don't even care, happy he isn't pushing me away. Finally, I feel the warmth of hands coming nearer to my face. They hold me gently, fingertips grazing the top of my cheekbones. My fingers find handfuls of hair and pull him close. His lips meet mine in a caress of longing and need and loneliness. We stay that way for a long time, making up for lost time.

His eyes are still closed, face barely an inch from mine, when he says, "I'm so glad you didn't listen to me just now."

"I asked politely and said please. Twice," I whisper in an exhale. Then, I breathe him in remembering his smell of spice and wood.

"I tried to forget how good kissing you feels." His forehead meets mine.

"I couldn't stop remembering."

"I'm so sorry, Cass."

Tears spring to my eyes. "Luckily for you, someone taught me a little something about forgiveness." When the corners of my mouth lift in a smile, the tears spill over. I reach up to wipe them. Half-laughing, half-crying with elation and disbelief together in a crazy cocktail of emotion, I reach out both hands toward him. He takes them in his. The contrast of black on my white wrist catches his eye and he slowly turns it over to examine it. Looking at the new tattoo on the inside, he catches my gaze.

"I needed something permanent. To remind me who I wanted to be."

He brushes his lips against the lotus flower in a kiss. "Even with roots in mud, every day a new, beautiful flower blooms."

I nod. He understands. "So, what finally did it? Why are you here?"

"Sneak peek of the message tonight. From Liz. I got it yesterday when I was with Cecil. He gave me your message, and one of his own."

I'm sure I look curious.

"He said I'd be a fool to lose something so beautiful. Since he had a hand in swaying me to be here, I invited him to come along. The message tonight is about second chances, silver linings and living life. It's for everyone, but especially applies to us. You'll understand. So, you can thank Liz, and Cecil, and Charlotte, and Chris, Maggie, Matt and Samantha, my parents, and of course, Alexandra. I love that woman. Of course, not like I love you. I love you, Cassandra."

"If I haven't said it enough this month, I love you too."

I want to show him every day that he is worthy of everything good. I want to start making up for lost time and lost hope. Right now. And so I ask, "Want to get out of here?"

"We can't yet. You really have to hear what's coming. But don't worry, I might have another surprise in store for you. At the same time I was swearing I wouldn't leave here with you tonight, I was planning it, so I guess it's official that you have won. Don't even say it, because I know what you are thinking."

He smiles, mischief in his lips, twinkling in his eyes.

Ryan is back. Happiness seizes my heart.

We share another kiss, and my right-shouldered angel wins. It's about time. I wouldn't even think of gloating.

RYAN JOINS us at the table with Cecil beside us. Alexandra wraps her sling-free arm around him from behind and kisses him on the cheek, "I knew you couldn't stay away forever."

I see Peyton slump into her chair, however. I haven't planned for this. She looks scared. I am scared for her. And Ryan. I whisper into his ear, "Peyton hasn't had it easy either."

"Thanks, babe," he says with a kiss to my cheek. He waves Peyton to our side of the table and she walks over to us. "I owe you an apology. I should have accepted yours. None of this was your fault."

She responds by throwing her arms around him and he hugs her back. When she finally lets go, Ryan winks at her. "I think you might have been the only person Cassandra didn't suck into her Operation Rescue Ryan. If this went on any longer, you might have ended up my only friend."

"Don't think I didn't try," I laugh, along with Peyton.

Ryan's laughing too, "Frankly, I'm surprised you didn't steal my kidnapping tactic."

"Well, I don't exactly have a private plane to whisk you away on. But don't think for a second that it didn't cross my mind," I tell him sincerely, because in fact, it had.

"Thank you for not giving up," Ryan says taking my hand.

My lips spread into a wide, coy smile as I look into his eyes, "Sometimes obstinate and headstrong comes in handy."

. . .

WE ARE among the first to make our way to the exit, not to skip out on Liz but a girl can only be expected to wait so long. The snow falling makes us our own perfect snow globe.

Cecil is waiting with a black limousine.

"I told you I had another surprise for you. Couldn't really go with a white horse. Horses and snow don't work out so well."

"White horse. Black limo. Same difference. I love you," I tell him, perfectly content with anything that carries us off into the proverbial sunset.

Within seconds Ryan has pulled me fiercely close, our tongues reacquainted, picking up where we left off a long time ago, making plans for the future. Together.

"Make good choices, you two!" Cecil laughs, and it reminds me of kissing with Chris as our cheerleader. So many memories, but more to make.

As soon as the divider closes us off from the front seat, Ryan's hand sneaks beneath my coat to find my covered breast. When we finally come up for air a couple of minutes later, it's for him to speak, "We should do that, you know. It would be fun."

Breathless and confused, I ask, "What?"

"Go horseback riding. Sometime."

"Okay. Sometime." I have something else in mind right now besides riding a horse. But I appreciate his sentiment, because he's dreaming forward. He is making plans for a future. With me by his side.

# RYAN

*I* made future plans tonight. Plans with Cassandra by my side. Horseback riding, maybe on the vacation she's made me feel ready to take. I'm alive and breathing so I'd better be dreaming. Tonight, I had to make the choice to take this chance when I wasn't sure that I could. I showed up, just like she did for the wedding. Showing up is where we all start.

The future will have to wait a few more minutes, however, because I want to fully experience this present. Staring at her mouth, soft and pouty pink lips beckon for mine to find them. Eyes closed, poised to kiss back before I have even reached her, she waits for me. Just as she's done for the longest thirty-four days of my life. Yes, before her, I thought I'd lived my darkest and loneliest ones after the accident, but I was wrong. Losing her was worse.

I take her in another first kiss. This one says I'm never letting go. I crash hard against her mouth, knowing everything I need is here. With her. In her. The sweetness of her taste, her warmth, the feel of her tongue parting the intermingled flesh of our lips, the softness of hers mixing with mine, the moan in her exhale, and her fingers dancing at the nape of my neck make me feel everything, everywhere.

When I know her lips are happily attended to, I find her neck, caressing its length with kisses before tracing her collarbone with my tongue. My fingertips traverse the curve of one shoulder, then move across her chest to the other, before my palm finally cradles the flesh of her breast.

Her breath hitches, audible, a sound I will never tire of hearing. Her body arches beneath my touch and my kiss then relaxes into mine, a delicate dance I remember the steps to. We have many more dances to learn, and we have time.

Thinking of time has one eye opening. I stop kissing Cassandra. I peek at the clock. 11:42 p.m. I gently push against her shoulders as she reluctantly separates from my lips.

"What's going on?" she asks, not hiding her irritability. I wonder if she knows she's started to wear every emotion on her sleeve.

"There are still a few more minutes in January. We never had a New Year's toast."

"Um, okay."

Her feet are already on the floor. She accepts I can't do anything quickly and is willing to help. I take a moment to be grateful I don't have to do everything alone any longer. Life is easier for anyone in a pair, but especially for me.

She returns, her delightfully curvy naked body before me, with two highball glasses of something bubbling.

"I might have gone with the top shelf," she says smirking cutely. "What was that again? Solo il meglio?"

"Yes, solo il meglio."

"But I couldn't find the champagne glasses so these will have to do."

She tucks her legs beneath her and sits on the bed facing me. "Tonight, you made my last New Year's resolution come true."

"Last resolution?" I ask.

"I made five."

"Always overachieving, my Cassandra."

"Yep. Your Cassandra resolved to survive the days without you, make girlfriends, and do yoga."

She's only shared three, so I ask, "And the other two? You said there were five."

Looking up at me, her long lashes flutter over slow, wide-eyed blinks, "The fourth was to get you back."

"You can cross that one off the list. And the fifth?"

"Shoes instead of sweets if I couldn't." She looks upward, shaking her head as if in disbelief.

"How many pairs?"

"A lot."

"How many donuts?"

"More."

"I'm sorry."

"I know." She leans in for a long kiss that says I'm forgiven, then with a smile says, "I'm thirsty."

I lift my glass. "To everything that's happened to get us here."

"Hey, I said that!"

I see and hear her childlike innocence again, the colorful sparkle beneath the hard exterior.

"I know. And I mean it. Falling down that mountain was the worst thing that ever happened to me, but maybe your worst is what brings you your best."

She lifts her glass to meet mine, and repeats what I have said, "To everything that got us here."

We clink our glasses and gaze at each other as we take a sip.

Her lips curl upward, a smile so big I can see it in her eyes. A different kind of beautiful. "Maybe we belong together, Ryan Steadman."

"Maybe we do," I return, setting my glass down and then hers as well. I'm going to make love to her now. Maybe not as spontaneous as I'd like, and never the way I wish I could, but still, the best we can give each other.

.  .  .

233

I'M HOLDING a sleepy and sated Cassandra safely in my arms. She seems custom-sized to fit me, just like her heart beating against my chest is the perfect complement to mine.

The fireplace glows across the room, crackling orange yellow flames whipping around, tamed by their cage of glass. It's the same for my heart inside my body. There are dreams and possibilities wildly thrashing about, enclosed in a broken body.

Haven't we all been broken by love and life? Haven't we all fallen?

Yes, falling can break us, but it can also prepare us for when we have the chance fix someone else's broken.

Maybe it's being broken into pieces that teaches us to love others.

Maybe we have to be broken to learn to let love in.

Fate knew better. It gave us the chance to put our pieces back together. Tonight, I took the chance, and made the choice to fall again. For Cassandra.

We can't do it alone. We can only do it together when we make the choice to fight for love. Because only love can fix us, after we have fallen.

# EPILOGUE

## RYAN

*I* skid to a stop on the mountain alongside my daughter, who's just fallen down flat on her back, skis tangled and pointing straight up toward the sky. Luckily, she's laughing so I can keep breathing. I know she's okay.

"I fell down, Daddy!" She smiles up at me from the ground, her wide grin, made even cuter with two missing front teeth, melts my heart, each and every time.

"You don't say, sweetheart." I offer my hand to help her up, but she has a healthy dose of her mother in her. She is already on her feet and dusting the snow off her pant legs. It's nice that she is fiercely independent, but if she did need help that I wasn't able to offer, I've learned there will always be plenty of back up.

J.T. arrives next to us, spraying me with snow from his snowboard. I'd like to call him a few expletives, but I will hold back for my daughter's sake.

"Sorry, man." He says with a laugh.

"You hardly are."

"You're right. I hardly am." He's still laughing.

Men are childish, but the kids do love our playful sides.

"That was a nice yard sale, girl! You alright?" He leans forward with his hands on his knees, face to face with my daughter.

"That was epic!" She gifts the adorable grin to J.T., flashing the same toothless smile.

"Yep, pretty epic! Next thing you know, your Dad and I will be trying to keep up with you on black diamonds!"

When that happens, I can't wait to tell John about it. By then, he'll probably be jumping out of helicopters with his teens, but that's okay, I'm grateful for his head start on everything. He is one of the reasons I am where I am today. And I don't just mean on this mountain.

J.T. slaps my shoulder, "Brave girl you got there."

"I like diamonds!"

It's my turn to laugh. Of course, she does, she's female. And luckily, when the time comes, I'll be able to buy her plenty of them.

My beautiful wife arrives on the scene. "Charlotte Alexandra Steadman, you need to slow down! You are giving mommy heart attacks!"

Cassandra earns a wrinkled-up nose, but she has plenty of practice with Charley's seven years of sassy since birth and doesn't flinch. She narrows her eyes and tilts her head at Charlotte, who responds with her bottom lip poking out in a pout. "I know Mommy, you love me so much you don't want me to fall down."

"Exactly," Cassandra offers in a soft tone.

Peyton finally joins the mix, having been behind the others with Shawn, our four-year-old, in tow. I send up a little prayer to the heavens, as I do each time I lay eyes on my vivacious son. I pray for peace for Shawn's mother who lost first her husband, then her child.

"Charley do you have any boo-boos?"

There is plenty of sibling rivalry between the two, mostly for who gets to ride on my lap in the wheelchair, but it's nice to see he's worried about his sister.

Charlotte's chest juts forward, "Nope! I kicked the mountains booty!" she beams with pride toward her little brother.

"I want to kick the mountain's booty too!" Shawn's little snowboard starts moving away from us.

"I got him," J.T. starts off after him.

"I can't keep up with these kids, honey!" Cassandra says with a laugh, followed by several pants and gasps, her exhales forming puffs of white exhalation in the cold. Her cheeks are pink from the wind, and she looks extra gorgeous with their hint of color and long chestnut locks flowing behind her as when she skis down the mountain.

"Don't worry. We got this, Cass. Together." I push off because Charley is already moving forward to follow the others.

"I'm going to need a massage tonight," Cassandra says next to me as we make our way down the mountain together, side by side. "A good, long one," she adds with a radiant smile that I know reflects her remembering the one from our wedding night.

"It would be my pleasure," I return, thinking of the memory myself. My hands spent plenty of time wandering over all those curves of hers after our perfect day.

We got married in Florida, on the patio where we'd eaten dinner after the kidnapping incident. Cassandra had her girlfriends there in Liz, Peyton, and Alexandra while I had my brother, John, and of course Chris, by my side. We toasted to our new beginning with a backdrop of the perfect sunset. Cassandra couldn't stop saying how romantic it was, and I was thrilled to have shown her the meaning of the word.

As the purple, pink, and orange hues reflected off the ocean, I was able to dance with my bride, to the same song we had the first time we held each other in my living room.

Our first dance taught us to hold on to one another. Eight years and two beautiful children later, we've never let go. The broken road has since been paved with dreams and countless memories I never expected to have the chance to make. And night after night, I make love to a woman I respect, admire, and crave.

Despite the odds, our broken led us to each other. I almost let my broken tear us apart once, but thankfully it was no match for headstrong and obstinate. From the beginning, fate was on our side, and forever after I don't need to be reminded, Cassandra and I were meant to be together.

# ACKNOWLEDGMENTS

Proceeds from this book will benefit the Christopher and & Dana Reeve Foundation. Since 1982, the foundation has awarded over $138 million to labs around the globe to accelerate scientific breakthroughs across the field of spinal cord injury research.

Thank you again for reading After Fallen, and raising money for a good cause by doing so.

**Our mission**

We are dedicated to curing spinal cord injury by advancing innovative research and improving quality of life for individuals and families impacted by paralysis.

## ALSO BY WHITNEY WALKER

Thank you for reading! I hope you enjoyed After Fallen.

Reviews are always welcome.

**Other books in this series:**

After Never

After Broken

Coming in 2021...Alexandra's story

& A short story series 'Hope for All Seasons.'

Just in time for Valentine's Day!

Get **Liam & Riley's** Second Chance Christmas short story **FREE** for subscribing! www.whitneywalkerwriting.com

Follow @authorwhitney on Instagram

Like & Follow on Facebook

www.facebook.com/authorwhitneywalker

Until next time - fight for love,

XOXO

# ABOUT THE AUTHOR

Whitney Walker starts and ends each day with gratitude to the tribe who has helped her realize the serendipity of our stories.

She writes for all the hopeless romantics who believe tears and laughter are best friends, second chances are better than firsts, and true love is worth fighting for.

With faith, wine, and chocolate by her side, she aspires to be the best mother to two, girlfriend to "the one", daughter, friend, and yogi she can be. It's a work in progress, and she appreciates the chance to share her life learning through writing.

She was born & raised in Detroit, then chose to reside there, even before it was cool.